MAIN STREET

ALSO BY DIANNA WILKES

DEDICATION

In memory of Florence Chaney Holley

Wish you were here to share this moment, Mom.

ACKNOWLEDGMENTS

Few efforts are a solitary endeavor. *Main Street* would not have become a reality if not for the support of so many wonderful people:

- My sisters Lin and Toni, whose help gave me the time to devote to writing.
- My critique partners Dena and Heather. Your feedback and tough love kept me on track.
- My longtime friends and early readers, Donna and Margie, whose encouragement kept me motivated.
- My editor, the amazing Dana Delamar, who helped me reach the finishing line.

Chapter One

As much as she loved Uncle Toddy, Dana Canfield was ready to stuff a napkin down his throat by the time dessert arrived. She detested the Harmony Hills Country Club, having spent too many evenings accompanying her late husband James to dinner with his clients.

The club was Toddy's second home. He savored the rich, decadent food, relished the posh Old World ambiance, and accepted the fawning from the staff as his due. Above all, he cherished flaunting his mere decades' affiliation among the multigenerational members.

The man had been James's godfather, but to Dana, he was charming, debonair, irreverent Toddy. Her stalwart support through those dark months after James's murder, when whispers had burst into full-bloomed gossip: the shooting wasn't merely due to a violent escalation of a custody case; James had been the primary target; the Canfield's twenty-five-year marriage wasn't as solid as they pretended.

She could have dismissed the speculation except for the small kernels of truth that had filtered into those stories. By the end, her charming, easygoing husband had morphed into a stranger. What was passionate had turned platonic, and his good humor had given way to a short temper.

I loved you, but during that final year I didn't know you.

Dear loyal Toddy had dispatched the stories with a fierce

1

vehemence that dared any rebukes. She couldn't have survived this past year after James's death without him. So she'd resigned herself to another meal at the club.

"Sure you won't try the cheesecake? Henri has outdone himself tonight." Toddy swiped the dessert fork from her place setting and cut off a small bite from his dessert. He extended the offering and winked.

She slid the fork from his grasp and set it on her own plate. "Avoiding the subject will not change the outcome."

"Might as well talk since my appetite's disappeared." Toddy glared at his plate before shoving it to one side. His expression brightened. "If it's those infernal gossips again, I'll handle them. A few words in the right ears." He wiggled his fingers. "Pow! Financial ruin."

"That's not necessary." The corners of her mouth twitched, spoiling the effect of the scolding look she sent in his direction.

"You're no fun." With a pout and a shrug, Toddy slumped back in his chair. "Let's hear the details."

"It's an incredible opportunity. Renovation of a four-block retail area on Providence Island. I fell in love with the area from the beginning."

She'd learned about the proposed revitalization project by chance, but afterwards couldn't stop thinking about it. The idea thrilled her and, at the same time, terrified her. Canfield Designs was a one-woman show, and the Main Street renovation would be the largest endeavor she'd ever handled.

She'd traveled to Providence Island, walked the Main Street area, shopped and chatted and explored. She'd polished her résumé and sent it off with a digital portfolio. When project architect Rhys McCall had contacted her a week later for an interview, her spirits had soared with an elation she hadn't felt since before James's death.

To her surprise, Rhys was only a few years older than her son Joshua. Rather than a sit-down interview, he'd escorted her on a tour of the area and explained the project in detail. He'd asked questions, sought her opinions, and challenged her answers.

She'd met each of those challenges, sharing sketches uploaded to her tablet to illustrate her points. The surprised look on his face had shifted to intrigued excitement. At the end of the interview, he'd extended his hand along with a job offer. She'd accepted on the spot.

If only she could make Toddy understand as easily. She met his concerned gaze with a smile. "I need to start living my life again."

His blue eyes clouded over with doubt. "Including selling the family home?"

"Toddy, we lived there seven years. It's not like it's been in the family for generations. It was too big for us, but James insisted."

"What about Joshua?"

"Joshua...." Grief strangled the edge of her composure, and her voice wobbled to silence.

Tall, handsome Joshua, with his runner's build and athletic grace, his quiet smile and quick wit. The curly haired moppet gripping her hand on the first day of kindergarten, the college graduate in cap and gown swinging her around in exuberant celebration.

The son who'd left a year ago without a word.

"He won't e-mail. He won't call. How could he not even come home for the funeral?" Another spark to the flames of gossip. She toyed with the handle of the cheesecake-laden fork. Nausea surged through her stomach, and she pushed the plate to one side. "I've lost both of them."

Toddy's hand closed over hers. "Whatever caused the fallout between him and James had to have been serious. Give Josh time. He'll come around." Toddy's silver hair glistened, the soft glow from the lights above haloing his head. "A boy always needs his mother."

Hope, ignited by Toddy's melodic tones, flickered briefly in Dana's chest. But like the magical voices he'd created for the storybook characters he'd read to Joshua long ago, the spell was temporary.

"How can I break through this impasse if I don't even know where he is? The police were no help. They said he was an adult and left voluntarily." She blinked back the tears swarming to the surface. "Every day I wonder if he's safe. Is he warm? Is he hungry?"

Toddy gave her hand a light squeeze, his firm grasp providing the anchor that had sustained her so many times over these past months. "Our boy is smart and strong, but he's also

3

stubborn. Maybe ashamed to come home, worried he wouldn't be welcomed."

"That's ridiculous. Every e-mail, every voice mail, I tell him how much I love him, how much I miss him."

"And you'll keep doing that until he believes in himself again." Toddy withdrew his hand and settled back in his chair.

"I'll never give up on him, but I can't put my life on hold either." She took a deep breath. "And I can't keep leaning on you."

His body stiffened. A second later, his expression crumpled and his voice thickened with his own grief. "It wasn't one-sided. I leaned on you as well."

"You've been my rock." Another deep breath. "But it's time I stand on my own again."

His mouth puckered in a brief pout. "But I'll miss you."

As adorable as Toddy could be, she couldn't succumb to his manipulations. "I'll miss you too. Thanks to your love and support, I have the strength to move ahead with my life."

"Well, damn my hide," he muttered, sliding his dessert plate back in front of him.

She hid a smile as Toddy raked the tines of his fork through the remainder of his cheesecake. His momentary pique ended with a jerk of his head.

"Sweetheart, are you sure this isn't a midlife crisis? Women have those too, you know."

Her jaw dropped. "Excuse me? I'm only forty-five." *And three-quarters.*

Toddy nodded. "Exactly. Current life expectancy for a female in this country is approximately eighty years. Forty-five is well into middle age."

Dana bit back a retort and reminded herself she loved the old coot. "It's not a midlife crisis. I need a good challenge, and this project is a godsend."

The lines on his face eased, and his head dipped in a brief nod. "There is one obstacle you might want to consider."

Dana glanced over her shoulder to the table he'd indicated.

Center stage in the dining room sat a coven of Harmony Hills socialites. Old money married to old money. Lineages going back to the settlement days of Hampton. Queens of society, purveyors of gossip, godmothers of Mean Girls.

Botoxed, highlighted, and hungry for drama. And over the past year, they'd fed steadily on James's death and its aftermath.

Until the wrath of Toddy had descended.

Dana turned back to Toddy, not wishing to risk eye contact with any of the women. "I'm happy to be leaving those witches behind. What's the problem?"

"Honey, have you been so involved with that little commerce street endeavor you've ignored the other construction taking place?"

A sick web of realization spidered across Dana's euphoria. She crumpled the linen napkin into a tight ball. If she could stop the words from coming out of Toddy's mouth, perhaps the ugly truth wouldn't be real.

"Vacation homes. Providence Island has become quite en vogue with that set." Toddy touched the corner of his napkin to his mouth, then sent a gentle smile in her direction. "Not too late for second thoughts."

Providence Island's shoreline came into view not long after the mainland coast of Virginia disappeared. Hands cupped around the wooden railing, Dana gazed at the churning waves as the ferry chugged through the water. The spray glistened, dancing momentarily before taking a bow back into the depths of the Atlantic. Beneath her feet, the metal deck swayed, and the morning's warm sunlight caressed her skin.

Leaving hadn't been as uneventful as planned. Toddy had pulled out every ploy during those months since her announcement. Debating if her decision was the result of unresolved grief versus a midlife crisis. Suggesting introductions to suitable gentlemen. Even offering to relocate his own business concerns.

Receiving no word from Joshua regarding her decision, she'd proceeded with the sale of the house. The deal had sped through escrow in record time. The furniture and other belongings had been shipped, sold, or stored.

The terminal came into clear view, and Dana pushed away from the railing and walked to her car, a sporty BMW convertible. After a final gaze at the approaching landfall, she settled into the vehicle. She'd lost count of the number of trips she'd made over these past few months for consultations and meetings. When she drove off the ferry this time, Providence Island, or PI, as it was called by the locals, would be home.

"Toddy, my dear, I don't need a therapist. I don't need a babysitter." She started the ignition, lowered the top on the convertible, and shifted into Drive. A chuckle escaped as she eased the car into the line for debarkation. "And I certainly don't need a man."

She shot a glance at the dashboard clock as she drove down the ramp. Doing well on time. The drive from the ferry to her office would take less than twenty minutes. She'd easily make the meeting with Rhys McCall for a final walk-through of her office and handoff of the keys.

Renovations to the building had been handled by McCall Construction. While Rhys owned his own architecture firm, he also seemed heavily involved with the construction company owned by his father. Though Rhys may not have intended to reveal any issues, hints of underlying tension between the two men had filtered into several of their discussions.

Something not uncommon when a father and son worked together.

Dana turned left out of the terminal facilities, choosing to take Ocean rather than the Old Main Street route. With the exception of Main Street, none of the other streets or roads had a designation after their names, an oddity she'd noticed during previous visits.

Halfway down Ocean, she braked for a red light. She tapped one thumb in an eager beat on the steering wheel and looked around. To the left, beyond the wrought-iron fencing and walking path, the tips of the ocean waves glistened diamond-like. She recognized by sight several dedicated walkers. To the right, the fitness center bustled with patrons. A warm rush of familiarity swept through her. PI was starting to feel like home.

On the opposite side of the cross street, the two overhead doors of a small garage were rolled up. A man stood between the entrances. Slightly spiked dark hair suggested he'd just rolled out of bed, and a day's growth of beard darkened his jaw. Tall and broad shouldered, he lingered in a hip-shot stance proclaiming he owned that piece of the sidewalk.

Hmm. Haven't seen him before. She glanced at the signal light, then back to the man. Might as well enjoy the scenery while she waited.

He took a deep swallow from the coffee mug wrapped in his left hand. A slow grin creased his lips as he pointed in her direction, right hand moving to his chest to play out a heartbeat motion.

What...? Garage... mechanic.... *Oh, right.*

She flashed a smile back at him. *Yes, I love my car too.*

The signal changed to green, and she accelerated. Once past the garage, she darted a quick glance in the mirror.

He'd stepped away from the building. Stood midway in the sidewalk, watching.

Car guys. Really.

Canfield Designs sat midway in the block between Ocean and Federal. Two stories tall, oxford white and renovated with subtle touches of art deco. She'd exchanged several spirited discussions with the work crew over that design choice. Rhys McCall had also voiced his doubts initially, but after viewing the final work, he'd admitted the building "popped" in a good way.

Standing on the sidewalk across the street, Dana pulled a digital camera from her tote bag and snapped several shots. Day One had to be commemorated.

She dropped the camera back into her leather tote, then glanced at her watch. Several minutes remained before she was due to meet with Rhys. Seeing his truck parked in front of a small brick building down the street reminded her of the text message he'd sent that morning.

Working at Carson's down the street. Call on way from ferry. Will meet you at your ofc.

In the excitement, she'd forgotten to call. Easy enough to walk over. A cool breeze carrying the faint scent of the ocean swept past her. Overhead, a seagull squawked. A bubble of laughter, so unexpected that she stopped in the walkway, rose in her throat.

Signs and symbols of her new life surrounded her, lifting her spirits and healing her soul. She was reborn, and it was time to charge into her new life.

Nick Warden watched until the vehicle turned out of sight. It wasn't the first time a car had bumped his pulse up a couple of beats. A BMW Z4 convertible would do that to any guy. But a woman jump-starting his heart the way that brunette just had? Too long to remember.

He had to admire a woman who didn't mind getting her hair a little messy. The wind had been on the mild side, but strong enough to toss those dark curls into a disarray he wouldn't mind seeing some early morning. Too far away to tell the color of her eyes. Not that he could have anyway with those oversized sunglasses she wore, but he figured they had to be brown. He hoped so. There was something gut-punching about a brown-eyed woman.

He walked to the back of the garage and set the near-empty coffee cup on the desk. The move to PI eighteen months ago along with the outlay for the garage had been more expensive than expected. He'd made up for it by converting the second floor to an apartment. The convenient location on Ocean helped build business faster than he'd expected, and a year-long contract with the sheriff's department for emergency call-outs added an additional tidy sum to the bottom line.

A contract due for renewal today.

Nick picked up the contract from the wire bin on the desk, then folded and tucked it into his back pocket. Slight bump in rates, nothing to boast about, but a solid income he could count on for the next year. More so if several of the other garages continued to opt out of their turns at rotation.

He'd planned to run it over to the sheriff's office at lunchtime. With only a few jobs on the day's schedule, no reason he couldn't take care of it now.

And see if the hot brunette is anywhere in sight?

Well… yeah.

He locked up the shop and cut through the back lot to the alley. The buildings on either side of the alley were high enough to block the wind off the ocean, but the brisk tang of salt drifted around him. Another plus for the garage's location. With both bay doors open, he had access to fresh air and a view of the water while he worked.

He rounded the corner onto Federal and came to a dead halt. The hot brunette was standing at the crosswalk a bare half-block ahead.

She was taller than he'd expected, slender but nicely curved. His mouth eased into a smile as the hem of her dress fluttered in the wind, teasing him with a glimpse of shapely thigh. She shifted a large tote—*What did women carry to need something that big?*—to her other shoulder and pressed her free hand against her dress to prevent a second exposure.

Damn it.

Traffic cleared with the exception of Abe Clancy's truck idling a half-block away. Strange to see the old guy in this part of town. His usual hangouts were in lower PI.

"Hey, Warden!" Sam Wallace's voice hailed him from the entrance to the Providence Island Sheriff's Department building. The lawman stood in the doorway, a wide grin on his face. "You gonna stand there all day soaking up the sunshine?"

Nick lifted one hand in response as he walked toward the entrance to the station. He drew even behind the woman, favoring her with one last glance as she stepped off the curb.

The rough cough of an out-of-tune engine shattered the stillness. Nick pivoted, glaring back at Clancy's truck.

What's that crazy fool...?

His breath caught as the vehicle leaped forward. The truck wasn't out of control. The increase in speed was too deliberate.

"Shit!"

Behind him, he heard a similar oath from Wallace.

Nick bolted forward and grabbed the woman's flailing arm as she tumbled into the path of the oncoming truck. He swung her into his arms and, with a slight stagger, backpedaled onto the sidewalk. The odor of burnt fuel polluted the air as the truck raced past them. The pickup shot through the next intersection, horns blaring in its wake.

A cry of distress dragged his attention back to the woman. Soft breath brushed the curve of his neck, and dark curls tickled the side of his face. The racing of her heartbeat matched the frantic pace of his own. Despite the fear that he could have been too slow, too late, he couldn't ignore she felt good—damn good—in his arms.

He lowered his brow onto those soft dark curls. "It's okay. You're safe."

Her trembling subsided, and her grip on his shoulders loosened. She stiffened, shifting enough to put a miniscule amount of space between their bodies. When she lifted her head, a faint blush feathered across her cheeks, and her eyes widened in what he suspected was recognition.

Brown eyes. He'd called that one right. Deep, dark brown eyes holding a myriad of mysteries he wouldn't mind exploring. Reluctantly, he broke their shared gaze as the sheriff joined them.

"Called out an BOLO on the truck. Crazy thing. Clancy reported it stolen about twenty minutes ago." His gaze shifted to the woman. "Mrs. Canfield, are you hurt? Do I need to call an EMT?"

Mrs. Canfield?

Nick glanced down as the woman pressed a palm against his shoulder. No ring on her left hand.

That same hand—without the ring—tapped his shoulder.

"You can put me down now."

If her eyes hadn't already hooked him, that caramel sweet voice surely would have. He shifted his weight, just enough to make her wrap her arms back around his neck, then met her startled gaze with a grin. "I'll hold on at least until we find your other shoe."

Running the gamut of emotion from terror to relief was enough to send any woman into shock. Finding herself in the arms of the handsome mechanic shattered the remainder of her composure. From twenty feet away, she'd found him attractive. Up close, he was devastating. Dark slashes for eyebrows, sharp cheekbones, and a mouth on the generous side of thin. Humor reflected in his tobacco-brown gaze, echoed by the slight crinkles around his eyes. And if her heartbeat still careened out of control, she credited it to the strong arms and broad chest that cradled her.

He might not meet Toddy's definition of a "suitable

gentleman," but he broke ten-plus on her personal scale.

"…shoe."

Shoe? She turned her head to see five toes tipped with Carnal Crimson reveling in their freedom. *Oh, wonderful….*

"By the way, I'm Nick—"

"How's the ankle feel? Looks like you twisted it when you started to fall." Sam Wallace approached, holding the missing shoe in his right hand. He leaned forward to examine her ankle. "Don't see any swelling, but let's have an EMT check it out to be sure."

Dana wavered. The time cushion she'd allowed herself before meeting Rhys was ticking away. On the other hand—foot—she didn't want to risk further injury. She rotated her ankle, relieved when only the slightest twinge followed the motion.

"Let me try standing."

Wallace lifted an eyebrow, but he set her pump onto the sidewalk. She swung her gaze from the sheriff to… She searched her scattered thoughts for the name he'd said just before being interrupted.

Nick.

It fit. Solid, sexy, strong….

Strong. Oh, good grief, how long had he been holding her? He had to be getting tired, though there was no wavering in his stance or the arms that embraced her. She shook those thoughts away. "I'm ready."

"No rush." The easygoing note in his voice allowed her to relax as he lowered her onto one foot. "I'll hold on until you get your balance."

She slid her foot into the shoe, paused, then stood firm on both feet. Slight twinge. Nothing major. Good to go.

She gave a nod. "It seems fine."

"If you're sure." With a final look at her ankle, Wallace held out her tote. Beside her, Nick lowered his hands and took a step back.

She took the bag from the sheriff's hand. "I'm certain. Thank you both."

"Nick's the hero." Sam nodded in the other man's direction, then pivoted toward the department building. "Take care, Mrs. Canfield. Nick, I'll see you inside."

She turned to face the man who'd rescued her. Her gaze swept over the broad chest that had nestled her seconds ago before traveling on to his face. Concern radiated from his dark eyes.

"Thank you seems so inadequate." Her heart thumped several hard beats as the reality of that close call set in. "You saved my life, or at least kept me from being injured."

He leaned his upper body forward in a slight bow, his mouth curving into a slow, easy smile. "I'd love to know your name."

The gentle teasing dissipated her lingering tension, and she extended her hand. "Dana Canfield. I'm here to work on the Main Street renovations."

Her hand nearly disappeared as he layered his other palm over hers for brief moment.

"Nick Warden." The crinkles around his eyes deepened. "I own a garage over on Ocean."

Her face grew warm as she recalled their flirtatious eye lock minutes ago. "Mr. Warden—"

"Nick."

"Nick, I feel horrible rushing off, but I'm late for an appointment." She started to stammer, then stopped herself. She never stammered, never rambled. Either the near miss by the truck or the close proximity of this man had scrambled her brains. "I'm truly grateful—"

"Understood. Maybe we'll run into each other again on one of your trips back here?" A smile tugged at one corner of his mouth.

If she hadn't made plans to move to PI before now, Nick's smooth as molasses tone would have been seductive enough to plant the idea in her head.

She tugged the strap of her tote bag onto her shoulder. "Actually I've moved to PI. I'm here for good."

He stood in that same hip-shot stance as she'd first seen him, hands shoved in his back pockets. His grin widened. "Well, this makes it my lucky day."

Whether he meant it or not, the light flirtation dissolved the lingering trauma of her close call. Even provoked her to feel a little daring. She favored him with a smile of her own before she turned to leave.

"My lucky day too."

Nick suspected Dana Canfield might not appreciate it if he watched until she safely made it to her destination. He settled instead for a slow stroll into the station, pausing by the front window until she entered the brick building at the end of the block. Once or twice she favored her left ankle but otherwise moved like a sleek gazelle.

His "lucky day" quip could have gotten him shot down in a heartbeat. Saving her life didn't necessarily mean she was open to breaking bread... or other endeavors. As it turned out, her saucy response left him grinning long after she'd walked away.

He paused at the front desk to take the visitor pass Sam's secretary, Molly Kincaid, held out to him. "Go on back. Sam's expecting you."

Nick clipped the pass onto the pocket of his jeans as he made his way to the sheriff's office. He tapped on the open door and, receiving an answering wave, entered. He pulled the contract from his pocket and dropped it onto Wallace's desk before seating himself.

"Mrs. Canfield get on her way?" Sam asked as he smoothed out the pages.

"She was walking okay, but she'll probably be sore tomorrow."

"Sorry we couldn't bump up the rate a little more." Sam retrieved a pen from the desk caddy. He scrawled his name onto the document, then extended the pen to Nick. "Thanks for taking those extra call-outs."

"Not a problem. Helps me out too." He took the pen and flipped the contract to face himself. "Any word on Clancy's truck?"

"Not so far. Anything that loud and ugly can't stay hidden for long. We're heading into Senior Week, so we might start seeing a rush of incidents."

Nick scowled as he signed his name. "I don't call a near hit-and-run a prank."

"No, but I figure the driver saw me and panicked." Sam heaved a disgusted grunt. "Regardless of what he intended, his actions put Mrs. Canfield in danger along with other drivers."

"Mrs. Canfield mentioned moving here to work on the Main Street renovations." Nick met Sam's curious stare with a blank expression. He knew how to bluff at cards. With cops too, when necessary.

Sam picked up the discarded pen, twirling it between his fingers. "That renovated building down the street is her office, and she bought a house over on Magnolia." He held out a hand for the signed contract, then pushed his chair away from the desk. "Let's head up front so Molly can make a copy for you."

Nick rose, mulling over the news as he followed the sheriff out of his office. The houses on Magnolia were large family homes. Mrs. Canfield might not be married, but she might be a *mom.*

Good thing he liked kids.

Sam paused at Molly's desk. "Make a copy for Mr. Warden, please." He turned back to face Nick. "Seems like a nice lady. Shame about her husband."

"What happened to her husband?"

"Shooting victim. Wrong place, wrong time. Happened about a year ago." Sam gave a slight shrug. "It got some press because Canfield was an attorney."

Shot. Holy hell. Stunned by the news, he barely registered when Molly returned, holding out the stapled set of papers. "Here's your copy, Nick."

"Looks like we're good for another year," Sam said.

"Looks like." With a nod, Nick headed toward the exit. He walked to the end of the block and paused at the mouth of the alley. Had the driver panicked when he'd seen the sheriff, not caring about the pedestrian in his path?

Wrong place, wrong time.

Maybe not.

Chapter Two

Dana paused outside Carson's Pizza and Sandwich Shop to study the brick structure. The restaurant occupied a sweet piece of real estate, where the end of the downtown business section fed into the Main Street retail area. The red-and-white striped awning and black ironwork projected a unique appeal compared to the more traditional structures along the street. The other exception being her own building.

She glanced back across the street. Her rescuer was nowhere in sight. She groaned, remembering her impetuous response to his teasing remark. She owed him more than a hasty thank you, but what? An idea bloomed in her mind, and her lips curled into a smile. *Perfect.* She made a mental note to take care of that task after meeting with Rhys.

Dana pushed the door open and stepped inside. The room was unfurnished with the exception of a semicircular counter extending from one wall. A workbench sat to one side, several tools neatly organized across the top shelf.

"Sorry, we're not open yet." A young woman stood behind the counter flipping through the pages of a thick catalog. She grinned and gestured to the nearly empty surroundings. "Obviously."

The friendly humor sent a warm welcome rushing through her. "I'm looking for Rhys McCall. He said he would be

15

working here today. We're supposed to meet at my new office down the street. I'm—"

"Dana Canfield." Brown hair shot with cinnamon swung around the woman's slender shoulders as she circled from behind the counter. "I was supposed to remind him fifteen minutes ago to meet you. I'll let him know you're here. By the way, I'm Paige Carson."

"Nice to meet you, Paige." She set her tote onto the floor next to the workbench. "I take it this is your restaurant?"

"Work in progress, but all mine." Her smile faded as she took a step back. "I know you'll be busy with Main Street, but are you available for consultations?"

Dana gazed around the expanse. With setting up a new office and home plus Main Street, her spare time would be miniscule. Still, the nearly blank canvas cried out to her designer soul for some TLC. She nodded. "I didn't have immediate plans to do so, but I can schedule some time for you."

A whoosh of relief passed through Paige's lips. "I can't afford more than a consultation. Maybe ten minutes?"

Dana burst out laughing. "Can we cover everything that quickly?"

"No, but if you can suggest a fix to the problem I have with Glaser's regarding my booths, I'll be happy."

Dana bit back a retort at the name of the commercial furniture company. While she'd never caught the vendor crossing the line of ethical behavior, she'd fought several battles when Glaser had blurred the boundary close to obscurity. Helping Paige would be a pleasure.

"How about a trade for the consultation?"

A cunning gleam flickered in the girl's eyes. "You mean food?"

Dana laughed. "I'll keep that in mind, but I was thinking more along the lines of advertising. A small sign with my company name in the window during the remodeling. A blurb on your menus. My business cards at the front counter." She opened her tote and pulled out an electronic tablet. "How about tomorrow, nine o'clock? I'll need to see your paperwork with Glaser."

With Paige's agreement, she tapped a reminder into her calendar. She placed the tablet back in the tote, then withdrew two business cards from a side pocket. "One for you. On the other, give me your cell number in case I need to reschedule."

Paige scribbled her number onto the card. "Call me if you need a helper for unpacking. I'm a firm believer in the barter system."

"She's paying me in pizza and beer." A male voice called out from the open doorway just beyond the counter.

The metal door swung shut as the tall, dark-haired man crossed the room in a long-legged stride. "Dana, I apologize. Lost track of time."

Dana returned Rhys McCall's welcoming smile. "I was delayed as well. I saw your truck out front and decided to walk over."

"I know you're eager to see your office. If you're ready, let's head over." He turned to address Paige. "The exit lights should be delivered this afternoon. I'll be back tomorrow to install them."

Dana lifted her tote from the floor. "Paige, call me if you need to reschedule."

"I'll be here." Paige bounced on her toes, tapping the card in her hand. Her smile held a lightness that had been missing when Dana had first arrived at Carson's.

From previous conversations, she'd learned Rhys was doing a great deal of the work on Paige's restaurant. If taking on some of the design work would lessen the load on his time, the Main Street project would benefit as well. And she'd get the opportunity to help Paige avoid future mishaps, such as the one she suspected was occurring with Glaser.

PI was home now, and she wasn't about to let Glaser or anyone else take advantage of her new neighbors.

Dana and Rhys stopped in front of the private parking lot next to Dana's office. A low stone wall ran along the frontage with an iron gate spanning the entrance. A twinge shot through her ankle as she stopped, making her wobble. Rhys's hand shot out, cupping her elbow as his gaze scanned the sidewalk for an obstruction.

"Are you all right?"

She held back a sigh. What the heck. Might as well tell the entire story rather than look like a klutz. "It happened earlier on my way to the restaurant. Someone stole a Mr. Clancy's truck. When the driver saw Sheriff Wallace, he gunned the truck down the street, which I happened to be crossing at the time. Other than a slight wrench to my ankle, I'm fine."

"Not the best start to your first day living on PI. If you're sure you're okay…." With her answering nod, he lowered his hand from her elbow, then gestured to the building beside them.

"Remotes for the gate are on your desk inside. The back entrance is controlled by an electronic lock. The key cards are on your desk as well." He slid his sunglasses onto the top of his head. "Thank you for agreeing to help Paige. After your consult, you might want to hold out for at least a pizza or two."

She glanced in the direction of Carson's. "She's a good friend, isn't she?"

"The best." His features relaxed, and she discerned a gentle fondness in his eyes. "We grew up together. She's been my best friend for almost as long as I can remember… and she makes great pizza."

"I'll definitely consider that with any future negotiations. So, what next?"

"I've been covering for my father while he's been on an extended leave. He returned this week, and I'll begin transitioning his work functions back to him." His attention shifted to a point behind her. "Speaking of my dad—"

A sense of familiarity shot through Dana as she watched the man approach. The flicker of recognition had to be due to the familial resemblance. Though their features differed, and the older man's hair was shot with gray, father and son shared the same tall, lean physique. His eyes, hidden behind aviator-style shades, may or may not have been the same dark green as his son's. The gleaming smile aimed at Rhys dissolved into a scowl in her direction.

"What's going on?" Gravel harsh, his voice teemed with suspicion.

Grateful for the sunglasses hiding her reaction, Dana shifted her gaze to Rhys. Other than a brief lifting of one brow, the young man maintained a calm demeanor.

"Dana, this is my father, Erik McCall. Dad, this is Dana

Canfield, the designer on the Main Street project. She'll also be working on the redesign of our building."

Dana extended her hand. "I'm pleased to meet you, Mr. McCall. I'm looking forward—"

McCall's hand remained at his side. His lips twisted into a thin line as he jerked his head toward the building beside them. "If this monstrosity is any indication of your taste and talent, I don't want any part of it. My advice? Sell the place and go back where you came from. As for Main Street, you're fired." He shot a final glare at Rhys. "My office, five minutes."

Dana's mouth dropped open as she stared at the man's retreating form. Her stomach churned, and a cold sweat swept over her body. Her new office. A house she'd yet to occupy. Leaving everything behind for this move. Would she lose it all the very first day?

She gave herself a quick mental jolt. *Get a grip, Dana. You have a signed contract, and Erik McCall is not the one calling the shots.* She looked at Rhys for his response.

He stood, hands on hips, staring at his father, already halfway up the block. A ruddy hue stained the back of his neck. When he turned to face her, the tightness around his mouth dissolved. "I apologize. I have no idea what brought on that reaction. I assure you, your contract stands, and the project continues as planned. However, I do need to clarify certain matters with my father."

The last vestige of her panic faded away. "There's no need for you to apologize for his actions."

His shoulders relaxed, though the apology she said was unnecessary still reflected in his eyes. He pulled a set of keys from his shirt pocket, jingling them in one hand. "Would you mind doing the walk-through yourself and noting anything that needs to be corrected? If there's anything urgent, you can call Jake Matthews."

Dana smiled at the name of the burly foreman who'd managed the renovations on the building. His "little lady" attitude had quickly morphed into admiring respect when he realized she had more than a layman's knowledge of construction.

"I don't mind at all." She extended her hand for the keys. "I have Jake's number in my phone if needed."

19

Rhys hesitated a second before dropping the key ring into her palm. "Do you have plans for those empty offices on the second floor?"

She shook her head. "No immediate plans. Why do you ask?"

"I'd like to rent one of them." Before she could speak, Rhys continued. "It makes sense since we'll be working together. Everything under one roof."

She understood immediately. "How about meeting back here tomorrow? Other than an appointment with Paige at nine, I should be here all day."

"Perfect." He flashed her a small smile before taking off after his father.

She watched him for a moment, then walked to the door of the building. Obviously, more than mere differences of opinion existed between the two men. Erik McCall showed no hesitation in insulting her or disrespecting his son in public. It was possible they'd caught him in a bad mood, but she doubted it. That abrupt reaction seemed too natural to be a momentary lapse in manners or business etiquette.

Up until the time Joshua had walked away, she'd never witnessed anything other than a loving relationship between him and his father. Whatever had caused the estrangement between them, she knew James had grieved over the separation. Now James was dead, Joshua was somewhere unknown, and their relationship could never be repaired.

Whatever was going on between the McCalls had to be fixed. If not, the Main Street project might be doomed from the start.

Early in the interview process for the Main Street project, Rhys had realized finding a designer to complement his vision without diluting it would be a challenge. Although Dana Canfield had presented an extensive portfolio, she possessed little experience in that type of project. And yet, only minutes into the interview, he'd recognized she was the best candidate.

"Art and science. Science to make it safe and solid. Art to make it breathe and live." Her eyes had sparkled as they'd toured the retail area.

"So much history and tradition. It needs a strategy and some TLC to bring it back to glory."

It came down to heart, and with each word, each observation she'd made, he'd known Dana was the perfect fit for the job.

So what the hell was his father's problem?

Rhys halted in front of the headquarters for McCall Construction. The two-story structure was painted the same oxford white as many of the other buildings along the street but was trimmed in a dark vintage blue that his father claimed denoted stability and trust. Stone flowerboxes, filled with blood red geraniums, flanked either side of the front entrance.

Definitely not art deco.

He jogged up the front steps, through the door, and across the width of the lobby. With a one-handed wave to the receptionist, he bounded up the staircase to the second floor. He let the heavy tread of his footsteps announce his arrival as he entered his father's office.

Hands in his pockets, Erik turned from the window. Anger lingered in the stiff set of his shoulders. "I told you five minutes." He walked to his desk and, with a grunt, lounged back in the plush leather chair.

"I was handing off the keys to Mrs. Canfield's building." He held up a hand in warning. "Yes, she's staying."

"Where do you get off deciding to renovate our office space?" Irritation bristled across Erik's lean features. "I own this building. You don't make changes without my approval."

Rhys bit back the response burning at the end of his tongue. Damned if he'd stand like a schoolboy summoned to the principal's office. He bypassed the guest chairs and settled on the couch, forcing his father to turn to face him.

"I returned to help you keep McCall Construction out of bankruptcy. Not long after I get it back on track, you take off for several months. I still don't have the full story behind that. As for the remodel, it's a capital expense. I approved it because I needed the work space and had the authority to do so."

"You agreed to come back after I allowed you a percentage of my company—"

"For which I paid market price." His insistence on partial ownership had proved to be a wise decision. Today being a prime example.

Erik waved a dismissing hand. "Now you want more? Erase all my hard work to put your stamp on everything? Not going to happen, son. I'm back, and you have only the authority I give you. As for that damn woman, where the hell was your brain?" His fist gaveled the desktop. "You want to pay someone to pick out paint colors, get Stacy to do it. She's on the payroll. Keep the money in-house."

"This animosity seems a bit personal." Rhys narrowed his eyes. "Do you know Mrs. Canfield?"

Anger flickered in Erik's gray eyes. "This is about your lack of respect. As for that woman, don't know her, don't want to know her. Get rid of her."

Rhys pushed to his feet and paced to the front of the desk. He leaned forward, palms pressed against the glossy surface. "You know what, Dad? The Main Street contract isn't with McCall Construction. It's with McCall Architecture. Hiring contractors is my decision, which means as far as this project is concerned…" He paused, knowing that his next words would be taken as a declaration of war. "…you work for me."

Erik bolted from his chair, his face white with fury. "You'd put that woman ahead of the family business?"

"I hired Mrs. Canfield in good faith, and I'll honor my word." Rhys straightened, stepping back. "And the office renovations? No longer an issue. I've found somewhere else to work."

He wheeled and walked away.

"Rhys, get back here! Damn it, boy, I'm talking to you!"

The tirade followed him down the corridor, fading away as he entered the back stairwell. He paused on the landing, struggling with his father's vehement reaction to Dana. If it even was about her. Knowing his father's temperament, the cause had more to do with not being in control.

Not this time, Dad. He'd worked too hard to restore McCall Construction to financial security, and he wasn't about to let his father's ego put the Main Street project in jeopardy.

Dana leaned back in the executive chair in her office. She'd completed the walk-through this morning without adding a single entry to the punch list. A first in all her years of experience. If her building was any indication of the work Rhys's crew could perform, the Main Street project was destined for success.

On paper, it hadn't made sense pulling her business from the mainland for what was a limited length project. In reality, moving to PI gave Canfield Designs an aura of exclusivity. She was setting the rules this time. With the vacation-home construction Toddy mentioned, she might pick up new clients sooner than expected.

The incident this morning with Erik McCall was a mere blip. Same typical behavior as with other ill-tempered contractors she'd dealt with in the past. She knew the type all too well. This morning's encounter had taken her by surprise, but going forward, she'd set Mr. McCall firmly in his place.

She arranged a thank-you gift for Nick Warden, then spent more time than she could spare debating her selection. Would he find it amusing? Ridiculous? Or rather a pathetic plea for attention?

Don't be silly. He flirted first. Show him you're interested.

Am I?

She groaned and dropped her head into her hands. For years, she'd maneuvered through society and business, both with their own rules of etiquette, rarely making a misstep. Now, she was dithering over a simple thank-you gift.

For a man who was anything but ordinary.

For reasons she wasn't quite ready to admit.

"For Heaven's sake, this isn't getting anything done." She'd made a decision—right or wrong. Done. Just one more thing to do before getting back to work.

Call Toddy.

Not a text. Not an e-mail. Nothing less than a personal call would be acceptable to Toddy, and she reached for the desk phone. After a short round of second-thought denials and a strong affirmation of her choices, she ended their exchange with a promise to call again in a few days.

She stretched, heaving a giant yawn as she returned the receiver to the cradle. "Oh, Toddy, I love you, but sometimes you wear me out."

The alarm on her cell phone chimed. Time to meet the realtor at her new house. She slipped on her shoes and pushed out of the chair, wincing slightly. Between the near fall this morning and unpacking her office this afternoon, her muscles protested the sudden move.

She flipped off the lights and closed the door. A soft golden glow from the afternoon sun bathed the reception area. All was quiet and calm. Perfect... for now. She couldn't wait for the first scuff mark on the lobby tiles, smudges on the glossy surfaces of the tables, phones ringing. All the signs proving Canfield Designs was open for business.

A cast-iron hummingbird sat on a small table just outside her private office, an impulse purchase she'd made the day of her interview for good luck. She gave the statue a fond pat before heading to the back exit. "You had your work cut out for you today, didn't you?"

The graceful symmetry of the Federal style house had captured Dana's heart at first sight. Set back from the two-lane road by a circular driveway, the brick home included clapboard siding and a wide front porch with an intricate wrought-iron railing.

Four bedrooms, two and a half baths, dining room, breakfast nook, patio, bricked-in garden with pool. Inside, a bounty of work awaited, some required, some cosmetic.

What were you thinking?

I thought it looked like home.

Even if home was one person, she could make this house a haven. Toddy, no doubt, would hoot with laughter, especially in light of her concerns about James's insistence on buying an oversized house.

The realtor pulled into the driveway, parking behind her BMW. April Davis, a tall, slender blonde, exited the car. Clad in a cream-colored suit and her hair caught back in a simple knot, she looked cool and elegant.

"No buyer's remorse, I hope?" April asked as they walked up the brick steps to the front door.

Dana restrained the majority of her sigh. "No remorse, but

I'm feeling a little overwhelmed."

"I can't imagine setting up an office and a house all at once." April gestured toward the doorway. "If it helps, your furniture arrived yesterday. I made sure the movers placed everything according to your instructions, and all the boxes are in the rooms as marked."

Yes! Relief ran a victory lap through her veins at the news. She held out her hand as April dropped a collection of keys into her cupped palm. "You are my new best friend."

She unlocked the door and stepped across the threshold. The late afternoon sun shone through the stained-glass fanlight over the front door, bathing the foyer in multicolored bands of light.

"You're wearing the 'I'm home' look," April said as she closed the door behind her. "That look lets me know I've done my job."

Hands pressed to her chest, Dana spun around to face the other woman. "Oh, I am home. And thank you for not letting me talk myself out of this."

April waved a delicate hand. "You knew it was meant for you the moment you saw it." She took another glance around, then nodded. "In case you didn't have time to shop for groceries, I picked up a few things at the deli. Shrimp salad, cheese, crackers, bottle of wine."

The unexpected kindness stunned Dana. The last thing on her mind had been groceries. Warmed by April's generosity, she gave in to a sudden rush of impulsiveness. "Stay and have dinner with me. You can be my first guest."

April's slight hesitation turned into a warm smile. "I would love to join you for dinner."

Dana kicked off her shoes, then headed toward the kitchen. She waved a hand over her head for the other woman to follow. "You mentioned you've been here only a few months?"

"About six weeks. Growing up, I spent summer breaks here visiting my grandparents. PI was as much my home as Fredericksburg."

Dana pulled the salad and cheese from the refrigerator. Her eyes widened at the collection of tableware April began unpacking from a basket sitting on the island countertop. "You brought china?"

April stared at her for a moment, then resumed setting plates, silverware, glasses, and napkins into position. "I knew you'd return them. I certainly wouldn't expect you to eat off paper and plastic. Especially not the dessert I brought."

A familiar craving tickled her stomach. "Chocolate?"

April laughed as she glided onto a barstool. "Of course. Decadently so with whipped cream and raspberries."

"You really are my new best friend." Dana poured a glass of wine and handed it to the woman. She poured one for herself then slid onto a stool.

April smiled. "I'm earning points toward getting you to work me into your schedule once I find a house."

Her house, her office. Carson's, Main Street. What was one more project? "Where are you living now?"

April rolled her eyes. She even did that elegantly. "My parents' vacation home."

Dana's fork hit the side of her mouth, and a morsel of shrimp plummeted onto her plate. Toddy's warning echoed in her mind. Was April's mother a member of the Harmony Hills coven? No Davises that she could remember, though that probably was April's married name.

She dabbed her lips with the peach linen napkin. "Do your parents visit here often?"

"They'll be here in a week or two and stay for part of the summer. I'm staying there only until I find *the* house. My son Kevin moved here as well. It'll be nice having all of us together again."

Dana struggled to push aside the sharp pang shooting through her heart as April chattered on about *location, location, location.* April's son was here with her while Dana's son was... wherever.

Would you have moved here, Josh? Shared this new life with me? She shook the treacherous thoughts away and forced her attention back to the conversation.

April's casual laughter confirmed her lapse had not been noticed. "Short-term for that living arrangement is probably best for everyone's sake."

The wine must have kicked in. Dana changed the subject before April could share any more observations of her family dynamics. "Tell me what you envision for your house. I'd love to start getting ideas together."

Dana walked through the main floor of the house, checking locks and flipping off lights. In each room, stacks of boxes waited for her attention. She walked up the stairs and entered her bedroom. Ignoring the boxes lining one wall, she went through her nighttime routine. Living out of a suitcase would work for one more day.

From the beginning of her house hunting, she and April had formed an immediate connection, strengthened tonight by their impromptu dinner. April seemed eager for friendly company as well.

Grabbing her tablet from the side table, Dana sank down onto the chaise lounge. Flipping open the cover, she logged into her e-mail account and began to type. She kept the tone light, encouraging. Just as she'd done all those years he'd been away at college.

Hi Josh. I made it here to PI. See, I'm already sounding like a native. My office is gorgeous. It's quite a change working on a project like this, but it feels great to be a part of something that affects so many people. Years from now, I'll look at that street and know I'm part of its history. The house is larger than what I need, but I love it. It'll be a work in progress for some time. Can't wait for you to see it. Let me know how you're doing.

I miss you.
Love always, Mom

She closed the cover and rose with a sigh. "Josh, where are you?"

Moments later in bed, she stretched, wincing as several sore muscles reminded her of her close call and the man who'd rescued her. She didn't have second thoughts about coming to PI.

But a man in her life?

That decision deserved reconsideration.

Chapter Three

"Totally unacceptable answer, Mark. Glaser is eight weeks overdue with the delivery. An additional six weeks is out of the question." Dana nodded in thanks as Paige set a cup of coffee in front of her. "According to the purchase order, cancellation without penalty hits at forty-five days if delivery is not met. We're canceling the order, and my client wants her deposit refunded in full."

Paige snorted. Dana shot a warning glance across the table, and the girl slapped both hands over her mouth as her eyes sparkled with suppressed laughter.

"Forest green in three weeks? What's the price?" She ignored Paige's furious nodding. "That's not a discount, Mark. That's a discontinued line, according to your catalog."

Dana held the phone away from her ear as a furious retort blasted the air. She took a sip of coffee and when the line fell silent, returned the phone to her ear. "E-mail the confirmation to my client, and cc me. She'll expect her deposit to be returned to her account within the next fifteen days, as specified in the contract."

She hid a smile as Paige bit her lip and swiveled on the stool. "I'm living on PI now, working on the Main Street renovations. We can have a conversation about that after this order is resolved."

Dana concluded the call with a few pleasantries, then

expelled a deep breath. "Sorry for cutting you off, Paige. I wanted to keep the pressure on until he agreed to process the refund."

Paige clasped her hands together, propping them under her chin. Her face glowed with admiration. "I want to be you. Teach me to be you!"

Dana chuckled at the enthusiastic praise. "All in good time. While you were delayed this morning, it gave me time to research alternatives. Look over the items I've marked in those catalogs, especially the table and chair options. You'll have greater flexibility with seating and large events if you opt for tables rather than booths. Also, check the brochure from Morgan's Woodworks here on PI. The cost is a little higher, but you'll save on shipping and delivery. Plus, no installation."

"At least something is going right this morning." Paige looked up from flipping the pages in one of the catalogs. "If the garage guy tries to snow me with my car, will you Canfield him for me?"

Canfield? Dana thought it over, decided she liked it. "Didn't you say it was a dead battery?"

"That's what I thought and what he suggested. I didn't have time to wait. I gave him the keys, told him to call if there was anything else. I rode my bike over here this morning."

Dana lifted one eyebrow. Paige's shoulders slumped in response. "I *know.* I should have gotten it in writing, but I was in a hurry. You were waiting."

Kids. Excuses. "I was at my office unpacking. Not a problem if I'd had to wait."

A rush of air swept through the room. Paige bounced to her feet, her gaze aimed toward the front of the building. "There he is."

"I'm here if you need me," Dana murmured as the girl raced away.

Nick tapped "Print" on the monitor to generate the statement for Paige Carson's Jeep.

The emergency call had come in moments before he was scheduled to open. He'd immediately recognized the area where the address was located. An older residential neighborhood midway south toward the Point. He'd looked at houses there before deciding to convert the upper floor of the garage to an apartment.

By the time he'd pulled up in front of the cottage, the girl had worked herself into a frenzy. He'd wavered between sympathy and amusement. Sympathy over her obvious distress; amusement when she tossed the keys to him, shouted an address, then hopped onto a ten-speed and pedaled away.

He should have called her back. Could have left the car sitting until she'd had time to deal with the details. He would have done exactly that except…

…except she reminded him way too much of his daughter.

Or stepdaughter, as his ex-wife Callie insisted now that she was remarried—again—and living halfway across the country.

Noticing he'd omitted the towing charge, he tapped the touch screen again, then paused a second before lowering his hand. The drop-off address she'd given him was just a few blocks from the garage. Close enough to walk over for a quick lunch once the restaurant opened. No doubt the girl had a pretty penny invested in opening her business, and anything more than a dead battery had to be bad news.

Give the kid a break.

He'd deliver the car, but make it clear to her drop-offs weren't part of his usual service.

He folded the statement and tucked it into his shirt pocket. Standing up, he nabbed the key ring from the pegboard on the wall. A figure appeared in the left bay entrance as he was reaching for the remote to close the doors.

Macy Montgomery strolled into the garage, clipboard in one hand, a mixed floral arrangement in the other. "Hey, Mr. Warden. Delivery for you."

He considered the colorful arrangement through a narrowed-eyed gaze. "I think you have the wrong place, Macy."

"Nope. Nick Warden. Warden's Garage." Her arm shot out. "Wanna take these for me?" She didn't give him a chance to refuse and shoved the container into his hands.

The earthy scent of a summer day filled his senses with a riotous bloom of daisies and carnations clustered in the bed of a…. He hefted the container to eye level.

1950 Ford Thunderbird.

"Cool, huh?" Macy said. "It'll make a great keepsake after the flowers die."

He gave the front tires a gentle spin with his forefinger. Cool indeed.

"Secret admirer?"

He set the car on his desk, then pulled his wallet from his back pocket. "Ah—probably from my daughter Megan."

Macy's right eyebrow quirked upward. "Sure. I do things like that for my dad all the time."

Nick returned the skeptical gesture and held out a bill. "I'm certain you do."

She tucked the tip into her pocket, laughter trailing behind her as she departed.

He pressed the button to close the front bay doors, then sat back down at the desk. A gentle tap sent the car into an experimental glide across the desk into his cupped hand. The flowers swayed in a subtle reprimand as he tapped the car into a reverse path.

Yeah, cool.

He pulled the card from the plastic pick and slid it out of the envelope. At least the flowers were generic enough to avoid being girly. The car though was primo. After all, who knew him better than—

Dana?

He rolled back in the chair, a wide grin stretching across his lips. *Looks like I'll be making a stop at the Canfield building.*

The door swung open with a touch of his hand. Nick walked into Carson's, pushing his sunglasses to the top of his head. Nice brickwork on the walls, refinished wooden floors, and—his heart thumped up a notch—Dana seated at a table toward the back of the room.

He took an automatic step in her direction, halting when the spitfire from this morning bounced up to greet him. "Tell me it's not bad news."

"Problem was the battery." He unfolded the work order, flipping the paper to the opposite side. "You're coming due for an oil change and the tire treads are worn, plus some routine maintenance is needed. I noted all of it on the back of the bill. Wherever you take it, don't let them talk you into a lot of unnecessary work. The Jeep's parked in the lot next to the building."

He handed her the invoice, shooting a glance toward the back of the room as Paige read the list of needed maintenance. She turned over the paper, and her whoosh of relief made him smile.

"Not bad. Hold on while I get my checkbook." She whirled, headed toward the door to the kitchen, then stopped. "You take checks, right?"

"Yeah, I'll take a check." He held back a grin. "If it bounces, I'll take it out for trade in lunches."

Paige blinked, her expression as bewildered as he'd hoped. A nervous laugh escaped through her parted lips. "That's funny. Sure. Not a problem... I mean, there won't be a problem... with the check."

"Good enough." He nodded to the table in the back. "Mind if I get some of that coffee?"

After one last curious look, she pushed the swinging door to the kitchen open and called over one shoulder. "Help yourself."

Nick strolled to the worktable. A coffeemaker, cups, and other accessories shared the space with a small assortment of pastries and fruit. As he poured two cups of coffee, he realized Dana wasn't ignoring him. She was just that engrossed in whatever was on that screen propped up in front of her.

She looked as good as she had the day before. The sweater and slacks didn't leave as much exposed as the dress she'd worn yesterday, but what he saw didn't disappoint him. Dark curls, pinned up, revealed the delicate line of her neck. She'd kicked off her shoes, and with a twist of his head, he spied the dark red polish decorating each toe.

Sweet.

"Looks like you need a refill," he said, setting one of the cups before her.

Her head jerked up, eyes widening in recognition. "Mr. Warden—"

"Nick." He hooked a foot around the empty stool, tugged it in front of him, then sat down. "Any woman who sends me flowers gets to call me by my first name."

A light pink tinged her cheeks. "Do many women send you flowers?"

"You're the first." He leaned forward, resting his forearms on the table. "So, when I thank you for the flowers, I guess we're even?"

The teasing light in her eyes faded. "What you did—"

He touched the tips of his fingers lightly, briefly against the back of her hand. "Thank you for the flowers. And the T-Bird."

"It seemed to fit." She puckered her lips and blew on the coffee, momentarily mesmerizing him as she took that first sip. "Did the sheriff locate Mr. Clancy's truck?"

"Not that I've heard." Her concern for a stranger's stolen property surprised him. Not many people would care, let alone think to ask. "How's the ankle?"

"Slight twinge ever so often, but other than that, good as ever."

"Good to hear. Sam mentioned the building down the street was your office. Sounds like you're settling in."

A dimple flashed in her right cheek. "That's the plan."

Spotting Paige returning to the main room, Nick stood. As much as he wanted to linger, he had three jobs scheduled, and the clock was ticking. "Dana, would you like to get together some time for coffee?"

A startled expression flickered across her face, and he recalled Wallace's comment about Dana being a recent widow. *Slow it down.* He reined in his disappointment, replacing it with a tip of his head toward the cups on the table. "We just did that, didn't we? I'll think of something else for the next time."

"In that case..." Dana reached into that humungous bag sitting on the floor by her feet. She pulled out a small white card and held it out to him. "Hold on to this while you're thinking."

Business card... with her phone number. Renewed hope kicked any doubts to the side of the road. Yeah, she was interested.

He slipped the card into his shirt pocket, giving it a one-two pat. "Right next to my heart."

Dana set another empty box in the hallway. The lobby and reception area were organized, and she'd managed to add the finishing touches to the office upstairs for Rhys.

She strolled back to the reception area, pausing to study the room. A cream-colored, wrap-around couch butted against an accent wall of peacock blue. A still life of a magnolia branch hung above the sofa, the gold frame echoing the metal sculpture of leaves on an adjoining wall. A large black and gold clock and a pair of art deco sconces broke the expanse of ivory on a third wall.

The area was exactly what she'd envisioned. Filled with serenity and luxury, a place to make clients feel inspired but not intimidated.

She walked across the room and sank down onto the sofa, reveling in a moment of relaxation. With so much to plan, so much to do, she didn't expect her thoughts to travel to Nick Warden. Seeing him again had been an unexpected surprise.

And a pleasure.

She couldn't remember the last time a smile came so immediately to her lips. Some men would have been embarrassed by a gift of flowers. Nick, on the other hand, seemed appreciative. The keepsake car might have played into that reaction. Still....

Her respite ended as the front door opened, and a young blonde-haired woman entered the lobby. She halted, her gaze traveling around the open space. "This room is... wow."

Dana rose with a laugh, savoring the uninhibited response. "Thank you. I'm Dana Canfield. How may I help you?"

"My name is Jamie Danvers." The girl took a deep breath and pulled a sheet of paper from her tote. "I'm checking if you have any job openings. I have a degree in Art. I have office experience. I'm great on a computer, and I'm willing to run personal errands."

Dana took the paper from the slightly trembling hand and scanned the entries. Limited work history, most of it in the service industry, next to no experience in the design field. A staffing agency would have tossed the paper immediately, missing several important aspects Dana detected.

"I see your Art degree focused on marketing. Do you have a portfolio I could review?"

Jamie's shoulders sagged. "I didn't bring it with me."

Dana lifted one hand in reassurance. "Those cases are bulky. No need to carry one unnecessarily. I do have an open position. I'd like to discuss the specifics of the job in relation to your résumé and portfolio."

The girl's face blossomed with excitement. "My case is in my car. I'm parked a couple blocks away. I can run over and get it now."

"No rush. I'll be here at least another hour." Dana picked up one of her business cards from a pewter tray on a side table and handed it to Jamie. "If you're delayed or need to reschedule, call me, and we'll set up a meeting for another time."

"I'll be back in less than fifteen." She turned toward the door, then paused. A hopeful smile crossed her lips. "Thank you so much."

The door closed behind her. Dana watched through the window as the girl raced down the street.

Returning to the couch, she read over the résumé in closer detail, noting items to address during the interview. A shadow passed across the front windows. She looked up to see Rhys lifting a hand in greeting. Seconds later, he entered the building. He stopped to clean his shoes in a two-step shuffle on the entry mat before crossing the room in several long strides.

"Just the guy I wanted to see."

Immediate concern etched across his face. "Something wrong?"

"Not at all." She gestured toward the couch.

With a quirk of one eyebrow at the white sofa, Rhys eased himself down onto the coffee table, facing her. "I have something to say first, if you don't mind."

Uh-oh. Maybe her personal late-night pep talk wasn't on as solid ground as she'd expected. "Go ahead."

"I don't want you to have any doubts about the project or your role. Nothing has changed." He shrugged. "I spoke with my father. Didn't get a satisfactory answer, but my best guess is he resents not being the person in charge."

"Will this be an issue with using McCall Construction?"

"Shouldn't be. There were only two bids on the job. It wasn't financially feasible for any companies on the mainland to bid. We—McCall, that is—will subcontract as needed to Ashe

Construction. Jake Matthews should remain as the job foreman."

The knot in her stomach relaxed. Although she was familiar with the legal setup and had a good sense of Rhys's sense of integrity, father and son dynamics couldn't always be discounted. "Then business proceeds as planned."

"Exactly." With a deep breath, he relaxed, setting one ankle on the opposite knee. "What's on your agenda?"

"A young lady came into the office today asking about a position with my firm. I need to hire an assistant but wanted to check if you had considered an admin for the project. She left her résumé and is coming back shortly with her portfolio."

Rhys ran a hand through his short dark hair. "I'd intended to use the staff at McCall and cross-charge the hours. That's not a likely option now." He took the résumé, shaking his head as he read. "I don't know. Not a lot of experience in either of our fields." He shrugged again and handed it back.

"Consider the combination." Dana held up one hand, counting off the points. "Office skills, which we need. Retail experience, which gives her an insight with the merchants you and I don't have. And an art degree with a side order of marketing." Dana laid the résumé on the sofa beside her. "I didn't fit the exact requirements you advertised for, but you gave me an interview, and here we are. That's all I'm suggesting for her. If she doesn't seem like a good fit, we'll keep looking. Trust me?"

A surprised look crossed his lean features, followed by a slow grin. "Absolutely." He stood, backing toward the door. "If you think she's is a viable candidate, let me know, and I'll talk to her as well."

"I'll let you know later today."

The door to the street opened as Rhys reached for the handle. He stepped back, holding the door to allow Jamie to enter.

She stopped in her tracks. He froze in his. Her lips parted. His mouth dropped open.

Dana held back a smile as she rose to greet Jamie. *Well, this could be interesting.*

Sheriff Sam Wallace finally had a night off. Tonight, he planned on settling his boots under a table at the Lighthouse Cantina. His plan for the evening was simple. Listen to some music, have a little food and drink, and, with any luck, score a dance or two with a pretty girl.

The original lighthouse sat at the west end of the island, no longer operational, though it drew a number of tourists—and their money—to the island. A marina, built to the right of the lighthouse, provided ports for private sea crafts. Its gangway ran the length of the dockage, leading to the Cantina, which used to be the island's old fort. A connected pavilion provided outdoor seating in addition to the bar and dance area.

Beer bottle in hand, Sam gazed out over the waist-high stone wall surrounding the pavilion. The sun sat low in the sky, skimming the edge of the horizon as gold-tinted waves washed across the sands.

You're a long way from the streets of Norfolk.

Thanks to Mayor Wolfe. Save a guy's life, and you end up as sheriff of a sweet piece of paradise. His own good fortune, considering he'd just been dumped by the woman to whom he'd planned on proposing.

Timing was—as somebody once said—everything.

Since arriving on PI, he'd dedicated his efforts to upgrading the department and solidifying his position. And, nope, he didn't do things the way Sheriff Rayburn had. He didn't give preferential treatment to cronies. Those who complained to the mayor were set straight that things were no longer run the way they used to be.

His job now leaned more toward the administrative side of law and order, but he kept his hand in the game by taking the occasional patrol and filling in an odd shift every so often. It was up to his department to keep the citizens and tourists of PI safe, and he was willing to do what it took to provide that security.

Sam turned, backside planted against the wall. Music blared from the speakers, and the lanterns strung from overhead cross-beams glowed, gaining intensity as the daylight faded. The place was crowded, especially for a midweek night.

His gaze swept on, stopping as he spied Rhys McCall and his friend Paige occupying a four-top at the opposite end of the pavilion. McCall was a hard worker and a straight-shooter, based on the times they'd shot the breeze over a couple of beers or a round or two of pool.

Paige Carson, on the other hand, intrigued him. Girl-next-door type, radiating a weird mix of joy and orneriness. Cinnamon brown curls, soft brown eyes, and a tight, curvy body bursting with chaotic energy. A woman like her would be a comfort and a pain in the ass, both at the same time. Sam hadn't seen much of her until she'd claimed the next-door-across-the-street building for her business several months ago. When he did take notice, he also noticed McCall was on the scene much of the time as well.

Sam was still puzzling out that relationship. Depending on who was doing the talking around town, the two were best friends since childhood, like brother and sister, high-school sweethearts, or all but engaged.

His preference would be the sibling option. Since he considered McCall a friend of sorts, bro-code and all, he needed to confirm that status.

When Rhys lifted a hand, Sam followed the direction of the man's gaze to a blonde standing at the bar. With a smile, she pushed away from the counter and walked toward the table.

While Sam stood alone, Rhys sat with two women at his table. Now that was a crime.

As sheriff, Sam was duty-bound to address crimes in progress. Bottle in hand, he headed toward Rhys's table. Time to find out if Paige Carson was on the market—or not.

Paige's internal alarm signaled red when Rhys insisted on inviting the blonde to their table. Jamie was pretty—okay, gorgeous. Model tall, beachy blonde hair, ocean blue eyes. She seemed nice on the surface, but the company she was keeping suggested otherwise. Hanging out at the bar with Stacy Andrews didn't speak well of Jamie's choice of friends. Paige was just glad McCall's office manager hadn't decided to trot over on her stilettos and join them as well. Then again, with four men surrounding her and drinks flowing, why would Stacy bother?

Paige had barely had time to puzzle out why Rhys had invited Jamie over when Sam Wallace approached the table.

"Room for one more?" he asked, laying a hand on the top rung of the empty chair's back.

"Hey, Sam." Rhys swept a hand toward the vacant seat. "Sure do. Paige, you know Sam, don't you?"

"By sight." She offered a quick smile as he dropped into the chair beside her. "Since I'm a law-abiding citizen, we haven't had a chance to meet."

"Good to know." Humor reflected in his dark eyes. "Although as Sheriff, I do serve in many ways."

Hmm... just what was that supposed to mean? She spared another glance in his direction. By this time, he'd turned his attention to Rhys. Good. She had to sort out this situation with the blonde first.

The waitress appeared to take their dinner orders. Noticing Jamie's unease, Paige motioned her to remain seated. "Please stay so we can get to know you better. Besides, Rhys is buying."

"I don't know about anyone else," Sam drawled, "but that's the best offer I've had today."

Jamie cast a glance at Rhys. "If you don't mind."

"Absolutely. It'll give us a chance to talk."

While everyone gave their dinner order, Paige marveled at the way Rhys was able to multitask—a smile to Jamie, a quick nod to Sam, and a swift kick to her ankle under the table.

She kicked him back.

"So, Jamie, how well do you know Stacy?" Paige smiled, ignoring a puzzled look from Sam and a scowl from Rhys.

Jamie shifted in her chair, hands dropping to her lap. "I wouldn't call her a friend. We were roommates one year in college. I ran into her on the mainland a couple of weeks ago, and she offered to let me stay at her place while I looked for a job. I haven't seen much of her since I arrived." She cast a quick glance at the bar. "She stays busy."

Paige mulled over that answer. Jamie wouldn't have been the first person Stacy had taken advantage of or made empty promises to. "Did you know she works for Rhys's dad?"

Jamie's eyes widened. "I knew she worked for McCall Construction, but she never mentioned who she specifically works for. Is that where you work, Rhys?"

"I worked there the past couple months while my dad was on leave. He's back now. I'm transitioning out to concentrate on the Main Street renovations."

"Mrs. Canfield discussed the project when she interviewed me for a position as her assistant. She also said there was an admin opening for the Main Street project." Jamie held up two sets of crossed fingers. "Two chances, but I'll be back out tomorrow putting in more résumés."

Paige noticed Jamie casting another glance toward the bar and the slight frown creasing her brow. Nope, she definitely wasn't from same mold as Stacy. Accepting Stacy's invitation must mean Jamie was desperate for a job and a place to stay.

A nudge against Paige's ankle told her to drop the subject. She ignored it, giving Rhys a steady glare in return. "When will a decision be made?"

"Paige, I can't discuss—"

Jamie stirred in her seat. "I'm sorry. I didn't mean to put you on the spot."

"Not at all." Rhys nodded in Paige's direction. "Hurricane here took care of that."

Sam snorted.

Rhys turned back to Jamie. "Dana came up with the idea that one person could fill both positions as a shared resource. Since her primary focus is Main Street, she won't need anyone full time on other projects for the immediate future. We decided the candidate would be hired by her firm. She'll direct the work and cross-charge those hours to the project budget." He lifted an eyebrow in question. "You haven't spoken with Dana?"

Jamie shook her head, distress lingering in her gaze. "I missed her call, but her voice-mail message asked me to come to the office in the morning."

Paige squealed as she bounced on her chair. "You got the job! She'd tell you over the phone if the answer was no."

Rhys's mouth dropped open. "I didn't say—"

"Give it up, buddy." Sam shook his head in commiseration.

He grunted and shook his head in defeat. "We need someone to start immediately. For now, the position is considered probationary until the required background check, drug test, and such is completed. Dana will go over the details with you tomorrow."

"Oh, my gosh! Thank you! Thank you so much!"

"You're welcome, but it was Dana's decision. She was

impressed with your interview, and we agreed a shared resource would be more practical."

Paige nodded to herself. The job took care of one of Jamie's problems, so they were halfway to a happy ending. Now they needed to do something about her housing situation.

Rhys started talking again, something about Jamie's role and responsibilities. Paige tuned him out and glanced to her left to check Sam's reaction. He wore a wide smile as well, but it wasn't directed at Jamie. It was aimed at her.

Her internal alarm went off again. Big time.

Jamie's good news broke the ice, allowing the conversation to flow freely. The mood remained light and friendly while they ate. Paige shared the story of her dead battery, garnering laughter around the table. She tuned out the subsequent teasing to mull over Sam Wallace's possible interest in her.

"I have a question." Sam swiped a napkin across his mouth, then jerked his thumb at a poster plastered on the pavilion wall. The image displayed a well-built man with curly dark hair down to his shoulders. He was clad only in gym shorts and demonstrating a bicep curl. "What the hell is MOM?"

"Poor Marco. His days are numbered." Paige slapped a fist to her chest as her face crumpled into mock sorrow. At Sam's and Jamie's puzzled expressions, she burst out laughing. "Not mom. M-O-M. It stands for Man of the Month. It's a promotion the Cantina started last month to draw in female customers. Marco's reign runs out at the end of this week."

Sam quirked a brow as he dipped his head in her direction. "Seriously?"

"He's a trainer at the fitness center. Membership supposedly went through the roof after the poster went up. Good for his business, good for the Cantina."

"Good grief." Sam shook his head.

Jamie scrounged one of the remaining taco chips from the basket sitting midtable. "How long before your restaurant opens?"

"The booths were going to take another six weeks." Seeing Rhys ready to jump to her aid, she rushed to explain. "Dana got

41

that fixed. I'm getting my deposit back. Depending on which of the options I go with, I can open maybe within the month."

Jamie looked up from her plate. "Is the construction completed?"

"The exit lights, final scrub down, and decorating are all that remains," Rhys replied. "A day or two to wrap that up. Then the inspection for occupancy."

"And the kitchen?" Jamie asked.

Paige dipped her own chip into the salsa and took a bite before answering. "Ready to go except for stocking my inventory."

"Got an idea?" Sam asked, glancing at Jamie. Sitting back, arms crossed over his chest, he looked well fed and at ease.

Jamie glanced around the table, her gaze landing on Paige. "What about take-out?"

"Eventually, but that's not—"

"With a promotion." She hesitated, then took a deep breath. "A drawing for first-night seating. Coupons in the take-out bags. Countdown-to-opening specials. That would grow your business until the dining area is completed."

Silence fell over the table. A flush crept over Jamie's face as she sank back in her seat. "Or not."

"Those are really good ideas." Paige studied Jamie with new interest, then turned her gaze to the two men. "We need girl-talk time."

Sam frowned. "Which means?"

"Find something to do. Go somewhere for ten minutes." She waved her hand toward the rest of the pavilion. "Dance."

Sam shrugged in Rhys's direction. "You did buy me dinner."

The men rose in unison, each taking his glass. Paige waited until they were beyond earshot before leveling her fiercest glare across the table. Despite her growing respect for the girl, certain conditions had to be made clear.

"I like you, Jamie. I didn't think I would because you were with Stacy. But I can tell you were in a pickle and maybe didn't have a lot of options. I'm picking up strong vibes between you and Rhys, which is fine. I have to warn you though. If you mess him over, you will feel my full wrath, and it will not be pretty."

Paige expected a furious denial, even a smart comeback. Jamie surprised her as the corners of her mouth turned up in a small, sad smile.

"I don't want to be your enemy. I like you too. I hope we can be friends. I am attracted to Rhys, but I don't have time for a relationship, let alone a romance. I need to focus on this new job and finding an apartment I can afford."

Not my problem.

But it was. Rhys was her friend, her best friend since—forever. With his mom deceased and his dad being... himself, her parents had become his parents. Secure in their bond, she'd never been jealous of any of his girlfriends. It was those other girls who couldn't handle a boyfriend having a female friend. Their loss. There was a definite spark between Jamie and Rhys. She saw the flirty looks, the smiles for no reason, the "checking you out" glances. Eventually they'd get a clue.

She could have discerned more between those two if Sam hadn't kept pulling her attention away with all his teasing comments and slow grins, laying his arm across the back of her chair....

Paige shot a look to the bar where Sam stood talking with Rhys. She barely knew the guy. Certainly never thought of him in that way before now. Maybe it was proximity? Flirting for the heck of it, like that killer smile he'd sent her way earlier?

She studied him with a new perspective. Older, early-to-mid thirties, which counted in his favor. More mature than most guys she knew and therefore less likely to irritate her. Tall, hunky, and doing total justice to those jeans he was wearing.

She shook her head. She didn't have time for this now, even if her internal alarm was sending hot flashes of the good kind all through her. Jamie's situation needed her attention first. She mulled over an idea a moment longer, then decided her instincts were on point. "I have an extra room. You can move in with me, and we'll give it a month's trial."

Unshed tears shimmered in Jamie's eyes. A small gasp grew into a shaky laugh. "Paige, you don't even *know* me. I should say no, but I'm selfish enough to say yes." She dabbed a napkin at a wayward tear spilling onto her cheek. "You don't know how much this means to me."

The escape of that single tear confirmed her decision. Paige glared at Stacy holding court at the bar. Rhys and Sam at least showed the good sense to stay at the opposite end of the counter.

"Trust me. I do. How fast can you pack? I hope you have a lot of luggage."

Jamie's mouth dropped open for an instant before she stammered a reply. "Not long. I didn't unpack much. Why a lot?"

"The boys need to work off their dinner." Paige lifted a hand, motioning for the two men to rejoin them.

While they waited, Paige considered Jamie's ideas for the restaurant. They had merit, but implementation meant incurring costs for the additional supplies needed for take-out orders. Money was always a problem. Her eyes narrowed as her gaze landed upon the MOM poster.

That could work. She just needed to convince a certain man to cooperate.

Chapter Four

Erik McCall barely glanced at the truck and car pulled over to the side of the road until a flash of blonde hair caught his attention. His eyes had to be mistaken, but his heart raced all the same.

April?

He halted his Lexus several feet in front of the disabled vehicle. Mouth dry, he swallowed, wondered if he'd imagined her. A glance in the side mirror confirmed she'd recognized him as well.

April.

He stepped out of the car and froze as she approached. Backlit by the morning sun, she glowed bright and pure, cool and elegant in a white dress that hugged her gentle curves. Her step sure, barely raising a trace of dust as she glided along the asphalt and grass. She smiled, and with that gesture, his breathing resumed.

"Are you all right?" Erik asked.

She lifted a hand to sweep back a lock of hair that the wind had dared to tease out of place. "I'm fine. When the dash light came on, I pulled over to check and saw the tire was going flat. Mr. Warden happened by as I was calling my son and offered to help." She cast a quick glance back at her car, lips curving in a smile he'd never forgotten.

He shot a glance over her shoulder at the man kneeling

beside her car. He recognized the guy. Owned a two-bit garage over on Ocean. Anger surged through him. Surely she wasn't impressed by a man in a T-shirt and faded jeans.

He drew a sharp breath. Except that had been him at one time.

"Do you remember?" April smiled. "About twenty-five years ago along this same road, I had a flat tire. It was a summer day, and the top was down in that blue convertible I had. I'd barely pulled off the road when this black pickup pulled up behind my car. Out you stepped, in T-shirt and jeans. You walked right up to me and said 'I can fix that.'"

He remembered. It had been hotter than any day in June had a right to be. He'd spent that day under an unrelenting sun, nailing shingles on a roof. Driving home with the windows down because they were broken and so was the A/C, all he'd wanted was an icy shower and a cold beer. Then he'd seen *her*, looking cool and fresh in snug white slacks and a pink-striped top. Blonde hair tumbling around her shoulders, framing a face sweeter than the convertible beside her. At that moment, anything seemed possible for a cocky, blue-collar SOB. All because April had smiled at him.

"You said 'Show me.'"

She'd shared an extra bottle of water from the tote in her car, sent Mitch Davis and his buddies on their way when they'd stopped, urging her to "lose the loser." Even written her phone number on the inside of his forearm.

"You never called me." A chill crept into her voice. "I waited two extra days before going back to college."

Erik fought back a scowl. He wasn't the villain here, and the time for keeping secrets had long passed. A lie might be kinder than the truth, but kindness wasn't a strong part of his nature. "I was in the hospital."

Her stunned expression hit him in the gut but not hard enough to stop his confession. "Got beat up pretty bad. Broken nose. Dislocated jaw. Busted leg, bruised kidney. Concussion. By the time I got back on my feet, you were gone. Word came back later you'd married the bastard who did it."

The horror on her face pinned him in place. He couldn't move.

But she did.

Her palms cupped his cheeks, and he closed his eyes for an instant as the cool touch of her fingers soothed his heated flesh. The heady scent of her perfume filled his lungs. Nothing like the sweet, innocent fragrance he once knew, but when mixed with April's own essence, it captured his senses once again. He bathed in the world of "what if" as her gentle fingers traced over his features, along his nose with the slight bump, down his jawline to the crease of his lips. The memory of the pain from that long-ago beating welled inside him, battling the benediction of April's caress.

"Mitch and his friends went after you. Because of me." Temper blazed in her pansy-blue eyes as she stepped back. The anger faded, replaced by something else. Regret, or perhaps "what ifs" of her own? "I wish I'd known."

Yeah, well, wishes counted for nothing. He swallowed back the dryness in his mouth. "Are you here visiting?"

"I'm surprised you hadn't heard I'd moved back. I'm working for Elliott Realty. My son Kevin moved here as well. I'm on my way to meet him for breakfast." She laid a palm on his forearm. "Will you join us?"

The soft sincerity of her invitation clashed with the lingering memory of his helplessness on that dark night. Meet the son of the man who'd stolen what could have been his life? Kevin Davis...

...could have been his son.

All the "what ifs" that never had a chance to become reality sucker-punched his gut. He took a deep breath and met April's gaze.

"I'd like that. I'd like to meet your son." He tucked his hands into his pockets to hide their trembling as he shot another glance over her shoulder. "The guy is finishing up. Why don't you take my car and go on? The key's in the ignition. I'll drive your car in case there's any additional problems."

"I'm meeting Kevin at the yacht club—"

"I'm a member." He hid a wince. A recent accomplishment for a McCall was a long-held tradition for someone in April's social set.

Lifting on tiptoe, she pressed a kiss to his cheek. "I always believed in you."

They walked back to her car. Warden had finished and was

47

returning his tools to his truck.

Erik wasn't a patient man, but receiving a kiss from the most beautiful woman he'd ever known knocked a dose of tolerance into his brain. He waited while April retrieved her purse, then paused to thank the man.

Warden smiled as he wiped his hands on a crumpled cloth. "Glad I could help."

To the man's credit, he didn't watch April walk away. Instead, he turned to Erik. "The tire can be repaired. It's in the trunk—"

Erik pulled a business card from his wallet. "I'll have my garage take care of any additional work. Send your bill to my office."

Warden accepted the card, gave a brief nod. "Have a good day."

Hand on the door handle of the Mercedes, Erik stopped to stare down the road. His own car was already out of sight. He settled into April's car, adjusted the seat and mirrors. A lightness he hadn't felt for over twenty years filled his heart.

April was home.

Erik didn't expect a hero's introduction when he met Kevin Davis, but that's exactly how April portrayed him. Twice he'd come to her rescue on the same road. She gave the story a humorous slant, leaving out all mention of Mitch. As an ice-breaker, it did the job.

Erik leaned back in his chair while the server refilled his coffee cup. He hadn't enjoyed a meal this much in a long time. Kevin's obvious resemblance to April made it easy to accept the young man as someone other than Mitch's son.

"By the way, Mr. McCall," Kevin said. "I applied for a job at your company. I didn't see any openings, but I'm hoping my qualifications might meet a need in your organization."

April shot a scolding look at her son. "Kevin, I didn't ask Erik to join us so you could discuss business."

"I don't mind." Erik offered a reassuring smile before turning his attention to the younger man. "Your résumé is on my desk. I asked my assistant to set up an interview. I guess she hasn't had an opportunity to contact you yet."

He took a sip of coffee, swallowing it along with the lie. He'd tossed the paper immediately into the trash for no other reason than the last name on the résumé. His mind ran over the course of the breakfast conversation. *MBA, Stanford, finance.* "If you have time, we can go to my office and discuss the position I have in mind."

"I need to leave for work." April pushed back her chair. "Stay and have your discussion here."

Both men rose. A pang shot from Erik's gut to his heart as April dropped a quick kiss on Kevin's cheek. The young man responded with a hug. The easy display of affection between mother and son mocked the crumbling relationship with his own son.

He managed a smile when April turned to say good-bye to him. A squeeze of the hand slipped her business card into his palm. It wasn't the same as writing her number on his forearm, but the intent was there. He gave a nod, his silent promise.

Erik slipped the card into his pocket as he eased back into his chair. He couldn't miss the way Kevin glanced from his mother's departing form and then back to him. No need for concern. He'd win the woman, and he'd win over her son.

He shifted, fixing a firm gaze on the younger man. "Twenty seconds. Tell me why you're the right man for McCall."

Kevin's good-natured visage sharpened into keen confidence. "I'll provide a solid financial foundation dedicated to growing your business. I have roots here on PI, so I'll be invested in your success as well as my own."

The boy was hungry. Eager to make his mark. McCall Construction couldn't match the six-figure salary Kevin could have scored elsewhere, but the job potential could feed that ravenous ego.

He gave a small shrug. "You know nothing about the construction business."

To his surprise and satisfaction, Kevin met that challenge without hesitation. "You have people now who fill that role. What I need to know, you can teach me. I'll apply what I know to help you determine what's best for McCall."

Erik's BS barometer registered a flat zero when he considered Kevin's response. Laying down a little truth at this point might help gain a greater measure of the young man's confidence.

"Telling you this might not be the best tactic from a negotiating standpoint, but I want to be straight with you. McCall is a family business. From small-time carpenters and jack-of-all-trades to what it is today. Father to son and so on."

He glanced at the coffee cup by his hand. The burning in his stomach convinced him to push it aside. "When my son went off to college, I expected him to return after he graduated. He didn't. Took a job on the mainland. I held out hope he'd come back home one day."

A frown creased Kevin's brow. "He never returned?"

"He did. About a year ago. I had let my pride get in the way. The company was growing, and I felt I had to keep a finger on every aspect." He rubbed a palm along his jaw as the truth became more recent and raw. "Things got bad. Bad enough I broke down and offered him an incentive to come home. I took a risk that a financial stake in the company would motivate him. Between the two of us, things rebounded. By that time, I needed a break as well. I took time off to show I trusted him. Gave him a chance to become emotionally invested in the company."

Erik saw the confusion on Kevin's face. God, he was talking too much. To April's son, of all people.

Kevin rested his forearms on the table and leaned forward. "How could he have turned his back on his heritage?"

Erik reached for the water glass and took a sip. The liquid had grown tepid, but it soothed the dryness in his throat. How was it this boy understood what his own son couldn't comprehend? He offered a small shrug in response.

"The company continued to do well, but during that same time, Rhys initiated this Main Street renovation project. I could foresee a repeat of the previous year. Only this time, it's Rhys and his pride trying to manage more than reasonable. I learned from my mistakes. I can't put sentiment over the welfare of my employees. McCall needs new blood." He paused long enough for his gut to give the go-ahead. "After hearing all this, are you still interested in the job?"

For a brief instant, a hint of barracuda washed across Kevin's all-American features. The young man smiled. "Even more."

Erik rose with a smooth fluid motion. "Let's go back to the office and discuss the job in detail."

The boy wanted to prove himself. With a father like Mitch Davis, no doubt he was aching for a paternal figure to lean on and learn from.

I can be that man.

Mr. Warden, could you come by the restaurant? I need your help.

For the second time in as many days, Nick traveled from the garage to the restaurant. The voice-mail message from Paige didn't seem urgent. Just cryptic.

No mention of her Jeep.

He bit back a snort of laughter. Maybe her bike had a flat tire. A twinge shot through his chest on the tail of that thought. The girl reminded him way too much of Megan.

And there it was. The reason he'd closed up shop again to see how he could help Paige.

He probably was going to regret it.

The jingle of a bell—something added since his previous visit—announced his entrance. The door to the kitchen area swung open. Paige scurried behind the counter, setting a package on the countertop.

"Hi, Mr. Warden. How are you?" She smiled. A bright, perky smile that tickled his suspicions.

He strolled to the counter. "Good. And you?"

"I'm good too." Her fingers toyed with the edge of the paper bag.

Nick swallowed back a grunt. Might as well get to the point. "What's up with the car?"

"Nothing. It's doing great. You did a wonderful job with the battery, changing it and all."

She pushed the bag across the counter. "Turkey sub. On the house."

He studied the offering in silence, then summoned his best "dad scowl." "Your check's going to bounce, isn't it?"

"Absolutely not! How could you think—" Paige halted, drawing in a deep breath. "That's not why I asked you here." She slid a plastic-wrapped sandwich from the paper bag, turning it sideways for his inspection.

Turkey, bacon, cheese, lettuce, tomato. Toasted bun and a hint of some type of dressing. To a hungry man coming up on lunch break, it looked damn good. A trap, but a tempting one.

"What's the going rate for 'on the house'?"

She eased the sandwich closer to him. "Let's call it a mutual business opportunity."

"I have all the business I can handle."

A noise from the adjoining room caught his attention. He turned his head and spied Dana through the open doors. She walked around the room while tapping on the screen of an electronic tablet. He settled an elbow on the counter to continue watching her move in and out of his view, half-listening as Paige blathered on.

"I want to open the restaurant initially on a take-out basis. I need extra cash for supplies, but my budget is limited. I thought about the monthly contest for photo submissions at the Cantina, which pays one hundred dollars if I win. I want to enter one of you in your garage… with your shirt off."

His automatic stream of "uh-huhs" stuttered to a halt. Heat rose in his face as he whirled to face the counter. "Are you nuts? You want that kind of picture, go ask your boyfriend."

He had to give her credit. Paige didn't back down in the face of his outrage. She met his glare with the same type of smile Megan would target at him.

"We have a great chance of winning. You're totally different from this month's winner. He's a pretty boy—gym muscles, long hair. You have that rugged, mature thing going on."

Ouch—mature. Nick shook his head. "Sorry, but fifty bucks isn't enough to convince me to change my mind."

Her smile faded so fast, he almost laughed. "Oh, right, you'd want a cut, wouldn't you?" she muttered.

Her disappointment guilted him into softening his tone. "Look, Paige, you're young enough to be my daughter. It falls into a creepy category for you to take pictures of me. Especially with my shirt off."

Paige nudged the sandwich to the edge of the counter. "Here's the deal. Win or lose, you get lunch for a week, your choice." She nodded toward the dining room. "I keep the prize money and get someone more appropriate to take the picture."

He didn't hesitate. "Deal."

"Everything's ready for the inspections tomorrow." Dana closed the pocket doors to the dining room section of Paige's restaurant. She set her tablet and digital camera to one side on the counter. "I'm glad you decided to go with the wooden tables and chairs from Morgan's. You'll have more flexibility in seating, especially if someone wants to reserve the room for a banquet or meeting."

"You think of everything. Thank you for taking over for Rhys." Paige leaned forward, forearms resting on the counter. "I know things are starting to get busy for you two."

"Not a problem." Really, it hadn't been. Working on the restaurant was a fun change of pace, even if she hadn't been involved from the beginning.

"Would you have any extra time this afternoon? I have a really, really big favor to ask."

Her mother-mode clicked on as she recognized that tone. And that innocent expression? Didn't fool her for an instant. "Let me hear the favor first."

"Taking a picture." Her hand eased the digital camera in front of Dana. "I need it by end of today to submit in the Cantina's monthly contest."

"What's the Cantina, and what kind of contest?"

"The Lighthouse Cantina. It's the restaurant located by the marina."

Dana nodded, recalling the festive structure that had caught her attention on previous visits. Time hadn't allowed her to try it yet. Maybe she'd call April for a girls' night out.

"So…" Paige's tone drew her back to the conversation. "The contest is good-looking guys in the area. The prize would cover the remaining cost for the extra supplies for the first couple weeks."

"I'm surprised Rhys agreed to this." Dana frowned as Paige focused her gaze on a stack of take-out menus. "You did ask him, didn't you?"

Paige ran a fingertip across the top menu. "I asked Mr. Warden."

"You asked Nick Warden?" A quiver ran through her stomach. "And he agreed?"

"In exchange for lunch for a week. Just some candid shots of him working in the garage. He didn't think it was appropriate for me to take the photos because of the age thing. It shouldn't take you even an hour." Paige beamed at her, even had the nerve to bounce on her toes. "I have a good shot at winning. I mean, look at him!"

Look at him, indeed. She knew better than to agree, but the beseeching plea on Paige's face persuaded her otherwise. "Don't *ever* ask me to do anything like this again."

"Promise." Paige drew an X over her heart with her forefinger.

Dana tucked the tablet and camera into her bag. She headed toward the door, calling over one shoulder, "Uncross the two fingers behind your back."

Paige's shocked "How did you know?" reached her just before the door closed.

Dana stood for a moment on the sidewalk. Why on earth had she agreed to Paige's request? Her gaze traveled across the street to the corner where Nick had swooped her into his strong arms, looking down at her with those teasing eyes and killer grin.

Oh, yeah. That's why.

"Couple of quick shots," Dana muttered as she parked her car in the lot behind Nick's garage. "Then I'm gone."

Nick Warden made her nervous. In a good way, but she wasn't prepared for the conflicting emotions raging inside her. He stirred up a deep craving, a yearning for something that had been missing from her life for a long time. And now to spend time up close, checking out every inch and angle of his body through the lens of a camera?

If it was just his body that attracted her, she could have admired it and moved on. But, Nick also possessed a smooth sense of humor and had a way of looking at her with his full attention.

With a groan, she flicked the A/C control to high. The blast of air shot across her face and chest, dousing the unexpected rush of heat brought on by her wayward thoughts. Paige knew what she was doing when she picked this man for the contest.

Dana savored one last blast of cool air before shutting off the engine. Stepping from her car, she took a deep, cleansing breath to shake away those dangerous thoughts. Purse over one shoulder, camera in hand, she entered the building.

The garage was on the small side, with room enough for two bays and a small alcove in the back where a metal desk nestled. A soft drink machine was tucked into the corner next to a utility rack holding an assortment of supplies and tools. A metal staircase against the back wall led to the second floor. The bay doors were rolled up, allowing a clear view of Ocean.

A midsize sedan, its hood open, occupied one of the service bays. A red metal cabinet on rollers stood nearby, several tools laid out on the top tray. Nick stood before the vehicle, clipboard propped on one hip.

She stopped and snapped a quick shot.

Nick's head shot up, swiveling in her direction. A slow and easy grin crossed his lips as he lowered the clipboard onto the front fender of the car. His gaze flicked to the camera. "I see you're ready."

"What can I say? Paige is persuasive. It was kind of you to help her out."

"Hope I don't regret it," he muttered. He jerked a thumb toward the front of the building. "Mind if I close the doors? I get armchair mechanics dropping by sometimes, and I don't care to explain what we're doing."

"Good idea." She moved to the side of the car, peering under the hood. "What are you doing here?"

"Points, plugs, a couple hoses, fluids. Guy bought the car for his kid. Not the one the kid wanted, but he'll live with it."

He punched the remote to lower the front doors. After a considering look toward the back of the building, he locked the customer door and flipped the sign to Closed. "Another garage told him the car needed the engine replaced, so he brought it by for a second opinion. Checked it out, told him what it needed, and he gave me the job."

Honest. But she knew that already from how he'd handled Paige's car problem.

"Where do you want me to stand or sit?" she asked as Nick returned to the work bay. When his gaze swept the full length of her body, she flushed.

"Stool is over there if you want to sit," he said with a nod. "You can move around as long as you stay out of the work area."

He sauntered across the garage and leaned a shoulder against the wall. His grin was more mischievous boy than hot sexy male as he looked down at her. "By the way, did our mutual friend mention she wanted the photo without my shirt?"

Without... that little brat!

"No, she omitted that information." Dana slid off the stool. "And you agreed?"

"No, ma'am. I figured you and I could negotiate that aspect ourselves. So tell me, Dana." He stepped closer, voice husky and full of suggestion. "How do *you* want me?"

Heat scoured all words from her brain. Where was the air conditioner when she needed it?

She stared into that ruggedly handsome face, catching a hint of uncertainty in his dark eyes. That small glimpse of insecurity reassured her. "It's best you leave your shirt on."

"Fair enough." He walked back to the work area, throwing an amiable grin over one shoulder. "For now."

Once Nick started working, he seemed oblivious to her presence. Occasionally, the *snick* from the camera shutter caught his attention, and he cast a quick glance in her direction. Otherwise he remained focused on his work as she moved around the perimeter of the bay.

The stretch of denim across his thighs as he leaned his long body over the open engine area to install a belt.

The careful way he wiped each tool before placing it back on the workbench.

One knee bent, both hands planted on the front of the vehicle as he studied his handiwork.

The smile of satisfaction as he listened to the purr of the motor.

He stepped away from the car, arms overhead as he arched his back, stretching. Snatching a water bottle from the workbench, he leaned against the cinderblock wall, shoulders and one foot braced against the cement surface. He took a deep pull from the bottle, throat muscles working as he swallowed.

Face and arms glistening with sweat, hair spiked with perspiration. The dark blue T-shirt clung to his damp body, inviting a second look for what was suggested rather than exposed.

He lowered the bottle. Head turned to one side, slightly lowered, eyes closed, he stood in quiet relief as the afternoon sun beamed through the window of the front doors. Dana lifted the camera for a final time, capturing the moment.

Money shot.

Hearing the rustle of Dana's movements, Nick opened his eyes. He pushed away from the wall, swiping one forearm across his brow. "Finished?"

Dana nodded, looking down as she fiddled with the camera. "You?"

"Needs a vacuum and wash, but otherwise, it's finished. I have a couple more jobs scheduled after this one." He set the water bottle back on the workbench.

"I'll get out of here so you can get back to work." She dropped the camera into her purse, then swung the strap over one shoulder.

He wasn't ready for her to leave. The quiet pace of the afternoon reminded him of his long-ago high-school days, working on a secondhand car in his dad's garage while his girlfriend cooed over his prowess. Not that Dana had verbalized any such admiration, but he had noticed a certain awareness in her eyes. An awareness that made him feel like a teenage boy again, in quite a few ways.

"Dana?" He waited until she looked up at him. "Will you have dinner with me tomorrow? I'm off call after tonight."

Once again, he saw that heartbeat of hesitation. When a slow, sweet smile broke across her lips, relief rushed through him.

"I'd like that, Nick."

Hot damn! "Let me have your address, and I'll pick up you. How about six-thirty?"

He walked to the customer door while Dana pulled a business card and pen from her purse. Flipping the lock and switching the sign to Open, he waited for her to finish writing and join him at the exit.

"Six-thirty's perfect." She held out the card to him.

He waggled the card between two fingers. "I'll add this one to the other one you gave me."

He swept the door open, anchoring it with his back as she exited. Fresh air and the scent of her perfume cleared away the smell of oil and grease from the garage. He lifted a hand in response to the wave she offered while driving off the lot.

Might be a good idea to put in some extra hours tonight. Get a jump on the next day's work so he could close on time.

Being a new guy in town had brought him a fair share of feminine interest and, in some cases, outright pursuit. But the dates he'd had so far had left him less than eager to proceed toward a relationship. Some concluded with the mutual decision to remain as friends. Others left him feeling like an entry on a checklist. Single guy, owns a business, no apparent baggage.

But this spark with Dana?

Instant and off the charts.

Honey, I don't think we have a choice in seeing where this goes.

Chapter Five

Rhys was on the way out the door to work when his phone signaled that a text message had been delivered. A frown crept across his brow as he read the screen display: *Dad*

"Better get it over with." He punched the button to display the message.

Need to discuss transition plan. My office 11am.

Calm. Reasonable. Either someone had stolen Erik McCall's phone or else a couple good nights' sleep had improved his father's attitude. Perhaps the request was that innocent and not an excuse to go another round about Dana's role with the project.

Admittedly, his own burst of temper hadn't helped the situation. His defense of Dana plus his defiant act of walking out had no doubt generated the immediacy of this transition plan.

The battle for control hadn't come as a surprise. The accusation that he was trying to erase his father's legacy rather than add his own contribution? That one had stung, hard and deep.

I thought we'd moved beyond all that when you took time away from the office. That you trusted me, looked upon us as partners. Equals.

He still didn't have the full story for that extended break. Exhaustion? Illness? The only reason his father had given was "I deserve a break, and I'm damn well taking it."

He'd even wondered if Dad had planned a romantic getaway with a mystery lady. Although his father's mantra was "never let yourself get roped in by a woman," Erik McCall definitely made time for female companionship, though none of them ever progressed past the casual stage.

Who was he to judge that decision? His own love life since returning to PI had been less than spectacular. If he wasn't working, he was… well, working.

He once dared to ask if his father's reticence to commit to another marriage had to do with mourning the loss of Rhys's mother. The question won a swift, vicious denial.

"Only thing good to come out of that fiasco is you, kid. Don't mention her again."

He had no memories of his parents living together. Always just him and his mom. Losing her when he had just turned four years old had left him with a man who was little more than a stranger. He'd learned two rules quickly: don't mention Mom, and be Dad's chip-off-the-old-block.

Thank God for the Carsons, who'd opened their hearts and home to him and had taught him what being a family meant. Not to discount all that Erik McCall had taught him as well. A love of building, a respect for doing a job right, and the knowledge and experience to do those things.

I want to us to have a good relationship, Dad, but I can't fix this breach by myself.

Not if it required sacrificing his own integrity.

Even though he'd decided to move his office to Dana's building, the process wasn't that cut and dried. Regardless of their argument, he wasn't about to walk off the job. Business as usual until the official handoff occurred.

He'd spent the previous day attending weekly project meetings with the foremen, a practice he'd implemented upon his return to the company. Following that were the field tours at each of the job sites. Rather than returning to the McCall building after completing the inspections, he'd taken advantage of one of the vacant desks in the work-yard office to update the project reports. With Dana handling the final setup at Paige's restaurant, he could concentrate on updating the job files during regular work hours rather than spending his own time in the evening.

Which had made for a long evening and too much time to think about Jamie.

Thoughts of her had darted through his mind ever since they'd met. Maybe once he relocated to the Canfield building, he'd have a better opportunity to see if this attraction was more than one-sided. With her working for Dana and moving in with Paige, it seemed they were destined to be in each other's orbit, one way or another.

He looked down at his phone again and typed a response.

Ok

His spirits lifted once he'd sent the text. Dad had reached out to him, even if it was about the transition plan. Fair enough. He'd go into the meeting with a cool head and an open mind, and with any luck, they'd be back on speaking terms.

Entering his father's corner office, Rhys was surprised to see another man sitting across from his dad. The transition plan was further along than he'd expected.

"There you are!" A hint of censure flavored Erik's greeting. He stood, motioning to the other man. "Kevin, this is Rhys. Rhys, this is Kevin Davis. Before he takes over the financials, I want him to become familiar with our daily operations. I need you to get him up to speed on the current projects. I expect a smooth transition."

"Glad to meet you, Rhys." Kevin rose and extended his hand.

A swift visual confirmed Rhys's suspicions. Collegiate, preppy, wearing the type of business-casual attire that Erik favored.

"Kevin." He accepted the handclasp before addressing his father. "Do you want to meet in here?"

Erik shook his head. "I'm not needed for this. Kevin, why don't you take Rhys to your office?"

"You got it." Kevin shot a thumbs-up gesture to Erik, then turned to face him. "Ready?"

With a nod, Rhys followed Kevin to the door. Both men halted as Erik spoke again. "Son, if you have time, let's have lunch today."

Rhys turned, on the verge of accepting, when Erik continued. "I can clarify any questions you have after your discussion with Rhys."

An awkward moment of silence passed before Kevin responded. "That would be great. I'll let you know when we're finished." He nodded in Rhys's direction. "I'll show you to my office."

Rhys fought back a blistering wave of anger. He'd fully understood Erik would assume the reins of leadership upon his return. Their conversation two days ago had clearly underlined that prospect. What he hadn't expected was that the handoff would be conducted in such a cold, impersonal manner.

He didn't know who the hell Kevin Davis was or how he'd come on the scene so quickly, but Rhys didn't intend to air a private dispute in front of the man.

"I want to talk with you before I leave, Dad."

Head lowered, eyes on the papers before him, Erik lifted one hand in response. Rhys shook his head and walked out to the hallway where Kevin waited.

He followed Kevin into his office and sat down in one of the guest chairs. A quick glance around the room revealed the man had already settled in. Clean desk, except for basic supplies. Framed diplomas on the wall. No unpacked boxes. The guy hadn't wasted any time. He looked totally at ease sitting in the black leather chair. Hands resting on the oak desktop, fingers interlaced. Ready to take charge.

"I anticipate this to be a smooth transition, Rhys." Davis's chin took an upward tilt, his blue eyes cool, his gaze steady. "I hope any animosity you have toward your father will not interfere with that."

Son-of-a— What the hell had Dad told this guy?

He swallowed the fierce response boiling in his throat. No need to give Davis additional ammunition. "I have no intention of sabotaging you, Kevin. I would have liked advance notice of this meeting. I could have provided you with status reports on all the projects beforehand for you to review. We could have spent this time discussing any questions you had about those projects. As it is, I'll have to give them to you cold."

He flipped open the cover to his tablet, bracing it on the leg he'd propped on the opposite knee. He glanced up, catching the other man's critical glance at his steel-toed work boots.

Well, tough shit, buddy. This job involves getting dirty.

He cheered slightly at that thought.

He swiped and thumbed the screen. "I'm sending you…" Tap. "…updates and timelines on the fourteen projects…" Tap. "…currently active." Tap-tap. "Also, a list of priorities to be initiated as the active projects progress."

He paused, looking up. "What's your company e-mail address?"

Kevin provided the information, then asked, "Why is this information not on the company network?"

"It is, but it's current only through last week. I met with the foremen yesterday to get their status reports. Stacy can show you where to load these new reports onto the network. After you review them, you can notify my father that they're available. Prior to next week's meeting, contact Jake Matthews, the senior foreman, to introduce yourself and let him know about the changeover."

Kevin glanced at his computer as a series of beeps announced the delivery of each e-mail. "Where are these meetings held?"

"At the work yard. It's more productive. There are three foremen in addition to Jake." Rhys glanced again at the tablet screen. "Will you be the lead on the Main Street project?"

"That's my understanding."

"All the reports are up-to-date on that project as far as McCall's involvement. I'm forwarding a couple of emails that will provide additional background."

"I'm sure I'll have questions about some of the projects."

Rhys hesitated. "I believe my father was going to clarify any questions for you."

"I won't have time to review any of these files before lunch. Since you're more familiar with the projects, perhaps we can schedule some time tomorrow or the next day."

He should let Dad deal with his half-assed way of handling the transition, but he couldn't let McCall's projects flounder. It wasn't fair to the employees, or to the clients, or to his replacement. He hadn't missed the note of trepidation in Kevin's voice.

I can't risk putting Main Street in jeopardy either.

The phone on Kevin's desk rang. After glancing at the

display, the man held up one hand as he answered. "Yes, Erik, we're finishing now, but I have some… Of course. I'll pass on your message."

Rhys closed the cover to his tablet and stood as Kevin ended the call.

"Your father says he has time now to talk with you."

Rhys gave a brief nod. "If my father can't answer your questions, he may prefer for you to discuss them with Jake. If not, then you can contact me to set up a meeting. Otherwise, I'll see you at the kick-off meeting. I sent you an invite with those other emails." He paused at the door, adding, "Good luck."

God knows Davis would need it. And thinking of the upcoming conversation with his father, so did he.

Rhys paused in the doorway to his father's office. Erik stood facing the window, his posture stiff and unyielding. Rhys tapped on the doorframe to announce his presence, then crossed the room to stand before the desk. "We need to talk."

Erik turned his head slightly, speaking over one shoulder. "Hand in your key card before you go."

Rhys stiffened, took a deep breath. He'd expected resistance, but not this stark dismissal. "Things don't have to be this way, Dad. Something is wrong, and I want to help…."

"Nothing's wrong, and I don't need your help."

He should have known his bold stance to relocate to another building would generate retaliation. Erik McCall didn't believe in getting even. He believed in getting ahead, and God help the person who got in his way.

Give it one more try.

Rhys sank down into one of the chairs facing the desk. Memories of those times when it was him and his father working together ran through his mind. Maybe reminding him of those days could break through this impasse.

"I was four years old when you put a hammer in my hand for the first time." As he spoke, the soft rolling Virginia drawl of his youth crept into his voice. "You did a lot of repair and carpentry work in those days. I was amazed how you could take lumber and a couple of tools and build something new or make something old like new again. You showed me houses you'd built with your father, others your grandfather had built. You told me stories of how they came to be. How the Fords and the Harpers had money and property. But the McCalls had dreams, and the hearts and the hands to make those dreams come true."

His father's shoulders began to relax. The older man shifted his stance, turning until he was almost in profile.

"Main Street is my dream. I want us to work together as partners. I want my children to have the same legacy you gave to me."

He fell silent. His father had remained calm during the entire speech. Perhaps he'd listened with his heart, heard Rhys's desire to push aside the animosity and mistrust and repair their fractured relationship.

When Erik turned to face him, all those hopes crumbled.

His father's visage could have been carved from stone, his gray eyes as icy as the ocean tides in January. When he spoke, his voice held no hint of emotion. "Turn in your key card. You may own part of the business, but not the building."

Time stopped for an instant. His reality shifted and would never be the same. The harsh rejection should have devastated him. Perhaps that was what his father expected, even wanted. But he too was a McCall and made of stronger stuff. An unnatural calm flowed over him. In that moment, he understood the ice-cold control his father wore like a badge. Rhys rose, savoring the freedom as he severed that final emotional tie.

I'm done.

Something in his eyes must have conveyed that message, for a glimmer of uncertainty flickered across his father's face. Without breaking his gaze, Rhys unclipped the key card from his belt and laid it on the desk. He walked out, shutting the door behind him with a quiet finality.

For the first time in ages, Rhys played hooky. After leaving McCall headquarters, he debated, then rejected, going to the Canfield building to discuss his new office with Dana. It wasn't fair to inflict his mood on her. Though a part of him felt that talking with her, if only about work, might make him feel better.

Instead he went home, ate a quick lunch, then stretched out on the couch for a nap. Several hours later, he awoke, bored and restless. Changing clothes, he headed out for a run along the beach.

He ran until he was physically spent. Three miles. Not bad, considering how much he'd slacked off on jogging lately. If nothing else, he might regain a measure of balance back in his life.

As excited as he was about Main Street, it had the potential to become a behemoth. Dana's presence was a godsend. And now he could make time to follow up on that bolt of attraction with Jamie. Then again, it might be wise to go slowly on that. If things didn't work out, it could make for very awkward working conditions.

As for Dad, he couldn't… what? Give in? Force him to change? He might as well wish…

He caught his breath as a long-forgotten memory soared to life.

"I wish I had a magic wand."

His mother's hand stroked the hair from his brow, followed by a light kiss. "What would we do with a magic wand?"

"Make wishes come true."

"You know what's more fun than having a magic wand?"

He shook his head.

"Making wishes come true ourselves. Like the storybook we made together. We could have bought one. Even wished for one. But we made one with our own hands."

He grinned. "It's the best book ever!"

It had taken them days and days to put it all together. They'd had so much fun with markers and glue and stickers, deciding which shape or color or word was just the right one to use until it was finally finished. That night, Mommy read the book to him from beginning to end. Then a second time just because he'd asked.

In their own ways, both parents had instilled in him the tenets of dedication and hard work. The difference being that his father's edicts had come from ego and the need for acknowledgment; his mother's guidance had come from the heart and seeing the value not only in what they accomplished but in how they did it.

"I wish I remembered more, Mom." In quiet times, he could

recall her voice, her scent, her touch. He just wished—that word again—he could remember her face.

No chance of that, since his father had destroyed any photographs from Rhys's childhood that included her.

A sudden chill penetrated the warmth around him. Would Dad try to destroy the Main Street project too?

The specter of the threat left as quickly as it came. Probably not. Dad's pride wouldn't allow McCall's reputation to suffer, and the company certainly couldn't survive a financial hit so soon after recovering from near bankruptcy.

Money and ego. Those two reasons ensured Dad wouldn't sabotage the project.

Standing calf-deep in the surf, Rhys closed his eyes, struggling with the emotions swamping him. The sun warmed his bare chest and shoulders, the water cooled his legs. Overhead, the cries of a seagull echoed while behind him came the occasional rush of a passing car. Farther down the beach, distant voices rumbled, but none so distinct as to disturb him.

Solitude, peaceful serenity. Exactly what he needed. He took a deep breath, tranquility seeping into his soul, revitalizing him in a way he hadn't experienced for months. He sensed someone nearby. He kept his eyes closed, struggling to hold that peaceful core, but the powerful scent of jasmine perfume wiped away any chance.

He opened his eyes to see Stacy Andrews standing about a foot away. Barefoot, clad in denim shorts and a plain white tank. Her auburn hair, absent from its usual tangle of curls, fell in a soft cloud around her shoulders. Without makeup, she appeared softer and almost vulnerable.

He didn't buy that illusion for an instant.

"The old man was in a mood when you left."

He shrugged. "The old man was in a mood when I got there."

"Tell me about it. Sorry you got canned." She scuffed a foot in the sand. "It won't be any fun without you there."

"You thought I was fun?" His eyes narrowed as she sashayed closer.

"Absolutely. You didn't come in with an attitude. You let me do my work, and you didn't let me get away with anything."

A sudden thought struck him. "What are you doing on the

67

beach at this time of day?"

"See. You caught on right away." Stacy bumped her shoulder against his arm. "I worked over a couple of evenings, so I told Kevin I was taking off early."

"You *told* Kevin?"

"I certainly didn't *ask* him. I'm training him from the start on how things are run around that place."

The unrepentant sass almost won a smile from him. But giving Stacy any kind of leeway was never to anyone's benefit. Instead, he shrugged again. "Not my problem."

Her hands came to rest on his forearm. His gaze dropped down to them then back up just as Stacy batted her lashes. "We still have Main Street."

Her croon washed over him like the water paddling around his ankles. She stepped away, palms sliding off his arm. "See you at the kick-off meeting." With a flip of her hair and a swivel of her hips, she walked away.

So much for an escape.

He walked to his vehicle, snatched his T-shirt from the front seat, and pulled it over his head. Settling behind the wheel, he pulled out his cell phone.

"Sam, you on duty tonight?"

"Nope. Planning on watching the game. You in?"

"I'm in."

Uncomplicated guy time. Just what he needed.

Chapter Six

Dana stood in front of the open closet, sliding hangers along the rod as she considered, then discarded each option. Nick didn't seem like a suit and tie guy. For a first date though, he'd certainly dress up.

What am I doing? I just met the man. I hardly know him.

She hardly knew Rhys McCall, and she'd accepted his job offer on the spot. She didn't know anyone on PI, but she'd sold her home and relocated her life here. A first date was nothing compared to all the other changes she'd made recently.

However, Nick Warden was in a category all his own.

Remember, Dana, you said you didn't need—

A man? Had she expected to spend the rest of her life with work as her only companion? It was a date. Nothing more, nothing less. A chance to have fun and enjoy herself.

She decided on a flowing print skirt that fell to midcalf, pairing it with a lavender sweater that softly draped her body. Fun, feminine, and completely the opposite of her usual professional clothing. She seated herself at the vanity. Opening the lid, she considered the array of jewelry before selecting a long string of pearls. She wound the strand several times around her neck, then threaded pearl studs through her earlobes. Leaning forward, she checked her reflection in the mirror. The faint crow's-feet and the slight creases on either side of her mouth were offset by the sparkle in her eyes and the smile on her full lips.

Middle-aged, my ass.

The front doorbell rang, and her heart skipped. She stepped into bone-colored slingbacks and snatched up her envelope purse. After a final glance in the cheval mirror, she exited the bedroom and rushed down the stairs.

She opened the door to find Nick lounging against the frame. Leather jacket, jeans, polo shirt, polished boots. Dana caught a glimmer of alarm in his eyes as he straightened.

Casual night it is.

"Hi. Come on in. I'm running late." She waved him into the house then closed the door. "I'll run upstairs to change and be right back down. Jeans okay? Shouldn't take me more than ten minutes. Have a seat in the living room."

His guilty look shifted to a knowing gleam. "Are you fibbing to me, Ms. Canfield?"

She blushed. "I believe I am, Mr. Warden." She trotted up the stairs, his laughter following her.

Back in her bedroom, Dana tossed her purse onto the dresser and opened the closet doors once again to search for a pair of jeans.

Stupid, stupid, stupid.

Lamebrain idiot moron. Did you stop to think she might expect to go somewhere fancy?

Well, no. He knew where he wanted to take Dana, dressed accordingly, and… forgot to tell her.

You've been out of the game too long, boy.

Still, she didn't seem upset. Maybe he hadn't blown it altogether. He glanced up the stairs, snorting.

Ten minutes, right.

He spied a dining room to his left, a living room on the opposite side, and the hallway in front of him leading to the kitchen. He chose to go to the right.

The arched doorway led into a spacious area. Two large windows at the front of the room provided an abundance of natural light. A fireplace flanked by bookcases, still empty, occupied most of the outer wall. The sofa facing the fireplace was long and plush, the type of couch where a man could stretch out comfortably after a hard day's work. Matching chairs, tables, and other furniture had been carefully positioned. The room looked fine as it was, but the stack of sealed boxes sitting in the far corner swore otherwise.

He wondered if the furniture had come with the house. It all seemed to have been selected with a man in mind. Nothing dainty or pastel. Or maybe that was what she liked. He hadn't been the most perceptive so far when it came to Dana's preferences.

French doors at the opposite end of the room looked out to the back of the property. He strolled to the exit, resting his hand on the door handle. The patio was wide and spacious, paved in bluestone, with steps leading to a kidney-shaped pool. He spied a deluxe gas grill set into a stone island at the far end of the patio, and his heart beat a little faster.

Beyond the pool, a half wall of traditional house brick enclosed the entire back lot. Plenty of space to landscape a kick-ass garden.

Garden.

"Damn it. Flowers!" He gave himself a hard mental kick. *Jeez, Warden, you're oh-for-two tonight.*

He leaned forward for a final look at the grill, then frowned as the door handle jiggled loosely in his hand. Flipping the latch, he opened one of the doors, then crouched to examine the frame and deadbolt.

The lock itself was a piece of crap. The bolt was less than an inch long, the strike plate wiggling easily under his touch. Chips of wood were missing around the plate. The framework didn't show signs of being replaced recently. Which didn't explain the scratches around the exterior of the handle.

Someone had tried to force the lock, and those marks looked new. Dana had moved in recently, so the attempt might have been made while the house was still vacant.

Nick rose, relocking the door. Hearing Dana's footsteps on the stairs, he returned to the foyer. "The lock on your...."

She'd traded her previous outfit for stonewashed jeans and a pink sweater along with a pair of sandals. She looked trim and vibrant, and he reconsidered his opinion about things dainty and pastel. Swinging the strap of a floral denim bag over one shoulder, she threw a smile at him that chased all coherent thought out of his head. "Ready?"

"Yes, ma'am." He reached for her hand, then halted. "You like seafood, don't you?" *God, please, don't let her be allergic!*

"Love it."

Nick heaved a sigh of relief. He hadn't screwed up the night completely.

Eddie's Sea-Shack was located at the tip of lower PI. All new territory to Dana. The drive took about thirty minutes via the coastal route, and along the way Nick pointed out various landmarks. Spying a silver bullet of a diner, Dana asked, "Pop's? Is that the restaurant Paige's father owned?"

Nick shot a quick glance to the right then back to the road. "Yep. He'd passed on before I came to PI. Best burgers on the island. Saw her there several times, but we never met until the other day."

"Now she's pursuing her own dream."

"Kids have a way of doing that, don't they?"

Dana turned her head to look at Nick. He seemed at ease, both hands on the steering wheel, left elbow resting on the ledge of the open window. Sunglasses hid his eyes, but a slight tightening around his mouth and jaw gave him away. There was a story there, though not one he seemed to want to discuss.

"You mentioned seafood." Her prompt earned her a quick grin.

"Eddie's Sea-Shack. Used to be a warehouse back when commercial fishing was a concern on the island. The original icehouse was torn down ages ago for parking while the rest of the building was converted into the restaurant. No frills, but the food more than makes up for it. Lot of history down this part of the island. I thought you might enjoy it."

He pointed to a large building just ahead on the left. "Over there."

The exterior of the converted warehouse looked weatherworn but solid, as if the old structure had combatted many a storm.

Nick pulled the SUV into the parking lot. He shut off the engine and opened the door, giving her a quick nod. "Be right around," he said before shutting the door.

Dana unlatched her seatbelt as Nick rounded the vehicle. He seemed off his usual confident self, making her wonder if he'd been out of the dating scene for long. If so, it had to be by choice.

The door beside her opened. She placed her hand into his palm and stepped out of the SUV.

"You can stow your purse in the center console. It'll be safe there. Or you can check it inside if you want."

Dana stared down at the cloth satchel then back to Nick. "Is this like a gun check or something?"

Nick chuckled. "Nothing like that. I thought that we might have a dance or two while we're here, and you wouldn't have to worry about it."

"Dancing, hmm?" Without hesitation, Dana stowed her purse in the console. She stepped forward to let Nick shut the door.

His hand enveloped hers. Fingers entwined, they walked toward the restaurant.

"Welcome to Eddie's." The hostess, gray-haired and just a smidge past five-feet tall, threw a teasing wink in Nick's direction. "See you brought company today, Nick. Two in red okay with you?"

"That would be perfect, Bobbie."

As they followed the woman to a two-seater by the window at the far side of the building, Dana savored the light touch of Nick's hand on her back. She wondered if he even realized he'd made the contact. For all his teasing and humor, there was a courtly manner about the man, a consideration that transcended formal etiquette. When they reached the table, she slipped onto the chair he held for her before taking his own seat. Bobbie dropped two menus on the table. Within moments, their server Janis arrived to take their drink order.

As a first date, it wasn't what she'd expected. Eddie's Sea-Shack was a world away from Harmony Hills Country Club. It fit Nick, and strangely enough, it fit her.

Industrial lighting in the ceiling aided by cone-shaped lamps created a setting that was warm and inviting. Fish netting interwoven with colored lights swagged from the rafters while oars, life rings, flags, and other nautical objects decorated the walls. Colored stripes on the floor—red, green, yellow, and blue—delineated various dining sections. Picnic tables filled one of those areas, while booths lined the walls in another. Scattered elsewhere were farm-style wood tables with mix-matched cane and ladder-back chairs painted in whatever color might have been on sale at the time.

"What does 'two in red' mean?" Dana asked. "I'm guessing a table for two, but what does red signify?"

Nick chuckled as he pointed to the colored lines on the cement floor. "That enclosed section with the green strip at the entrance is family seating. It includes a door that leads to an outside playground. Yellow is general seating. Blue marks off the dance floor." He reached out, laying his palm on top of her hand. "And red is for couples."

Janis arrived with their beverages. "Sam Adams and a sweet tea. Ready to order?"

After placing their orders, Nick said, "Shrimp and dirty rice, nice. I expected something sophisticated like grilled salmon on arugula."

Dana lifted a brow at his observation. "What about you? I expected to hear surf and turf, and you order a Cajun Po' Boy."

"I became partial to Cajun food while stationed at Fort Polk many years ago."

A piece of the Nick Warden puzzle fit into place. "So, you're ex-military. What else?"

"What else?" He leaned back in his seat, a huff of air brushing past his lips. "Military, twenty years and out. Married ten years, divorced for seven. We met when I was stationed at Fort Riley in Kansas. Callie worked a civilian job on post. My daughter—stepdaughter—is in her final year of high school."

Dana ran a finger along the outside of her glass, catching a drop of condensation. "Do they live here on PI?"

A cloud crossed over Nick's face. "My ex remarried last year, second time since our divorce. This time to Megan's biological father. Gary walked out on Callie while she was pregnant. She and I met when Megan was about seven months old and got married a couple of months later. About five years after that,

Gary started showing up every so often, wanting to play the proud papa."

Dana swallowed a shocked gasp. "That must have been confusing for Megan."

"That's putting it mildly. Gary was a stranger, and she was told 'this is Daddy.' Megan wasn't buying it. As far as she was concerned, I was her dad." He smiled, pride—and a tinge of hurt—radiating from those memories.

"She sounds like a very loyal girl."

His grin widened. "She's a great kid. An old soul with a loving heart." His good humor faded. "I wanted to adopt Megan, but Gary would never agree to relinquish custody. They're in the Denver area now, living as, according to Callie, 'the family they were always meant to be.'"

Her mouth dropped open. "Ouch! That's cold."

"Politely put, but yes. I decided I needed a change too. I came across this opportunity to buy the garage and snapped it up." He tipped his glass in her direction. "And I'm glad I did."

A warm flush crept up her neck and cheeks, and she stumbled to change the subject. "You mentioned going off call. Do you have a partner who takes over?"

Nick took a sip of beer, then set the glass aside. "Emergency call-outs are through the sheriff's department. Sam set up a rotation with all the garages that are interested. Works out to be about once every four weeks, depending on whether any of the others opt out of their turn. I don't mind taking the extra shift when needed. It helped build up a reputation for my business."

The conversation halted as their dinner arrived. While Janis arranged their plates, Nick nodded to several diners at a nearby table, gave a wave to someone at the bar, and exchanged a laughing remark with a passing server. Dana envied the easy familiarity he'd managed to build within the time he'd lived on PI.

"Everything look okay?"

She snapped to attention, realizing Janis was addressing her. "Yes! Thank you. I can't wait to try it."

"Enjoy." With a nod, she stepped away.

Seeing Nick's curious gaze, Dana laughed. "Sorry. I was thinking how lucky you were to know so many people already."

"Has its pitfalls. I get hit up for car advice all the time. Which reminds me. That car of yours was sounding a bit rough. I'd be glad to check it out. You know, take it out for a test drive."

She nearly dropped her fork in exasperation. Exactly what she *didn't* need—car trouble. The vehicle was barely two years old. She'd had it checked thoroughly before leaving for PI.

Wait a minute.

Remembering the heart-pat he'd bestowed on the BMW the day she arrived, she shook her head. "Very clever, Mr. Warden."

"Just trying to keep you safe on the road." He favored her with another of his deadly smiles. "Your turn. What's the Dana Canfield story?"

She chose the safe version. "Married almost twenty-five years. My husband passed away a year ago. I have a son, Joshua." Echoing his words, she added, "And when I came across the opportunity to work on the Main Street project, I jumped on it. I was fortunate that Rhys McCall felt the same way and hired me."

"I'm sorry for your loss."

His expression softened in sympathy, but Dana discerned an uncomfortable knowledge there as well. "I get the impression you've heard the story."

He met her gaze full on. "Sam mentioned a shooting. That's all he said, and it wasn't my place to ask." He pushed his plate and his manners aside to rest his folded arms on the table. "Consider the subject dropped."

Her throat tightened. In the brief time she'd spent with Nick, she'd witnessed both his teasing sense of humor and his kind heart. She wanted—no, *needed*—him to hear the story. "James was murdered."

Nick's mouth dropped open, then snapped shut.

She pushed her own plate to the aisle side of the table. "James was an attorney. Mostly estate planning. We lived in Harmony Hills. He was asked to represent a woman in a child-custody case being heard in Sutton. As a favor, he agreed. The morning of the hearing, a man supposedly hired by the father-in-law showed up at the courthouse with a gun. The client, a friend who was with her, and James were all shot. Both women died instantly. James lived a few hours longer. The police never located the shooter, and they weren't able to make a case against the father-in-law."

"I moved here from Sutton." Nick shook his head. "That must have happened after I left. I don't remember reading or hearing anything about it. Probably most people on PI wouldn't know about it either."

Some might. She stirred in her seat, remembering the coven and Toddy's comments about vacation homes. "You mentioned how you and your ex-wife met. I had an accident a number of years ago." She tapped two fingers against her temple. "I suffered a head injury and was in a coma for a couple of weeks. I lost my memory prior to that time. I don't remember meeting James. I don't remember our wedding or when my son was born. Two of the most important events in my life, and I can't recall anything about either of them."

His brow creased into a frown as he asked, "You're all right now, aren't you?"

"Perfectly healthy. Just a blank slate before the injury. Although I must have had some crazy dreams during the coma. Remembering things that never happened. The doctors surmised I subconsciously heard other conversations and incorporated them into my brain."

"What about pictures? Did it help looking at photographs of those times?"

"There weren't any. We were in the process of moving, and that box got lost."

Nick shook his head. "Dana, no offense, but you definitely have not lived a boring life."

"I could have done with a different sort of excitement." Enough of the past and morbid memories. An impish thought nudged her. "Change of subject. Do you like cheesecake?"

"Ah... not really." He glanced around for their server. "If you want dessert, I can check."

Another point in his favor. "I didn't want cheesecake. I just wondered if you liked it."

His lips pursed then stretched into a grin. "You like to dance?"

"I love it."

He rose and held out a hand. "Let's hit the dance floor then."

Shoes kicked to one side on the floor of Nick's truck, Dana wiggled her toes. Wedge sandals had not been the best option for dancing. However, getting on the dance floor had broken the ice in a way she hadn't expected. Several Main Street merchants greeted her with welcoming smiles and friendly conversation. When one woman hinted for home-decorating suggestions, Dana caught the knowing wink Nick sent her way.

She hadn't achieved official PI status this evening, but being with Nick Warden had helped her gain a larger measure of acceptance.

She pressed her back into the comfortable leather seat, soothed by the gentle roll of the vehicle as it traveled the darkened country road. Twin beams pierced the darkness ahead. Neck resting against the high-backed seat, she rolled her head in Nick's direction. The dashboard lights shadowed and highlighted his strong features.

As if sensing her gaze, Nick cast a sideward glance in her direction, then focused back on the road. "Never expected to be part of the entertainment tonight, did you?"

"I can't believe I line-danced!" Despite her embarrassment at forgetting the steps, she'd loved being part of the group. It hadn't hurt that Nick was there, ready to turn her in the right direction.

Seeing the driveway for her house, she wiggled her much-abused feet into the abandoned sandals. A quick dive into her purse retrieved her house keys.

Nick turned onto the circular driveway, then parked in front of the house. He reached for the door handle. "Be right around."

She watched him cross in front of the vehicle. Of course, he would open the door. His manners had been impeccable, so innate even the simplest of gestures seemed natural.

Why do I feel so comfortable with you?

Maybe it was due to making a fresh start. She was at peace with herself. More open and ready to trust. Not totally though, not this soon.

The door opened, and Nick stood with hand extended. She placed her palm in his and stepped to the ground. They walked up the wide steps to the entrance. Turning her back to the door,

Dana looked up at the man beside her.

"Thank you for a wonderful evening. I haven't had this much fun in a long time."

"Same here." He propped a shoulder against the door frame. A brow lifted, a teasing smile hinted. "Ask me in for coffee?"

"Coffee?" She faked a frown. "We already had a coffee date, remember?"

A split second passed before he burst out laughing. He rolled his back against the wall, using the solid surface to support himself until he could control his mirth. She'd noticed that about him all evening. How he gave each moment his full attention.

Was he that focused in all the things he did? Did his dedication to detail, such as she'd witnessed in the garage, extend to other areas?

Did she have any coffee in the house?

The chuckles subsided. Nick straightened, shifting to face her. "In that case, Ms. Canfield, how about Friday night? There's a dinner cruise that goes out for a couple of hours. I'll even wear a button-down and a jacket. You can wear that purple thing you had on earlier."

That purple thing. God, he was adorable in a totally masculine way. "I have to say yes. I can't turn down a chance to see you in a button-down shirt."

He stepped forward, giving her a considering look. "What happens if I add a tie to that mix?"

She leaned into him, her purse and keys slipping from her fingers onto the wooden porch. Her palms slid along the soft cotton of his knit shirt, the cloth warming beneath her fingers, coming to rest on his broad shoulders. She lifted onto her toes, face tilted upward, and whispered, "Try it and find out."

The answer to her challenge gleamed in his eyes. "I think I will."

His hands slid from her shoulders, caressing down her back to rest along her waist. Their lips met. A shiver coursed through her body, awakening a long-slumbering part of her. Without a doubt, Nick Warden gave his devout attention to even the sweetest, simplest of kisses.

For now, a gentle kiss was all she could handle. She drew back, startled to see the same sense of wonderment on his face.

"Yeah. Me too." He stroked a fingertip down her cheek, then straightened with a reluctant shrug of his shoulders. "So… Friday?"

"Yes, Friday."

He dipped his head in for a final caress of her lips, and she did nothing to stop him. He took a backward pace, half-turned toward the steps. "Not bad for a third date."

"Third?" She bent down to retrieve the purse and keys that had tumbled from her hand. "What are you talking about?"

"Tonight. This was our third date." Taking another backward step off the porch, Nick held up one finger. "Our coffee date at Paige's."

"That was not a date. You sat down for less than five minutes while Paige got a check to pay you for her battery."

He reached the front walk. "Hanging out at my garage was two. Dinner tonight was three."

"I'm surprised you didn't count our eye lock on Ocean." With a smile, she inserted the key and opened the front door.

"Hey, Dana."

She turned to see that Nick had reached his vehicle.

"That day…" He pantomimed the heartbeat gesture. "…it wasn't for the car."

Words froze in her throat. She could only nod. A moment, long, silent, and powerful, passed between them.

Nick opened the door to the truck. "Night, Dana."

"Good night, Nick." She entered the house, knowing he wouldn't leave until she was safely inside.

Leaving her shoes and purse at the bottom of the stairs, she padded barefoot toward the kitchen for a bottle of water to take upstairs. A rush of air swept down the hallway, and she paused. She stood in the glow of the hallway light, listening.

The gurgle of water from a nearby brook, the rustle of leaves trembling in the wind, crickets chirping their nightly call.

All the sounds she should not have heard from inside the house.

She stepped quietly to the end of the hallway, glancing toward the exit to the patio. Both doors were open, broken glass strewn across the floor. Her gaze swept to the living room, where she saw boxes ripped open. Broken glassware and scattered books. Cushions uprooted, tossed aside. Furniture overturned.

"Oh, my God."

She whirled and dashed to the front door. Threw open the dead bolt, ran outside.

"Nick!" She raced down the driveway to the edge of the road. The bricks were cold and unforgiving against her bare feet. Only the faint glow of taillights in the distance remained. Though the attempt was useless, she screamed again. "Nick!"

What was dusky and romantic moments ago loomed now with hidden threats. The silvery glow from the moon cast the surrounding trees and shrubbery into ominous shapes. A cluster of bushes rustled though the wind was absent, and she sensed a piercing gaze from eyes that didn't belong to night creatures.

She whirled, stumbled up the front steps and into the house, locking the door behind her. Not that she felt any safer inside. *Cell phone!* She snatched up her purse, then staggered into the dining room, which appeared untouched. Backing into the corner nearest the exit, she sank into a crouch and upended the bag, her hands grabbing the phone when it tumbled out. She punched in the emergency number.

Answer, answer, answer.

"Sheriff's department. What's the nature of your call?"

Dana swallowed, choking back the fear that threatened to silence her. "A break-in at my home, 21 Magnolia. My name is Dana Canfield."

The officer's voice was calm and soothing. "I'm dispatching a deputy now. I'll stay on the line with you until he arrives. Are you somewhere safe?"

"Yes," she said, her voice barely above a whisper. But seeing all the dark areas where danger could emerge, she didn't believe that was so.

Chapter Seven

Dana huddled in the corner of the dining room. The hallway chandelier gleamed like a spotlight, waiting for whatever threat lurked in the recesses of the house to loom forward out of the dark. The voice on the phone no longer soothed her, the flat, impartial tone reminding her that help was that much further away. If the intruder was still in the house, she'd left herself vulnerable and exposed to his view.

Going elsewhere meant walking down darkened hallways and up dimly lit stairs, past open doorways and unlit rooms. She wasn't about to commit the classic movie mistake of locking herself in a room with no alternative means of escape.

The rotating blaze of red and blue lights through the window broke her paralysis. Dana jerked to her feet. "They're here." She disconnected the call and raced to the foyer.

Throwing open the front door, she charged barefoot onto the porch as deputies exited from two separate squad cars. Sheriff Wallace arrived immediately afterward, followed by Rhys in his own vehicle. Rhys headed immediately in her direction, while the sheriff paused to direct two of his deputies to either side of the house.

"Are you all right?" he asked, extended his hand.

She took his hand between her palms for a moment. The warmth reassured her; the contact grounded her. "Unnerved. How did you know to come?"

"I was watching a baseball game at Sam's when he got the call."

Sam, followed by two other deputies, joined them on the porch. He tipped a finger to the brim of his cap. "Mrs. Canfield. Sorry to meet again under these circumstances. Where did the break-in occur?"

Dana stepped toward the doorway and motioned the men to follow. Crossing into the foyer, she gestured toward the living room entrance. "At the back through the patio doors."

Sam motioned one of the deputies in that direction, indicating for the second man to remain on the porch. He pulled off his cap as he crossed the entryway. "Where can we talk?"

"The dining room. Nothing seems to have been disturbed in that room. I don't think the burglar got that far."

Sam lifted an eyebrow. "We'll check the rest of the house to be certain."

Spying the shoes she'd left at the foot of the staircase, Dana paused to slip them on. A small thing, but it restored some measure of her confidence. She continued to the dining room, flipping on the light as she entered.

Rhys lingered in the doorway. "I'm going to get supplies to board up the patio doors." He turned to leave, then hesitated. "Would you prefer I stay while you talk with Sam?"

"I can handle it." She threw a worried look toward the back of the house. "Getting the doors secured will take a tremendous load off my mind. Thank you for coming."

The corners of his mouth turned upward, a reassuring smile that settled the quivering in her stomach. "Glad to do it. I'll be back as soon as I can and take care of it." With a nod to Sam, he departed.

Once again, "thank you" seemed inadequate. When he'd heard the news, Rhys had immediately come to her house. His concern was for her, and not because of a potential risk to their project. It was the act of a good man showing consideration for someone else. He was her business partner, but for a moment... one brief moment, she'd felt as if it were Joshua by her side.

No problem, Mom. I'll take care of it.

"Mrs. Canfield?" The sheriff's tone was gentle, even kind.

Had he seen her tears? She blinked, taking a deep breath to steady her voice. "Yes?"

He gestured toward the dining table chairs. "Why don't you have a seat so I can take your statement?"

Dana seated herself as he took the chair opposite her. She recounted the events of the evening, watching the sheriff write each detail in the notebook he'd pulled from his jacket pocket. After going through the events for the second time, she bolted from the chair. "I wish I could give you better information, but I've told you everything I know. Repeating it isn't helping."

"Sometimes additional details are recalled on a second go-round. I understand this must be frustrating on top of the scare you had." Sam stood, tucking the notebook back into his pocket. "Excuse me while I go check on my deputies."

Dana followed the sheriff down the hallway. Stopping at the edge of the kitchen, she watched the crime-scene technician pack up his equipment. The two men conferred briefly before the deputy departed.

Sam returned to the kitchen. "Appears to be a random break-in. No indication of footprints outside. The ground's dry, so no surprise there. There's been a couple other break-ins over the past month." His eyes narrowed at he studied the destruction in the next room. "Nothing like this though."

Dana shook her head. "Boarding up the door fixes the immediate problem. But what are you doing to find the person responsible for these break-ins?"

She winced at the sharpness in her voice and immediately shook her head. "I'm sorry. I just…" She looked around her new home; the place where only hours ago she'd felt at peace now seemed anything but secure. The shattered doors and scattered boxes mocked her hopes for a serene new beginning.

She met Sam's sympathetic gaze. Softening her tone, she said, "Between the near hit-and-run the other day and now this break-in, I'm not feeling very safe. What are you going to do about it?"

Nick lowered the volume of the radio enough to provide a comfortable background. He hadn't felt this relaxed in ages. In spite of his irritation with Paige over those ridiculous photos, it had provided an unexpected opportunity to spend time with

Dana. Not to mention a perfect chance to ask her out.

He'd eaten at Eddie's enough times that he was known by name. Besides a meal, he'd often found a dance partner or two, and he'd certainly tossed back his share of beer. A man had to eat, and going to Eddie's was one way to pass the time.

Being with Dana, though, made all the difference. Her smile. Her laugh. Her hand in his. Despite the car, the big house, and the outward sophistication, she was as down-to-earth as a man like him could want. Been a long time since he'd felt that comfortable with a woman and never upon such a short acquaintance.

Maybe that was the reason no one else had captured his attention. He'd been waiting for Dana.

Everything about her pulled him in. When she looked at him with those liquid brown eyes, he felt like he could share his dreams. Listening to what she'd endured made him want to protect her. Kissing her, holding her body against his, made him want to possess her. No, not possess. He didn't want to own her. When they came together, he wanted it to be mutual. It didn't matter how much he might tease, cajole, or suggest, he had the firm conviction that Dana could hold her own.

I really did mean just a cup of coffee.

Or a glass of wine… bottle of water… any excuse to keep the evening from ending. Sitting out on the patio, watching the stars, talking.

Twin beams of light blasted into the rearview mirror, making him wince. Another truck judging by the height and spacing of the lights. He reached up to adjust the mirror. *Idiot.* Traveling way too fast on a dark country road. Nick tapped the brakes in warning as the distance between the two vehicles eroded.

The idiot wasn't slowing down.

Closer. Closer still until the headlights disappeared. Nick tightened his grip on the steering wheel, steeling for an impact. The driver slowed, backing off until the lights again blazed through the cab of his SUV.

No room to pull off the road, and the driver didn't seem inclined to go around and on his way. Less than a half-mile to the crossroads. He'd have room to maneuver there. Plus, those roads were illuminated, giving him a chance to get a look at the idiot.

The headlights flared into high beams, and the distance began to close again. The rattling roar of the other engine pierced the night. Just as Nick pressed down on the accelerator, the beams shifted to the left, and the truck swept into the oncoming lane.

Nick eased up on the accelerator just in time as the driver swung back into right lane. The truck barely missed the front of his SUV before speeding away.

In those few seconds when the truck was in the beam of his own headlights, Nick recognized the vehicle.

Abe Clancy's truck.

He reached the crossroads intersection seconds later. No sign of the truck or even taillights to suggest which direction the vehicle had gone.

Was it a coincidence the truck had been on this very road? Traveling away from the location of Dana's house?

At least she was inside behind locked doors.

Door.

Patio door...

"Oh, hell!" He slammed a fist onto the steering wheel, glanced in all directions, then U-turned the SUV. He nudged up the speed.

The glare of red and blue lights several miles ahead punched him in the gut. "No, no, no." He shoved his foot to the accelerator. The powerful vehicle leaped forward, eating away the remaining distance to Dana's house.

Nick steered the vehicle to the side of the road just short of the driveway and leaped out. Ignoring the warning shouts from one of the deputies, he raced across the front lawn and charged up the steps, two at a time.

"Hold it there, buddy." Deputy Mike Winslow stepped forward from his post by the front door, his hand lifted. "You need to move back."

He shot a *don't mess with me* glare at Winslow, side-stepped him, then bolted through the front entrance.

Dana stood at the far end of the hallway where the kitchen flowed into the living room. A pale version of the vibrant woman he'd left not long ago. She gestured toward the room as she spoke with Sam.

"Dana!"

She turned and saw him standing at the doorway. Color raced back to her tired features, and a smile spread across her face. Without another word to the sheriff, she raced down the hallway. He opened his arms and captured her in a tight embrace.

She was safe.

Dana savored the security of Nick's arms wrapped around her. For that moment, the terror, the unknown, the frustration of the night faded away. He was here, and everything would be all right.

A gentle hand stroked her hair. "Are you okay?"

"I'm glad you're here." She nodded against his chest, then pulled away, looking up. "Why did you come back?"

Nick stared over the top of her head toward the back of the house. "It was the patio door, wasn't it?"

Dana's mouth dropped open. "You knew?"

Deputy Winslow loomed forward. "Hey, Sam! This guy says he knew about the patio door!"

Seeing Winslow's smirk and Nick's answering glare, Dana sighed. She didn't need this on top of everything else. Before Nick could respond, she pulled him by the hand toward the kitchen. "Thank you, Deputy," she said firmly. "We'll talk to the sheriff."

Sam stepped forward as they entered the kitchen. "Nick, you have some information on the break-in?"

"When I was here earlier, I noticed the door handle was loose in its setting. I checked the outside and found indications someone had tried to force the lock. I meant to tell Dana, but forgot until I was on the way home."

Sam pulled the notebook out of his pocket, then gestured toward the dining room. "Sounds like there's more to the story. Let's talk."

Nick shrugged, turning toward the hallway. Dana moved forward, halting as Sam stepped in front of her.

"Rhys is coming up the front steps. Why don't you show him where the patio doors are?"

"Considering it's my house that was invaded, I'd like to hear what Nick has to say. But since that big gaping hole in the back of my house is so hard to find, yes, I will show Rhys where it is. I want a complete report when you're finished."

Knowing that one of the deputies would point Rhys in the right direction, Dana stormed into the utility room in search of her own hammer. She was in a mood to pound nails.

Nick hated the dining room—the cream-on-white walls with wainscoting, the antique cherry wood table with seating for eight, the ornate chandelier and wall sconces. Maybe she had other plans for the room, as there were no boxes in the corner waiting to be unpacked. He doubted Dana had picked a single thing in the room. Possibly Canfield's stuff. Heirlooms, passed down generation to generation.

Was she holding on to the set for her son? Or was she filling spaces in the house with things that reminded her of when she had a family around her? Whatever the reason, this room didn't provide the same feeling of comfort that the living room did.

The sounds of hammering and nail guns, along with grunts, laughs, and conversation flowed in from the other room. He wouldn't mind being out there right now, swinging a hammer.

"Sorry for the wait," Sam announced as he returned to the room. He seated himself on the opposite side of the table. "Tell me about the door handle."

"The entire unit was loose in its setting. The bolt was less than an inch long. Your tech probably noted there were wood chips missing from around the strike plate. Also, fresh scratches where someone had tried to pick the lock."

"What were you doing by the door?"

"Waiting for Dana. She was upstairs getting dressed for us to go out for dinner. I walked into the living room, saw the patio outside, and went to the door to take a closer look. The handle jiggled when I rested my hand on it, and I checked it out."

"So your fingerprints are on the handle. Did you touch anything else in the room?"

He had to think about that question, finally shaking his head. "No, can't remember anything else."

Sam thumbed the end of his pen. "We'll compare prints on

the handle to the ones we have on file for you."

"Something else you need to know. Someone driving Abe Clancy's truck nearly rear-ended me after I dropped Dana off this evening. I remembered the patio door and turned around."

Nick looked out the window at the dark night while Sam jotted the information in his notebook. He couldn't see the road and wondered if the driver had circled back. If he was lurking somewhere nearby until Dana was alone.

"It's no coincidence, Sam. The other houses were burglarized, but there was no vandalism. Plus, those break-ins occurred before Abe's truck was stolen. The same day the truck goes missing, the driver tries to run Dana down. Then he's on the same road as her house the night it's robbed."

Sam tucked his notebook and pen into his pocket as he stood. He paused at the doorway. "I noticed that too."

Noticing wasn't good enough. Sam might have to follow procedure, but Nick didn't. Not when it came to Dana's safety.

Rhys had the corners of the plywood sheets secured to the door frame by the time Dana returned to the living room. She watched as he popped several more nails into place.

"Nail gun! Let me do it." She laid her hammer on a nearby table and stretched out both hands.

Rhys thumbed the lock to off then pushed the safety goggles on top of his head. "Seriously?"

"I need to work off some mad." For any number of reasons. The break-in, the destruction to her belongings, the lousy end to what had been a romantic, fun evening.

He held the gun back, looking doubtful. "Ever used one before?"

Dana tapped the goggles hanging by their stem from her jeans pocket. Setting them into place, she reached again for the gun. "Not my first rodeo."

"Why did I doubt you?" He shook his head, laughing, then set the gun in her hands.

Dana fired off several well-placed nails before handing the gun back to Rhys. She whipped off the safety glasses, dropping them on a nearby table. "Okay. I feel better. Or at least good enough to start cleaning up some of this mess." She surveyed the broken glass, scattered books, and other destruction.

The reality hit her again. A stranger had invaded her home. Touched her belongings. Destroyed her treasures and keepsakes for no good reason. Her lips quivered, and she turned to hide her reaction from Rhys.

"I'll give you a hand in a minute." He stepped back to the door to finish securing the panels.

She pulled on a pair of gloves and began tossing broken glass and other debris into one of the now empty packing cartons. "I cannot begin to tell you how much that plywood offends my sensibilities."

She clamped her mouth shut, ashamed for her bitchy tone. *Way to go, Dana. The man is here out of the goodness of his heart, and all you can do is criticize.* "Rhys, I'm sorry—"

"No apology necessary." He shot a quick grin over one shoulder. "I figured Urban Distressed wasn't the look you were going for." He shot the last nail into place, then stepped back, giving the area a final look-over before locking the gun.

"Not even close." She examined a small porcelain box. The trinket wasn't particularly valuable, but she loved it for sentimental reasons. A "just because" gift from Toddy, and now it was destroyed beyond repair.

The darkness she'd set to rest wormed its way back to the forefront of her mind. *I'm not going there again. It's just a box. No one was hurt.* She dropped the shattered pieces into the carton and counted her blessings.

Dana and Rhys worked together in harmony, setting as much of the room to rights as possible.

"You aren't having second thoughts about moving to PI, are you?" Rhys asked, looking up from where he'd knelt to pack away his tools. "Between the near fall you had on the street, my dad, and now this…."

"Of course not. I certainly have no intentions of allowing a few setbacks to change my decision. What do they say? Bad luck comes in threes. I should be home free from this point."

His hearty chuckle swept away the remaining darkness from her mood. "Here's to 'they' being right." He gave a final glance at the boarded-over exit. "Any ideas about the door?"

"I planned on replacing it along with the windows. They're

already on order."

"Who's the vendor? I can see about getting it expedited."

Dana dropped onto the couch. "Believe it or not, I have clout with quite a few vendors."

Her gentle chastisement made him laugh. "I have no doubts about that. Speaking of schedules, I have an inspection at Carson's tomorrow at ten. Can we push our meeting up before then?"

"How about afterwards? I need to make calls about an alarm system." She counted off the additional tasks to her mental to-do list. "And the insurance company. How does one o'clock sound?"

Rhys pulled out his cell phone, tapped a couple times, then nodded. "Works for me. Sending you an update." He looked up as Nick stepped into the doorway leading from the kitchen. He nodded his head in greeting before continuing. "I'll head out unless there's something else you need."

Dana eased to her feet, fighting a wave of exhaustion. "You've done so much already. I can't thank you enough."

He picked up his toolbox, giving a quick look around for anything else he might be leaving behind. "Call if you need anything."

She walked him to the front door, thanked him again as he left, then leaned her head against the doorframe for a brief moment. The house was secured, the sheriff and his men finally departed, and she knew nothing more than what Sam had surmised. The joyful evening spent with Nick seemed so long ago.

Nick.

He was waiting in the next room. She pushed away from the doorframe and returned to the living room. Without thinking, she walked to him, wrapping her arms around his waist.

Safe. Safe. Safe.

The mantra kept time with the beating of his heart. She yearned to rest in that protected cocoon forever, but hiding never solved anything. Drawing back, she took his hand and walked to the couch. They both sank onto the cushions with a grateful sigh.

Nick nodded toward the front door. "That kid has a crush on you."

91

She sniffed. "Don't be silly. He may be my business partner, but he's also a friend."

He jerked a thumb toward the boarded-over patio doors. "Does your business partner rate 'thank you' flowers?"

Teasing or a touch of jealousy? She wasn't sure, but either choice coaxed a small smile from her. "I was thinking homemade cookies."

He gave her a considering look, then stretched out an arm and pulled her against his chest. "I like cookies."

She stiffened for a second, then decided resting against him was just what she needed. "Any preference?"

His fingertips traced down her arm, a soothing, gentle stroke. "I'm not particular. Except no raisins… or nuts…. Nuts don't belong in cookies. Not crazy about molasses either."

"Got it. No raisins, nuts, or molasses." His thumb caressed the inside of her wrist, easing the remaining tension out of her. "How does chocolate chip sound?"

"Perfect." He dropped a light kiss on top of her head.

"Hmm, how lucky for me you're not particular."

"Only about you, darlin'." He tugged his cell phone from his pocket. "That reminds me. I'm calling your number."

A few seconds later, Dana heard her ringtone. Nick tapped the phone again.

"You have my number in your call list now." He set the phone on the table beside the couch. Shifting onto one hip, he pulled his wallet out of his back pocket and set it onto his chest. One handed, he flipped it open and pulled out a plastic card. He closed the wallet, laying it and the card beside his cell phone. "The card is a security pass. It'll give you access through the gate and into the garage."

Her head shot up. "Nick, I can't expect you to—"

He cupped her neck, easing her against him once again. "I want you to have a way to contact me. If you can't reach me, you'll have somewhere safe to go."

She wavered between arguing and acceptance. Granted, accepting help from Nick wasn't a sign of falling back into old habits as she had with Toddy. Nick's offer simply provided a way for her to protect herself.

She probably should send him home and call it a night for both of them. Maybe she would do just that in a few minutes.

When she wasn't nestled against his shoulder with his hand stroking a soothing path up and down her spine.

"I hope this is the end of my bad luck. The flood in James's office, his car stolen, a fire at the old house, now this. All in just the past year."

His arms tightened around her, and she snuggled into the warm comfort of his embrace. Exactly what she needed.

Nick knew the moment Dana fell asleep. Her body relaxed, melding into his, and her breathing slowed into a gentle rhythm. Once he was certain she was deep asleep, he'd shift positions and stretch out. Taking advantage of the situation? Yeah, but he wasn't about to leave Dana alone while she was still dealing with the aftermath of the break-in.

Had tonight's break-in been committed by the same perpetrator as the other B&Es? Wallace seem to think it was more likely than not, but Nick wasn't convinced. From the accounts, there were more differences than similarities between the break-ins, and criminals didn't change their MO without good reason. The near hit-and-run the day Dana arrived and the very same truck that almost ran her down being on her road the night she was robbed was just too coincidental to be... well, a coincidence.

He was willing to bet tonight's break-in was connected to the other events Dana had named. And they were all related to James Canfield's murder.

He moved her hand aside, then stroked a knuckle across her cheek. She stirred briefly, a small smile drifting across her lips.

Was she thinking of him—or dreaming of James?

Chapter Eight

Dana squinted against the early morning light. Navy blue? Her sheets were sage green so why...?

Because it was Nick's shirt under her cheek.

Fully awake, she took quick stock of the situation. Legs intertwined, her head on his chest, his arm wrapped around her. The last thing she remembered was discussing the break-in. When she'd fallen asleep, the sneaky devil had taken it upon himself...

...to keep her safe.

She'd slept through the entire night. Resting with a peace she hadn't experienced since prior to James's murder.

Shifting onto her elbow, her other hand resting on his chest for balance, Dana studied Nick's face as he slept. Stubble decorated his cheeks and jaw, adding to his usual rugged appearance. His dark hair spiked in several directions.

There was nothing soft about him. Except for his mouth. The memory of the touch and taste of those lips rushed through her. Tempting her for a second course. She ran her hand over his chest, smoothing the wrinkles from his shirt. Her palm lingered, feeling his heartbeat. Strong and steady.

What an incredible way to start the morning.

Nick stirred. His body shifted against hers, and she drew back her hand. His eyes opened, a slow, lazy smile stretching across his face. "Good morning."

That gravely baritone was better than any alarm clock. While he lay there, all rumpled and sexy, Dana inwardly cringed, thinking of how she must appear—messy hair and any residual makeup not transferred to the front of Nick's shirt smeared across her face. She pushed back her wayward curls, then wiped a finger under each eye while considering their positions. Nestled between the back of the couch and Nick's body, there was no way she could make a graceful exit.

"Good morning." She gestured toward the space beyond them. "We should...."

He gave a tremendous stretch, then swung his legs to the floor and pushed to his feet.

Accepting his extended hand, Dana stood, weaving for a moment before she caught her balance. "Um, bathroom is down the hall past the kitchen. I'm going to run upstairs for a moment."

"Meet you back in the kitchen." With a quick grin, he headed off in the direction she'd indicated.

He totally confused her. She'd slept soundly, but would have been aware of any wandering hands during the night. Taking stock, she found there wasn't a snap, button, or hook disrupted. The only things missing were her shoes, which were on the floor at the far end of the couch, along with Nick's boots. A flutter coursed through her at the sight of their footwear tumbled together.

He'd had every opportunity. Could have carried her up to her own bed, settled down beside her, removed his shirt in addition to his boots, but he hadn't done that. Instead, he'd pulled the most insidious type of seduction.

Honor.

Mug half-filled, Nick switched the carafe back into place on the coffeemaker to catch the remainder of the brew. Backside planted against the cabinet, feet crossed at the ankles, he savored that first hit of caffeine. How would Dana react when she returned downstairs? Waking up together this morning had been awkward, as much on the physical side for him as the emotional side must have been for her.

The heartbeat gesture had been an instinctive reaction when he'd first seen Dana. Yeah, it was corny, but she'd set his heart racing from the get-go. And truth be told, love-at-first-sight was a punch in the gut to anyone. He'd been struck by that type of lightning only once before. Although the object of his affection at that time had been bald, toothless, and hadn't yet learned to walk.

Hardly the same thing.

He took a deep breath, waiting for... what? A knee-jerk reaction to his revelation? His doubts—and there hadn't been even a handful of those—drifted away along with any pressure to rush to the next phase. He could wait until Dana caught up to him.

Though if she came downstairs, plastered herself to his body, and licked his tonsils, he damn sure wouldn't turn down the offer.

He watched her enter the kitchen over the rim of the coffee cup. She stopped on the opposite side of the island. Back straight, shoulders squared. Forearms resting on the countertop, hands folded primly in front of her.

Well, hell.

Nick retrieved a second cup from the cabinet. He filled it from the carafe, then set the cup on the island. He figured making free with her kitchen might tick that polite look right off her face.

Instead she stared at the mug, then back at him. "I have coffee?"

He jerked a thumb toward the crumpled package on the counter. "Sample bag. Enough for a couple cups."

Confusion cleared from her features. "April. I'll have to thank her."

He took another sip, shrugged. Not bad, a little on the mild side for his tastes. "April Davis?"

"You know her?"

"Not really. Stopped and helped her out with a flat tire the other day." He hadn't planned on charging the lady for what was a simple job. Thanks to Erik McCall's attitude and his business card, a bill went out the very next day. "You know how to change a flat?"

"Gee, Nick. Seems like that's something you'd know. I'll tell you what I can. First, make sure the spare is inflated—"

Smart ass. He grinned, cutting off the unnecessary explanation. "Let me rephrase the question. Would you be able to change a flat tire?"

"Intellectually, yes. Physically, no." She gave the coffee another glance, then pushed the mug to one side. "Why are we talking about flat tires?"

"Just curious." He tapped a forefinger against the side of his cup. "We can talk instead about how we slept together on our first—excuse me, our *third* date."

Her exasperated groan told him he wasn't as funny as he thought.

"Nick, I appreciate you stayed—"

He set the cup onto the countertop with a solid thunk. "I did that as much for me as for you. You needed to feel safe. I needed to know you were. When I came back last night and saw those flashing lights in the distance, I didn't know what had happened. If you were hurt or worse. I blamed myself for not checking the house, for not remembering to tell you about the latch. It seemed like an eternity until I got to your front door and saw you standing at the other end of the hallway."

He leaned across the island and wrapped both hands around hers. "That's when I took my next breath."

"You overwhelm me." The soft confession spilled from her in a breathless rush.

"Back at you, Ms. Canfield. You seduced me the moment we locked eyes."

She shook her head, untamed curls dancing around her face and neck. "I don't know what to do with you half the time!" A small moan slipped through her lips. "How can you be so *sure*?"

Her question took less than a split second of consideration. "Because I'm smart enough at this point in my life to know what's real and what's right."

He circled the island, Dana turning in tandem with his approach, and planted a hand on either side of her. "I know good things can disappear in an instant. That could have happened last night, and I don't want to lose the best thing that ever happened to me without fighting for it."

A gentle sheen misted her eyes. Before he knew it, she was

on her toes, soft curves molding against him. He tightened his hold as she murmured his name. He wouldn't mind staying this way a while longer, but his better judgment advised him to step away before Dana retreated back behind those barriers.

"As responsible business owners, I suppose we should get started on our day." Reluctantly, he broke the embrace and held out one hand. "Walk me out?"

Disappointment flashed across her beautiful face, nearly driving him to pull back those words. Before he could backtrack on his good intentions, Dana accepted his hand. He detoured through the living room to retrieve his wallet, boots, and phone. He handed her the key card he'd left on the table the previous night.

"Make sure you keep this with you." He dropped a quick kiss onto her lips. "Lock up after me."

The moment wasn't lost. Just postponed.

Rhys figured he had twenty minutes from the time he called Paige to tell her the inspector had left until she arrived. She made it in fifteen, bolting through the front entrance.

"Where are my permits?" She bounced up and down with a vigor that exhausted him. "I want to see them! I want to hold them!"

Rhys shook his head, held his hands out to his sides. "I don't have them."

A storm of emotions whipped across her face. "Why not? What did he say? There is nothing wrong with this place. Is it because of the dining room? Did you tell him—No, wait. Give me his number. I'll tell him—No, wait. Ask Dana to call. She'll Canfield him before he knows what hit him."

"Hold on." He set his palms onto Paige's shoulders and turned her to face the wall behind the front counter. "Take a look."

Paige's lips parted. She stared for a silent moment at the permits, framed and mounted on the wall. Slipping from his grasp, she rounded the counter for a closer look. She stroked the frame, glided her fingertips over the glass.

Rhys tucked his hands into his back pockets. Buildings he'd

designed, structures he'd built, none compared to this small restaurant. This one belonged to Paige, and it was her dream. He cleared his throat. "I figured they needed to be framed and on the wall as quickly as possible. Otherwise, they'd end up smeared with tomato sauce or tucked into one of your recipe books."

Paige whirled around, pouted for an instant, then flew around the counter. "I don't know whether to hug you or punch you!"

He braced himself, ready to dodge a blow, until Paige decided on the hug option. He returned the squeeze. "I feel like I went twelve rounds with the inspector. He seemed disappointed he couldn't find something to cite. Keep the doors to the dining area closed. Otherwise, you're in business."

He gathered his belongings to leave, then paused. "What do you mean by 'Canfield'?"

"It's what Dana does. She's amazing." Skipping ahead of him, Paige blocked the exit. "Let's celebrate. Come over to the house, and I'll cook dinner for us."

He considered his schedule for the rest of the day. "What are you cooking?"

Scowling, Paige landed the promised blow to his arm. "Jerk! Your answer is supposed to be 'I'd love that, Paige. It'll give us a chance to catch up.'"

He rubbed his arm, damning the day he'd taught her how to throw a punch. "What are you cooking?"

"Lasagna!" She grunted in exasperation. "Does that meet your approval?"

"I'd love that, Paige. It'll give us a chance to catch up." Toolbox in one hand, tablet in the other, he circled around her. "Oh, I'd like dinner on the table at six sharp."

He shot her a quick grin, then hustled for the door before she could hit him again.

"Just like a man," Paige grumbled as the door closed behind Rhys. "Shoot off a smart remark then run."

Then again Rhys deserved to get the last word once in a while. She glanced at the permits on the wall. Actually, Rhys deserved a lot more than the last word or a hot dinner. She had her dream thanks to him, and she was going to make sure Rhys got his dream as well.

Right now, she had to tend to more immediate tasks. Like stocking the kitchen and purchasing supplies. She pulled the deposit ticket from her pocket for the one-hundred-dollar check from the Lighthouse Cantina.

Thank you, Mr. Warden.

Settled on the couch in the waiting area of Canfield Designs, Dana tapped away on her tablet. She looked up as the front door opened, and Rhys entered. She nodded to the toolbox in his left hand. "I see you're ready to work."

"I am on a roll," he said, walking across the room. He set the toolbox on the floor, then sat down on the edge of the coffee table. "Got the permits for Paige's restaurant this morning, and I'm ready to tackle my new office."

"Let's do a walk-through." Dana stood up and gestured toward the hallway. "There shouldn't be much that needs to be done."

"I'll take care of whatever is needed. I know you're weren't planning on using that space yet."

As they walked to the elevator, Rhys nodded toward the vacant receptionist desk. "Jamie not back from lunch?"

"She's out of the office this afternoon, but she'll be back tomorrow morning." The question seemed innocent on the surface, but the heat rising up the back of Rhys's neck outed his interest.

Cute. She punched the elevator button. "Can I give her a message?"

He tapped one toe, gaze fixed on the illuminated up button. "Just asking."

Dana hid a smile as they entered the elevator. She'd let him off the hook for now.

When they reached Rhys's new office, he tapped a knuckle against the door. "This reminds me. I have the brass plate from my old office. I want to put it up while I'm here."

"You could do that." Dana traced a fingertip across the area of the door where the plate would be located. "Or I can have one engraved that matches the other plates on this floor."

He grinned. "I'd hate to offend the building's sensibilities. Let's go with that."

"You chose wisely." She returned the grin and pointed to the doorknob. "It's unlocked. Go on in and see what needs to be done."

He opened the door, walked in several steps, then stopped. Dana slipped past him, eager to view his reaction.

His gaze darted from one area of the room to the other. Stopping, examining, moving on. He set the toolbox on the floor. When he laid his precious tablet next to it, Dana knew she'd succeeded. She stepped back, allowing him to savor the exploration.

The work area, complete with desk, credenza, and guest chairs, received an approving nod. A small conference table designated for meeting with clients to review designs, mockups, and blueprints achieved the same response. He ran a palm over the cherry wood desktop, along the back of the black leather chair, then veered toward a cozy nook nestled within the far wall.

Dana hid a smile as Rhys turned to face her, his expression similar to eight-year old Joshua's when he'd found a puppy under the Christmas tree.

She joined him at the entrance to the alcove. "I know you weren't crazy about the straw yellow color I chose for the walls. Anything you want changed—"

"It's perfect." He shook his head again. "How did you manage all this?"

Dana chuckled, patted his shoulder, then stepped back. "I told you I have clout."

"You must have called in some heavy-duty favors."

"Not really." While she loved the awed appreciation, she had to confess. "I contacted Jake Matthews. When he heard it was for your office, he and couple of other guys on his crew did some moonlighting. Mostly, it was moving furniture from the storage room. He said you owe them a couple of beers."

"I owe them a steak dinner."

Dana gestured at the back wall. "I left those spaces open for any plaques or degrees you want to display. After you decide where you want those, I can fill in the rest with artwork. I have several prints in my own stock that would work well in here if you want."

She stopped, took a deep breath. "It certainly won't offend me if you want something changed. Things are going to get crazy-busy soon, and you need an office where you can be organized and comfortable."

He looked stunned by the offer. "I love what you've done. No one has ever done anything this spectacular for me. I'm completely overwhelmed."

Today's the day for that.

She forced wayward thoughts of Nick aside and picked up a manila envelope from the desktop. "Lease agreement, which we both need to sign. Electronic pass card for the back door and new security codes. I also made arrangements to have your company name added to the front signage." She thought for a moment. "Yep, that's it."

He tucked the envelope under his arm, then retrieved his tool box and tablet. "Guess I don't need these right now. I'll bring in a check tomorrow for the rent. If you have time now, we can sign off on the lease."

"Would you mind if we took care of that later? With the kick-off meeting tomorrow morning, I'd like to get the conference area set up and could use some help."

"Absolutely! Jeez, Dana, don't try to do all this stuff by yourself."

Pausing in the doorway, Dana tapped her knuckle against Rhys's shoulder. "Between the two of us, partner, I think this project is going to rock."

Rhys parked next to Paige's Jeep in her driveway. Cutting the motor, he sat for a moment studying the simple frame house. Since Pop Carson had passed away, the interior and exterior had been updated, thanks to sweat equity from both him and Paige.

Most of his life had revolved around this house and neighborhood. He and Paige had ridden their bikes along this street too many times to count, sat on the porch eating popsicles, and climbed the trees that shaded the side yard. When he thought of home, this was the house he pictured.

Exiting the SUV, he followed the cobblestone path to the back door. Because that's what family did. The doorknob turned easily despite the number of times he'd told Paige to lock it. He entered the mud room and came to a dead halt when the aroma of baking lasagna hit him.

Home.

He stood at the doorway to the kitchen, watching as Paige pulled on a pair of oven mitts. He closed his eyes, and for one moment, he could make-believe that Mom Carson was standing there. That Pop was in the back yard. That he and Paige would be sent off to wash their hands.

The four of them would then sit at the simple wooden table, eating dinner and sharing stories of their day.

His family.

And now it was just him and Paige.

He opened his eyes, pushed back the memory, and walked into the kitchen. "Honey, I'm home!"

Paige tossed a smile in his direction, then turned to open the oven door. She removed a baking dish and set it on a trivet. "Good. Take out the trash."

He pulled a bottle of beer from the fridge. "Need me to set the table?" Leaning over Paige's shoulder, he inhaled the fragrant mixture of garlic, oregano, and tomatoes. "I'm starving, and that smells terrific."

"Wait!" Paige snatched the bottle out of his hand. "You can't have a beer yet." She shoved the bottle back into the refrigerator and planted herself in front of the door.

He could easily pick her up and retrieve the beer, but it wasn't worth the hassle. "Why not?"

"The lasagna needs to sit, and we need to talk. Now. In the living room." She pointed toward the front of the house as if he hadn't been in that particular room at least a thousand times.

Shaking his head, Rhys headed toward the living room. When he slowed to glance down the hallway, Paige chuckled. "Jamie's not here."

Geez. Was he that obvious?

"I know. Out of town. Back tomorrow."

He sank down onto one corner of the couch. Paige slid onto the cushion next to him, tucking a leg underneath herself. She gave him a wicked grin. "Keeping tabs on her?"

"Dana mentioned it. So what—"

"I gave her your old bedroom." She stretched her arms toward the ceiling. "Yep, your old room. Repainted. New mattress, new sheets, but still your old room. The one you slept in, the one you... remember how you used to sit in the closet while talking on the phone with a girl? Did I ever tell you I could overhear every word?"

A moment of panic gave way to suspicion. "There is no way you could have heard me talking."

"I could... but I had to sit in *my* closet. I learned so much from you."

No one—absolutely no one—pissed him off the way Paige could. "Is there a point to this?"

Her knee nudged against his leg. "Jamie's the one, isn't she?"

That damn heat rushed up his neck again. "I've hardly had a chance to talk with her."

"Doesn't matter. I can tell. I've seen the way you were with other girls. Never like this. I like Jamie. I didn't think I would, and I was ready to fight to keep you safe from her." She shifted until they sat side-by-side, legs outstretched. "Did you ever think of me in that way?"

He didn't even have to stop to think. "Nope. Not even when you asked me to teach you how to kiss."

"Me neither." She sighed. "And you were a fantastic kisser. I was so impressed with how much you knew at fifteen."

"That was a great year." He smiled with fond memories. "You got boobs that year."

She slapped the back of her hand against his thigh. "Hey! I had boobs before then."

"Those were pre-boobs. That year..." His hands cupped the air. "...you got real ones. Not that I got to see them, let alone touch them."

Paige giggled. "You had your chance and blew it, buddy. Your focus that year was Lucia, the Spanish exchange student. She was seventeen. As I recall, Pop gave you some advice about dating an older woman."

Rhys shrugged. "So did my dad. He threw a handful of condoms at me and said 'Don't knock her up.'"

Her expression grew serious. "How are things with your dad?"

He rolled his head against the back of the sofa. "Worse than ever. He hired some new guy. Kevin Davis. No idea where he found him. According to the diplomas on his office wall, his field is finances. Granted, McCall could use a CFO rather than our friendly accountant, but the guy knows nothing about construction. After handing off the projects to Davis, I tried to talk with Dad."

"It didn't go well?"

"He demanded my key card and ordered me out of the building."

Paige jerked upright, her cheeks flaming with indignation. "How could he do that? You own part of that company!"

"And he's never forgiven me for insisting on a share of the business." He sat up, rubbed both hands over his face. "He's not going to change, and I'm tired of the battle."

He swallowed back the searing pain clawing at his gut. He'd lived his life taking the best of what his father taught him while striving to be his own man. Time and again, he'd compromised; some hills weren't worth the battle. Others, such as his father's edict about Dana, demanded he sacrifice his own integrity, and that he couldn't do.

They'd fought before, but this estrangement hurt more than he'd admit even to Paige, because this time it seemed permanent. Even if he and Dad reconciled, he'd never have the same level of respect for the man.

"I should be sorry." Her hand slipped over his. "But I'm not if means you're free from his drama."

"I don't know about free. We'll still be connected through business. Maybe it's a good thing Davis is onboard and can deal with Dad instead."

They sat for a moment in comfortable silence. Only a moment, because Paige couldn't stay silent any longer than that. "Things are changing." A wistful note crept into her voice. "I don't want to lose you."

"You are never going to lose me. You're my best friend." He squeezed her hand. "Always have been…"

"…always will be."

He lifted their linked hands and dropped a gentle kiss onto Paige's knuckles. "Dinner?"

"Dinner." Paige bounded to her feet.

Their hands remained clasped as they returned to the kitchen. Because that's where family gathered to eat.

The table bore the scars of several generations of use by the Carson family. The placemats were Paige's selection, the stoneware dinner plates passed down from Mom Carson's grandmother, the casserole dish from Pop's mother. That sense of tradition carried on each time he sat at this table. Mom and Pop C were both gone, but their presence remained in this simple cottage. Family, by blood and by love. They joined hands again, this time to say grace.

They ate in companionable silence for several moments before Paige spoke again. "I love you, Rhys."

Rhys looked up from his place, smiling as Paige tipped her glass in his direction. He lifted his own in response and tapped the lip against hers. The clink was solid and clear. "I love you too, Paige."

Paige picked up her fork and shot him a mischievous smile. "So how was work today, dear?"

He shook his head, thankful for all those things that stayed the same. "Incredible. You'll never believe what Dana did."

Chapter Nine

Freshly showered, Nick pulled on jockeys and jeans, then padded barefoot back to the bathroom. Wiping steam from the mirror, he peered at his reflection and rubbed his jaw. A shave could wait until the next day.

Living above the garage was convenient, not to mention easy on the wallet. But it crossed the border into pathetic that at forty-six, he was living like a damn college kid. The bathroom existed because he'd thrown up two walls and a door to create the space, filling it with a sink, shower, and toilet. Apartment-size appliances and cabinets occupying one wall served as the kitchen. The wooden table and two chairs pulled double duty. One half for dining, the other half for his laptop.

He could boast a few pieces of kick-ass furniture that might meet Dana's critical approval—a king-size bed, a forty-two-inch flat screen, and a black leather sectional.

With two other garages opting out of rotation, he'd found himself handling evening calls the past three nights. When he'd returned home, the sofa had become a relaxing spot to settle down and spend the final moments of the day on a phone call with Dana.

The casual "How are you? Need me to come over?" inquiries had turned into thirty-minute conversations. Stretched out on the cool leather surface in a room illuminated only by the street lights outside, he'd imagined her right beside him. One arm tucked under his head, he'd closed his eyes while her honeyed tones had washed over him. Her soft laugh had seduced him, especially when she'd gently mocked him for asking if phone calls counted as dates.

He was hooked. No doubt about it. After spending a night with Dana in his arms, he felt lonelier than ever in these quiet, thrown-together quarters.

Someone else was missing in his life too. He nabbed his cell phone from the table beside the bed and thumbed through the contact list.

Megan.

Texting was a pain, but that method would get her attention quicker than a phone call.

How are you doing? Miss you, sweetie. How about a visit this summer?

He checked the time. It was too early for Megan to be awake. Still, the kid's hand was attached practically 24/7 to the phone and her ear attuned to the delivery of a text message in her sleep.

He shoved the phone into his jeans pocket, then pulled a clean T-shirt from the dresser. Tugging the shirt over his head, he walked to the windows facing southward over Ocean. The water was calm, and a few seagulls circled overhead searching for food. Along the sidewalk, early morning joggers trotted by. On the side street, several cars were lined up outside the parking lot entrance to the garage.

PI was waking up.

The phone vibrated. He jerked it out of his pocket and tapped the icon.

Nick. I'm doing well. Great to have a dad to do things with. M

He slumped against the window. The glass panes, not yet warmed by the morning sun, leeched the heat from his back and shoulders. After almost eighteen years of "Daddy" and "Dad," he was relegated to "Nick."

What was going on with his girl? Genetics aside, Megan had always seemed more his child than Gary's—or even Callie's. Level-headed, with a quirky sense of humor and not a bit squeamish about getting her hands dirty. Definitely daddy's girl—daddy being *him*. The kid had been disappointed too many times by Gary to buy into a temporary show of interest. Then again, maybe they *were* living that family vision Callie had created in her mind.

But he doubted it.

He glanced out again, saw several additional cars lined up. Going to be a busy day. He shoved the phone back into his pocket.

I will get answers, young lady.

Rhys stood in the alcove of his office and stared out the window at the seascape. Water, warmed to a cobalt blue by the midday sun, stretched to the horizon. He couldn't taste the salt in the air or hear the wind and the waves, but he knew they were there. Right on the other side of the glass pane. Those pieces of PI were as much a part of him as the color of his hair or eyes.

How could I have stayed away for so long?

Because it had been part of his plan. Finish his education, gain experience, then return home to build on the McCall heritage. Strengthen the foundation laid by his father and grandfather and those before them. Make his dad proud and be recognized as an equal.

Put your stamp on everything? Not going to happen, son.

Erik McCall's way or the highway. *Not this time, Dad.*

He turned his back on the seductive vista. His gaze swept across the room, marveling once again at the space. He hadn't been crazy about the shade of straw yellow Dana had selected when the building was under renovation, but nothing else would have brought in the light of day as well. It warmed the room and brightened the somber tones of the cherry and red oak furniture and black chairs. With the random accent pieces of Carolina blue and winter white, she'd brought the spirit of PI to the indoors.

Thank God for Dana. As prepared as he had been for the technical aspects of the kick-off meeting, Dana was the one who'd kept all the personalities on an even keel. She'd assuaged Mayor Wolfe's concerns about schedules and budgets, gently guiding the majority of those decisions to their team rather than risking them on the whims of the mayoral office. The grin he'd bit back during the exchange now came out full force. She'd not only gotten the mayor to agree, he'd thanked her for it, even came to think of it as his idea. It'd be more work for them in the initial stages, but maintaining control of those aspects protected them from delays later on.

She'd welcomed Kevin and settled Stacy into submission by seating herself next to the redhead. Jake Matthews, already charmed by Dana, had refrained from his usual colorful language. At least during the course of the meeting. Not long after the session ended, Jake hadn't hesitated to express his outrage at Kevin Davis representing McCall Construction.

"Little pup doesn't know squat about construction. He'd be lucky to pour rain out of his boot with directions on the heel. Your daddy almost ran the company into the ground before you came back and put it to rights. Tell you right now, a lot of the boys are getting nervous about you not being over there."

The burly foreman was the linchpin to keeping the work crews motivated and on schedule. His knowledge was invaluable, and his word carried weight. "Tell the guys to relax. This is a big project, and there'll be plenty of work for a long time. Dana and I are managing things, so no one needs to worry."

Jake grunted. "There's a lady with a good head on her shoulders. Looker too. Might be just the one to keep your daddy in line."

Picturing Dana's expression if he told her that Jake Matthews had given his blessing to her and his father, Rhys chuckled out loud.

His stomach rumbled. He should have accepted Jamie's offer to pick up lunch for him as well as for her and Dana. The outside beckoned though. A short jog followed by a quick lunch at home would keep him energized for the afternoon. He missed all the physical activity from when he'd worked at McCall. Once the Main Street project broke ground, he intended to get his hands dirty again.

Someone tapped firmly on the closed door, and he shook his head. *Go away.* The knock repeated. *Not here.* Both the mayor and Jake had left the building. Jamie or Dana would have called before coming to his office. That left either Kevin or Stacy as the likely person on the other side of the door, and he didn't want to talk to either one.

A third knock sounded, followed by the rustling of an

opening door. "Rhys?"

He swallowed an irritated grunt and stepped out of the alcove. "Over here, Kevin."

Kevin Davis entered, halting midway to pivot in one direction then the other. "This is a great office, especially that view. I understand why you didn't hear when I first knocked."

Rhys walked to his desk and gestured for Kevin to take a seat. "What brings you by?"

Kevin lowered himself into one of the guest chairs. He folded his hands across his stomach, the casual pose at odds with the tightness in his jaw. "Great start this morning. However, there are some issues that we need to resolve before construction begins. Easily mitigated with a simple solution. I'm issuing an invitation for you to return to McCall."

He hadn't seen that one coming. "No."

Kevin's mouth dropped open, followed by a shake of his head. "I can work things out with Erik—"

"Again, no." The exasperation on the other man's face was rewarding.

"Let me explain a few facts to you." Kevin slid forward in his chair, forearms resting on the edge of the desk. "McCall's difficulties began because Erik was trying to fulfill all roles, and you weren't there to help with the family business. After you returned, the company rebounded because of the dual management, and, fortunately, there was no regression during that period of time you were solely in charge."

Rhys rubbed the vein ticking at his right temple. His molars ached as he bit back the urge to correct the re-created history Kevin was spewing.

"I took the opportunity to look over the corporate structure. It makes sense for Erik to function in a strategic position as CEO. As CFO, I'll handle financials. That leaves operations, a position for which you are suited."

His first impression had been correct. Davis didn't want to get his hands dirty dealing with the physical side of the business. But that wasn't Rhys's concern. His father had made that abundantly clear.

When Kevin opened his mouth again, Rhys shot a hand up in warning. "I gave you my answer. It won't change regardless of how many times you ask. I will give you some advice. McCall has talented individuals who know their jobs. Let them be a resource for you."

Kevin sank back in his chair, shaking his head. "You mean Stacy? She's been great to step in, but she's an admin."

It galled Rhys to defend the woman, but honesty forced him to do just that. Regardless of Stacy's outrageous behavior, her knowledge couldn't be discounted. "Technically, she's the office manager, and she's familiar with every aspect of the business."

He wanted to say more. To tell Kevin Davis exactly what kind of man Erik McCall could be, but that wouldn't resolve anything. Davis was firmly in Erik's court and would discount anything negative as being driven by spite.

"However, I wasn't referring to Stacy. There is someone else in the company who has the knowledge to handle operations. You saw an excellent example during this morning's meeting."

"Jake Matthews?" The sour look on Kevin's face illustrated his opinion of that idea.

"Jake has the experience but not the authority to act in many cases. In the field, you need quick answers. I gave Jake that flexibility. If a situation occurred where it impacted the budget or schedule significantly, he ran it by me. Otherwise, I trusted his judgment in those matters."

"He's a senior foreman. I don't see him as management material."

Get a clue, Kevin.

The crease in the man's brow rippled away. "Superintendent of Construction. All field responsibility including personnel and equipment. Set up financial limits. It's effective, efficient. I can sell this to Erik."

"Give it a trial run. You'll have proof either way." Rhys stood, a hint for Kevin to leave. "Glad we got it worked out."

Kevin hopped to his feet, clearly buoyed by the solution. "I appreciate your time, Rhys. Even though you're not coming back to the fold, at least we'll be working together on the Main Street project."

Rhys crossed the room, opening the door to the hallway. "I'm on my way out—"

"For lunch." Kevin smacked the heel of his hand against his forehead. "I haven't eaten yet either. Come on, buddy. I found a great place just off Towne Square. My treat for all your help."

Rhys stepped into the hallway as Kevin headed for the elevator.

Buddy?

Was Kevin really that clueless, or just that self-absorbed? Then again, this might be a good chance for him to pick Davis's brain regarding what might be behind Dad's recent actions.

"It's been steady all morning." Paige set two take-out bags on the countertop. One for Jamie, one for Dana. She tapped her fingertips on the wooden surface, hips swaying in rhythm to the beat. "Nothing we can't handle so far. I'll have to hire at least one more person to help out. We're getting a lot of requests for delivery in the downtown area. Thanks to your suggestion to open with take-out service."

"You're lucky you won the contest money for supplies," Jamie said.

"I know! I made it just before the deadline. Abby took one look at the photo and yelled 'Winner!' She even sent an electronic copy over to the printer while we finished the paperwork. She really built up the suspense between Marco's poster coming down and the new one going up last night."

"Glad it worked out for you," Jamie said as she grabbed her wallet. "Exciting morning for me too. We had the Main Street kick-off meeting. Kevin Davis brought Stacy with him."

Paige wrinkled her nose. "Why?"

"Admin for McCall. Notes, organization, blah-blah-blah." Jamie fluttered the fingers on one hand in the universal sign for yakking. "She cornered Rhys. Had a big smile on her face, put her hand on his arm."

"That slut! She's going after him, and we're not going to let that happen! Did he talk with you?"

Jamie toyed with the top of her take-out bag. "We sat next to each other but didn't have a chance to talk privately. Enough about *her.* Do you know what happened over on Ocean this morning? We heard a lot of sirens."

"I heard them too. Maybe a wreck or a tour bus broke down." About to ring up the sale, she spied Nick Warden crossing the street toward the restaurant. "Here comes Mr.

Warden to pick up his lunch. Looks like he's in a rush. Can you run back and get his order from Karen?"

"On my way." Jamie pushed away from the counter and dashed into the kitchen.

Paige entered a note into her daily ledger for the cost of Mr. Warden's complimentary lunch. Despite Rhys's urgings to move to an electronic method, she preferred pen and paper. The door crashed open, the bell clanged in violent protest, and heavy boot steps pounded across the entryway.

Jeez, someone's in a major rush.

"Hi, Mr. Warden." She lifted her head, jerking backward as he gripped the far edges of the counter and loomed toward her.

"Do you have any idea what kind of morning I've had?"

Wow. Not even Rhys gets that cranky when he's hungry. Maybe it's an age thing? Edging back, she shook her head in denial. "No, but your lunch will be right out."

"My work day started with almost a dozen cars lined up in one direction to get into my parking lot."

"That's great! Business must—"

A warning finger shot up, silencing her. "Another eight to ten cars lined up from the other direction. A half dozen on the side street. All women drivers, and guess where all of them had dinner last night?"

Uh-oh. A sick feeling crept into her stomach.

"You said it was a photo contest. You didn't say a single word about turning it into a six-foot poster *plastered on the wall!*"

Jamie returned from the kitchen. Paige snatched the take-out bag from her hand and set it onto the counter. It wasn't much of a shield, but it was all she had at the moment. "I thought you knew."

"The sheriff's department spent over an hour getting traffic cleared up. I had to close my doors and put my phone on voice mail." His forefinger beat a steady tattoo on the countertop. "I'm not putting up with this for a month. Get it down today."

Her heart started racing. The check from the Cantina had been money in/money out of her bank account in record time. She grabbed Jamie's wrist, pulling her closer for protection. "I can't do that. The decisions are final, and I don't have the money to pay it back. Plus, you signed a release." She'd made sure of that the day he'd agreed while he was still mooning over Dana in the next room.

Jamie's arm wiggled out of her grasp, and she grabbed a handful of the girl's skirt, forcing her to remain close. "I'm really sorry, but there's nothing I can do."

Nick snatched up the lunch sack. "You see this? New deal. Every day that poster stays up, I get a free lunch. Longer if this harassment continues past that."

Sweet relief rushed into her lungs. "Absolutely. I'm sure this'll all blow over in a couple of days. Things will go back to normal. We'll laugh...."

She flinched at his final glare as he turned to leave. *Maybe not...*

...then again.

"Mr. Warden, can I ask one more favor?"

Nick jerked to a stop, shoulders stiffening. He turned, mouth moving, his stride slow and deliberate as he retraced his steps. She couldn't hear the words but the *Are you effin' kidding me?* look was unmistakable.

"Oh, God." The hot whisper of Jamie's breath burned into her neck.

"You *really* want to ask me for another favor?" His words, clipped and cold, dared her to agree.

She pushed one of the other lunch bags in front of him. "Since you're going that way, could you drop off Dana's lunch?"

His mouth worked furiously, then his gaze dropped to the paper bag. After one final heated glare, he grabbed the container and stormed out of the building.

Paige collapsed against the wall, gulping in a deep breath. "Wow. That was close."

"Paige, he's furious! And you sent him to Dana?" Jamie shook the wrinkles out of her skirt as she cast a worried look out the window.

"He likes her. It'll be okay. She'll calm him down." Paige swallowed hard, looking at the one remaining lunch on the counter. "You might not want to go back there just yet."

Project plan. Vendor list. Meeting schedule. Supply list. Work schedule. Dana sat back in her chair. She and Jamie had a full afternoon ahead of them.

Hearing approaching footsteps, she saved the master file to the hard drive of her computer. *Good timing.* Her anticipation for lunch changed to curiosity. That stride was too heavy to belong to Jamie. The half-open door to her office swung fully ajar as Nick barreled inside. He looked around, then headed to the coffee table on the other side of the room.

"I hope you've had a better morning than I have." The grouchy tone didn't quite match the care he took in unpacking the two meals. Dropping onto one of the chairs, he waved a hand in her direction. "Lunch."

He'd definitely had a bad morning if the clenched jaw and vein pulsing in his left temple were any indication. She eased onto the couch nearest to where he sat. "My morning was good. What happened with yours?"

"An invasion of women drivers, all of whom had dinner at the Cantina last night. Not a single legitimate car problem in the bunch. Flapping their eyelashes, flipping their hair, trying to be cute. 'Rotate my tires.' 'Look under the hood.' 'Check the fluids.' 'Charge my battery.'" He rubbed both hands over his face. "What is *wrong* with those women?"

She knew exactly why those women had stormed Nick's garage.

Face and arms glistening with sweat, hair spiked with perspiration, dark blue T-shirt clinging to his damp body.

She didn't know who those women were, but she detested every one of them. Nick was none of their business! She jabbed her fork into the salad, irritated at herself for being irritated. She cast a quick glance at Nick, and her mood brightened. The frustrated pout decorating his mouth was totally at odds with the rough masculinity of his muscular body slumped in the chair. She doubted he would appreciate her humorous observation, but that flare of vulnerability swayed her to sympathy.

"I'm sorry. I had no idea about a poster."

Nick shrugged and picked up his sandwich. "Not your fault. Megan rooked both of us into her scheme."

Dana studied him closer. Something else was going on. "You mean Paige."

"Yeah, Paige." With a *what can you do?* shrug, he bit into the sandwich, and gave a grunt of appreciation.

"You said 'Megan.' Did something happen with your daughter?"

Pulling the cell phone from his pocket, he thumbed the device several times before extending it to her. "After seventeen-plus years, I'm 'Nick.'"

A pang shot through her heart as she read the curt response. She thought about Joshua and wondered which would hurt her the most. His continued silence or a cold reply like the one she'd just read. How could one's child change so much? And why? The harsh message sounded nothing like the funny, spirited girl Nick had bragged about on their drive home from Eddie's.

Nothing at all.

She scrolled through several previous entries to confirm her suspicions. "Unless Megan has learned the fine art of punctuation and spelling, I don't think she wrote that last message."

Nick bolted upward in his chair. "What do you mean?"

"It's nothing like her previous messages to you." She passed the phone back to him. "Oh, and sorry for snooping."

His mouth curved into a grudging half-smile. "I noticed that but thought it was her way of flipping me off." With a disgusted grunt, he shoved the phone back into his pocket. "Damn it. I bet Callie wrote that. The dig about Gary being 'Dad' is her style."

"Keep calling Megan and find out for sure where things stand." His previous reference to Megan struck her with new meaning. "Paige reminds you of your daughter, doesn't she?"

A rueful grin broke across his face. "Yeah, she does. Enough that I was ready to ground her to her room over that poster." Giving a half-shrug, he changed the subject. "By the way, nice office."

Fork halfway to her lips, Dana smiled at the unexpected compliment. "Thanks. I like your garage."

Nick chuckled as he settled back in his chair, finally showing signs of relaxing. "So, you had a good morning?"

"It was wonderful!" The rush of the morning's success washed through her again as she launched into a recap of the initial project meeting. Seeing the grin on his face, she halted. "Are you laughing at me?"

He folded the sandwich wrapper and dropped it into the wastebasket next to his chair. "I'm enjoying your enthusiasm.

You're loving this, aren't you?"

"Absolutely! It's the largest project I've ever handled, but it's so invigorating." She stood, tilting her head toward the doorway. "I hear Jamie in the outer office, which means I need to get back to work."

They walked to her office door. Nick paused, favoring her with a smoldering gaze that sent her pulse racing. "Any chance of playing hooky instead?"

One look into his eyes, and temptation had a good chance of winning this round. She focused on his lips, but that only made her more aware of a mouth too talented to ignore. His chest reminded her of how comfortably she'd rested against him a few nights ago. His... nope, she had to stick with his eyes. Looking anywhere else was just too dangerous.

"As appealing as that sounds, we are responsible business owners—"

"Ow!" Nick slammed a fist to his chest.

She giggled—actually giggled—as he slumped momentarily against the door frame.

He straightened, took a half-step forward to drop a kiss onto her cheek. "You win. We're still on for tomorrow night, right? That dinner boat thing?"

"Yes, that dinner boat thing. And don't forget, you promised to wear a tie."

For the longest moment, she didn't move; neither did he. Gazes locked, something shifted between them. An awareness reaching beyond the physical ignited between them. She saw it on his face. She felt it in her heart.

"I'll give you a call tomorrow." A brief frown creased his brow before he turned and walked away.

She rested a palm on the head of the hummingbird statue, watching until Nick turned the corner. Her lips curled into a smile as she gave the metal bird a fond pat.

Returning to her desk, Dana dropped into the chair. Jamie would be in any moment, ready to start this afternoon's work. She needed to clear her mind. But it wasn't easy. Every interaction with Nick played on her senses. Lunch today was a perfect example.

Talking, listening, teasing. Confident enough to be silly. Ending with that weird flash of awareness. A connection that grew undeniably more insistent. It led her to one inescapable conclusion.

She was going to sleep with Nick Warden.

Chapter Ten

The rest of the group was seated when Rhys arrived at the Lighthouse Cantina. His step slowed as three sets of eyes followed his approach. Sam looked amused, Paige looked pissed. Jamie looked at him for a second, then stared off in another direction.

Oooo-kay.

"Hey, how's everyone?" He dropped into the vacant chair.

Paige shot a glare in his direction. "Peachy. Your beer's waiting for you. It's probably warmer than you like it, but that's because you're so late."

He shifted his attention to Jamie. "You want to take a shot at me too?"

Her cool stare guilted him more than Paige's bitchy remark. "You were supposed to be downstairs by five-thirty. I didn't think your meeting with Stacy would have lasted even that long. I waited an extra half-hour, then left and met up with Paige."

He heaved a deep sigh. "I apologize. When I saw that you'd left, I figure you'd done just that. But I should have called. Stacy had some questions regarding the last project reports I submitted. It got involved, and I lost track of time."

Receiving no response from Jamie, Rhys glanced at Sam, who threw up his hands. "No problem here, buddy. I'm just the guy who had to listen to these two until you showed up."

"We're waiting for a better explanation," Paige said. "When

it comes to Stacy, nothing's that innocent."

Jamie gasped, whispering, "Paige, no!"

Rhys stared at the bottle of beer before him. Drops of condensation ran down the glass. He caught one of the drops with his forefinger, his touch confirming that the beer had warmed to where it was no longer palatable. *Like me.* Working until he dripped with sweat, trying to please everybody else and meet the wants of everyone who needed him. At the end, he was just as depleted as that beverage before him. He pushed back his chair and stood.

"I'm not good company at the moment, so I'm going to take off. Jamie, I apologize. Paige, you should know better. Sam, good luck with the rest of the evening."

Sam caught his arm. "Not so fast. You sit down. Paige, be quiet. Jamie, accept his apology."

No one moved; no one spoke. Sam jabbed a finger in turn at each person. "Sit. Quiet. Speak."

Rhys eased back into his chair. Sam motioned to Jamie, who flushed under his glare.

She barely met Rhys's gaze. "I'm the one who should apologize. Stacy knew we were all going out tonight and probably delayed you on purpose. I was totally out of line to be upset with you. I'm sorry."

"Accepted." A smile broke across his lips, widening as she returned it with one of her own.

A hand landed on top of his. He turned his head to face Paige. A long look passed between them, Paige's eyes widening in unspoken understanding.

"I'm sorry too. I do know better." The contriteness lasted mere seconds. "But that woman makes me so mad!"

A rough laugh barked out of Sam's mouth. "Paige, quit while you're ahead."

"Okay, *okay*!" Turning in her seat, Paige held out her arms. "I am sorry, Rhys. Forgive me?"

"Always." A tight hug, a pat on the back. Forgiveness, however, did not rule out payback.

It took the rest of the meal before his plan fell into place. The dinner crowd thinned out, and the late-evening folks started to arrive. A clean line of sight to the far side of the restaurant gave him the perfect opportunity.

Rising slightly from his chair, Rhys nodded toward the far wall. "That's the poster that shut down Ocean for over an hour?"

"And closed down Warden's garage for the day." Reaching for a taco chip, Sam scowled when Paige pulled the basket out of his reach.

"Can we talk about something else?" Returning the scowl, Paige scooped a generous helping of salsa onto her own chip and popped it into her mouth.

Rhys pulled the basket back to the center of the table, ignoring Paige's demand. "I'm glad I didn't get pulled into that scheme of hers. Not that I would have agreed."

"Really, guys. Give her a break." Jamie glared at both men. "All she tried to do was earn money to help open the restaurant."

Sam snorted. "What she did was con Warden and Mrs. Canfield into doing the work for her. And Warden was rightly pissed off at our little friend."

"Excuse me! I'm right here!"

Rhys shot another look at the poster. At least a dozen women were lined up to have their picture taken in front of the display. "I don't see it."

"Those ladies do. So must Mrs. Canfield, considering the way Warden was hanging around the night of the break-in."

Rhys nodded. "He was still there when I left after boarding up the door."

"Wait! What?" Paige's fork clattered onto her plate.

Sam drained the remainder of his beer, then set the bottle aside. "We need to drop this topic."

"When it's getting interesting? I don't think so! Spill it!"

"Nothing to spill. They'd gone out to dinner earlier that night. Warden—"

Paige squealed and grabbed Jamie's hand. "It's working! I told you they were perfect for each other." She turned back to Sam. "What happened? Where did they go? What was she wearing?"

Sam stretched out his legs and locked both hands behind his neck. "Sorry, but I cannot discuss an ongoing investigation."

"Rhys?" Paige asked.

He threw up his hands. "He was talking with Sam while I boarded up the door and was still there when I left. That's all I know."

"Hmm." When Jamie avoided her gaze, Paige's eyes narrowed. "You *know* something!"

"Paige, I work for Dana. I can't—"

Sam shoved to his feet, grunting in exasperation. He cupped a hand under Paige's elbow. "Let's dance, sunshine."

Rhys and Jamie watched in silence as Sam pulled Paige onto the dance floor, not giving her a chance to protest.

"That's one way to handle it."

Jamie bristled. "Did it occur to you that Paige might not want to dance with Sam?"

"Believe me, if Paige wanted to avoid dancing with Sam, she'd put him in his place in a heartbeat."

Jamie studied the couple as they moved in time to the music. "I suppose you're right."

"Let's not waste the music." He stood up, holding out his hand. "Dance with me?"

She rose with a smile that wiped away all the stress of his day.

Seated at the table in his apartment, Nick searched the Internet for any stories related to James Canfield's murder. After reading the available articles, he still couldn't draw a full picture of the shooting. The articles focused on the divorced couple, the custody battle, and the suspected actions of the paternal grandfather. Canfield's death was more of a sidenote, deemed a "tragic loss to the legal and social community."

Wrong place, wrong time, as Sam had termed it.

The random result of handling a custody case might be all there was to the story, but it felt… *hinky.* Too many coincidences, too many unexplained incidents, had occurred to Dana since the shooting. Had Canfield been the intended target all the time?

He pushed the laptop away and sat back in his chair. Dana was in the process of rebuilding her life. Was it fair of him to thrust her back into a time she was trying to move beyond? Was it his own paranoia attempting to put pieces from different puzzles together to make one picture?

His cell phone rang. That damn well better be either Megan or Callie returning his call.

He gave a quick glance at the display. Area code was mainland Virginia, but he didn't recognize the number. Not unusual if it had been his work number, but not the norm for his personal phone. He tapped a forefinger on the screen to answer the call.

"Nick Warden."

"Nicky, buddy. Getting tired of the laid-back life yet?"

Keg Lansing's voice boomed through the receiver, making Nick wince. The Sutton police detective was hardly a friend. More an acquaintance of a friend and a former customer. Interesting guy though. Full of stories that were fifty percent bullshit and the rest crazy enough to be true. Sure made taking his money at poker games enjoyable.

"I'm keeping busy, Keg. What's up?"

"Tony's trying to get enough guys together for a game. Told him I'd give you a call."

"When?"

"Next week. Wednesday. In or out?"

Relieving Lansing of some hard-earned cash would be worth the trip over to the mainland. About to accept, a sudden thought occurred to him.

"Yeah, I'm in, but I have a question for you. About a shooting a year ago. James Canfield. Can you give me something more than what's in the news articles?"

The following silence lasted so long Nick glanced at the display to confirm the call had not been disconnected. The *whisk* of a cigarette lighter sounded over the line, followed by a puff and a deep-chested cough.

"Wasn't expecting that. Care to tell me why a grease monkey wants a gander at an open case file, and why I should put my ass on the line to let him?"

Nick bit back a retort. "Not over the phone."

Another long silence followed. "Meet me tomorrow evening at Parton's, and I'll tell you what I can."

Cancel his date with Dana? Not happening. "Can't tomorrow. How about Saturday?"

"No can do. Offer's on the table for Friday night only, and you're buying."

Asshole. Taking his money next week would be sweet revenge. "Tomorrow it is."

"Be there at six. I'll be up for a second drink by then."

Nick disconnected the call. He pushed the phone and laptop to one side. Hunger begged for his attention. Maybe he should start ordering a larger lunch and keep part of it for dinner. If Paige didn't like it, too bad.

Too early for bed. He could catch up on paperwork or he could mindlessly flip channels on the TV. Then again... Plopping onto the couch, he hit the speed dial for Dana's number on his cell. Stretching out on the cool leather, he counted the rings until she answered.

"Hi, Nick."

Ah, yes, that honeyed voice was just what he needed. "Hello yourself."

"How was the rest of your day?"

"Worked on inventory. Listen, I need to reschedule tomorrow's date."

He held his breath, not sure what reaction to expect. He was batting minor leagues when it came to guessing how she'd respond.

"How about Saturday instead?"

That was easy. Too easy? Maybe she wasn't that enthused about the date?

"Nick?"

"Saturday would be great."

"It occurred to me that the boat for the dinner cruise boards near the Lighthouse Cantina. With all the reaction from your poster, we might want to go somewhere less crowded."

Smart woman. "Good idea. There are a couple places in lower PI I think you'd like."

"Or we can have dinner at my house."

Nick shot upward on the couch. *Say what?*

"The new patio door was installed today. You can check it out and give me your approval. I thought you might want to check out the grill as well."

Dinner at Dana's. The bad-ass grill. He went for the trifecta. "Can I drive your car?"

Sweet laughter spilled into his ear. "Maybe. Someday. So it's a date. I'll see you Saturday about six."

A few more words, and they ended the conversation. Twilight washed the room as Nick lay on the couch, cell phone resting on his chest. He hadn't expected that invitation.

Simmer down, Warden. Don't blow it. If slow and steady is what it takes to win Dana's trust, that's what she'll get.

Chapter Eleven

Some days just sucked. A pissed-off voice-mail message from Kevin, twice the time beyond what Rhys had expected to spend with Mayor Wolfe, and now Jamie wasn't at her desk.

On the plus side, the mayor was so pleased by the status update that he'd guaranteed full cooperation in coordinating tasks between the city crews and McCall Construction. On the not-sure-what-to-expect frontier, Rhys had received a text message from Dana to meet her in the conference room when he returned.

Whistling under his breath, he headed for the stairwell, taking the steps two at a time to the second floor.

The doors to the conference room were open. Dana was seated at the far end of the massive oak table, her head bowed as she sketched. Several colored pencils were threaded between the fingers on her left hand. She flicked one pencil out with her right hand, made a few quick lines on the paper, then switched that pencil for another.

"You look industri—wow!" Rhys halted midway into the room, transfixed by the photos and drawings that lined the length of the side wall.

He strolled to the far end. Dana rose, falling into step beside him. She beamed at his surprise. "Like it?"

"That's our project." Main Street now, alongside Main Street to-be, visually represented along the stretch of wall.

"Each segment represents one of the four blocks we've targeted for Phase I. The center strip is the street. Above and below that strip are current photos of the shops, along with illustrations representing the finished design. Along the far top is the timeline marking the milestones."

Rhys walked the length of the wall. "This is incredible. How did you think of this?"

"It's difficult for some people to make the leap from concept to reality from a digital drawing. They need something tactile." She tapped the board with one knuckle. "Plus, it packs a punch when you're dealing with the money guys."

"The mayor will love it. Wish I'd seen this before our meeting this morning. That's what took so long. He wanted to walk the length of Main Street and back while looking at our projections. Then debrief over lunch at the club."

Dana's nose wrinkled in sympathy. "Ouch."

He scanned the length of the display again, noting the missing dates at the far right. "Is there a question on the schedule at that point?"

"We ran out of time. I let Jamie go early since it's Friday, and I'm not good with ladders."

He stared at the blank area for a brief moment. "Does that bother you as much as it does me?"

She picked up a marker and waved it in his direction. "If not more."

He held up one hand, and she tossed the marker. He caught it, then climbed up the stepladder. Holding out his free hand, he wiggled his fingers. "Give me the schedule."

Rhys glanced at the paper Dana handed to him, then started recording the dates onto the whiteboard's painted surface. "You always had a problem with heights?"

"As long as I can remember. Maybe before that."

He hitched a hip onto the top step of the ladder, twisting to look down at her. "Before you could remember?"

A slight flush colored her cheeks. "I was in a car wreck a number of years ago. Ended up in a coma for a couple of weeks due to a head injury. Since then, I noticed I became dizzy when it came to heights. Before that?" A shrug. "Who knows?"

Rhys shook his head. Dana always seemed indomitable. He couldn't imagine her as less than her usual vital self. He turned back toward the wall to record the remaining dates as she continued.

"I was driving on Old Militia Road in Chesapeake. May eighth. I don't even remember why I was on that particular road that day. I don't remember anything prior to the accident except for a few seconds just before it happened. The sun was shining, the hood of my car was red, the dash was black. Another car, blue like the sky, was passing mine. Then nothing. Isn't it strange to remember just those isolated images?"

Her words wrapped themselves around him, piercing his consciousness with a nearly forgotten memory. Sweat broke across his brow, and he swiped a forearm across his face. "When did this happen?"

"Over twenty years ago. Twenty-three actually."

I was four years old.

He stared at the numbers he'd written. They matched the numerals on the paper, but as hard as he looked at them, they were meaningless. He descended the ladder, automatically passing the paper and marker back to her. She patted his shoulder as she passed.

His gaze followed her as she returned to the table. She gathered the markers, straightened her papers, packed her briefcase. All so normal, but in his heart, Rhys knew nothing would be normal again.

"Perfect plan. I design, you build. It'll be fun. A massive headache, but fun."

He couldn't look at her, couldn't meet her eyes. He folded the ladder, setting it against the wall, and forced himself to respond. "Why don't you take off? I want to take pictures of the layout."

Dana waved her tablet in his direction. "How about I send you an electronic copy instead?"

He managed a smile, a small one. Of course, she would have anticipated that. "Great. I'll put the ladder away and lock up."

He hefted the ladder, murmuring a response to her "Have a good weekend" as he walked out of the room. By the time he returned from storing the ladder in the utility closet, Dana had departed. He heard her footsteps on the stairs followed by the closing of the back door. In the quiet of the building, he sank into a chair.

"Will Mommy be at our new house?"

"I told you, buddy. You're not living with Mommy anymore."

Rhys squirmed in his car seat, leaning to see his father as he drove them to their new house. "Why can't she live with us? I always live with Mommy."

Daddy came and went, but Mommy was always there. She wouldn't leave him.

An angry grunt came from the front, and Rhys sank back in his seat. He bit his lip as the car moved over to the side of the road and stopped.

Daddy unlocked the seatbelt and turned around to face him. "You crying, son?"

He shook his head. The tears were still in his eyes so that didn't count. If he blinked fast, maybe they'd go away.

"Good, because you're a big boy now. You have to be brave."

"I am brave. Mommy says so all the time."

That look again. The one Daddy gave whenever he talked about Mommy.

"It's a different kind of brave. Your mother was in a car wreck. She's not coming back."

"She's hurt?" He struggled with the straps holding him. He had to get out. Mommy needed him.

Daddy made another one of those grunts. "She's dead, Rhys. You know what that means, don't you? Like your friend Cody's puppy. Up in Heaven, I guess. But you and me—we're here, and we're together."

Daddy turned back around. "Settle back. We'll be at our new place soon. Got a friend there. Tom Carson. He has a daughter about your age. Name's Paige."

Rhys turned his face toward the window. He blinked faster and faster, daring any tears to fall. He didn't know where Heaven was, but wherever Mommy was, she needed him. He had to be brave until he could find her.

Rhys lifted his head, staring at the empty doorway. He knew only the bare facts about the wreck that had taken his mother's life. The location, the date. The exact same facts as those Dana related. His mother had died, and Dana had lived.

Was that the reason for Dad's hostile reaction? If so, why didn't he explain that to me? What do I do now? Confront him?

Hardly. As obvious as it seemed, he didn't have proof, and when dealing with Erik McCall, he'd learned to have all the facts before approaching him.

He couldn't talk to Paige. Couldn't ruin the growing

relationship between his best friend and Dana. Nor Jamie either.

Why should I care about that? This woman drove the car that killed my mother.

Or had she? What if his mother had been the one at fault? The one who'd nearly killed Dana?

He pushed out of the chair, paced to the window, then back to the wall. The meticulous beauty of the Main Street rendition mocked him. He traced a finger over one of Dana's drawings. The care she took in her work was evident, each line professional but passionate. The drawings could have been created by his own hand, but it was her touch that had given life to these images.

All his dreams were tied to this project. The McCalls would make a permanent mark on PI. Their work would become a part of the history of the island and stand for generations.

A relationship with his father appeared impossible now, and the woman he'd deemed the perfect business partner might be responsible for the greatest loss in his life.

The door to the past was open, and he couldn't ignore it.

The boxes taunted Rhys. Stacked in one corner in the spare bedroom of his cottage, untouched for years. He knew exactly the carton he needed. The one sitting topmost on the stack, daring him to touch it, to open it and explore its confines. With one deep breath in, then out, Rhys shifted the box to the floor. He dropped to his knees and rested his palms on the cardboard surface.

Leave it alone.

But he'd never forget. He owed himself—and his mother— the truth.

He flexed his trembling hands, pulled the lid off the box, and laid it to one side. Inside the container lay stacks of photograph albums. Thanks to his father's vindictiveness, all photos of his mother had been destroyed prior to the albums being stored away. Within one of those books, a certain picture existed that might resolve the terrible suspicions he'd had since his conversation with Dana.

The book he sought was the final one in the box. He opened

the volume, flipping past each page. Forcing himself to bypass those long-ago images of his childhood until he found the photo that would give him answers.

Fingers shaking, he pulled it from the plastic sleeve.

The gentle blur of his memory sharpened as he studied his younger self. The rear passenger door of the car was open, and he sat with his legs dangling. Navy plaid shorts, a white polo shirt, and a wide grin. An Easter basket sat on the ground in front of him. His mouth quirked to one side. Thank God she hadn't dressed him in a dorky suit with a bow tie.

"No more pictures! We'll be late and all the eggs'll be gone!"

"I would never let you be late to the egg hunt. Hop in the car so I can buckle you."

"I can do it myself."

He climbed onto his booster seat and fastened the seatbelt. He didn't huff or puff when Mommy checked. It was okay. She wasn't used to him being a big boy yet.

He closed his eyes for a brief moment and reveled in joyful nostalgia.

With a silent sigh, he flipped the photo to the other side. His breath slowed, his heart clenched. He glided a fingertip over the inked letters inscribed on the blank side as he mouthed the words.

Rhys. 4 Years Old. Easter.

His name... her handwriting. He was holding what she had touched so many years ago.

The dam broke. Memory after memory slammed into his consciousness. Hugs that kept him safe, kisses that ended his day and started the next. Gentle tones lulling him to sleep. The smell of her skin, the soft brush of her hair against his cheek, the way she'd laughed...

Oh, God... the way she'd loved him.

He sank to the floor, cradling his head in one hand. Deep, heaving sobs broke free. He slammed a fist to his chest to halt the pain ripping his heart to pieces as tears spilled down his face.

Grief swelled inside until he could hardly breathe. Grief for the child who'd never had the chance to say good-bye, grief for the man who now understood all he had lost.

The storm waned, then passed. Slumped against the wall, he swiped a forearm across his face. Another moment passed before he stirred enough to tuck the snapshot into his shirt pocket. He drew in a deep breath and stood, centering himself back in the present.

As he lifted the photo album to return it to the storage box, an envelope tumbled to the floor.

He picked up the packet, frowning at the logo of a photo printing service. The flap was still sealed. The name *Catherine McCall* was written on the front with a receipt dated mere days before the automobile accident stapled to the top.

Tucked away for more than twenty years, this small packet had escaped his father's wrath. A prayer swept to his lips. He rubbed a damp hand against the leg of his jeans, then peeled back the adhesive flap. A deck of photographs tumbled into his waiting palm. One by one, he flipped through the stack. One by one, each image stabbed at his heart.

Memories, faded in his mind but alive in his heart, flooded back. Her face. Her smile. He never knew joy could hold such pain, but the power of it brought him once again to his knees. Tears rolled unchecked down his cheeks. He stroked a finger over the surface, and in his soul, he remembered her touch.

I never forgot your love.

He gathered his courage, rose with determination. Time for justice.

Rhys rang the doorbell and within seconds, the door swung open. His throat swelled at the welcoming expression on Dana's face. He was about to tear her life apart, and she had no warning to prepare herself.

"Rhys! Come on in. Can you get the door? I have cookies ready to come out of the oven. Oh, and check out the new patio doors!" The oven timer chirped from the kitchen, and Dana dashed down the hallway.

Rhys stepped inside and closed the door behind him. He detoured through the living room, pausing to lay the packet of photographs on the table next to the couch, before continuing to the French doors that led to the patio.

The doors didn't match the existing windows, but he knew Dana planned to replace those as well. These were attractive, secure, and—he couldn't hold back a rueful smile—totally unlikely to offend her sensibilities.

Can I go through with this?

There was no other choice. If he was wrong... he couldn't bear to think about the consequences. Unable to linger any longer, he walked into the kitchen just as Dana set a plate of freshly baked cookies onto the table in the breakfast nook. Her laugh, joyful and innocent, cut a knife through him.

"I baked these for you as a 'thank you' for boarding up the doors the other night. There's two kinds. Try each and let me know which one you prefer."

Her kindness was killing him. Words stuck in his throat as he stared at the plate. The scent, rich, sweet, and buttery, shot through him. He sank down into the nearest chair as the aroma swept him into another time.

"Can we play outside after snacks?" It was raining, but that didn't matter. He had the best mom ever. She loved playing in the rain as much as he did.

"We could or...."

His head shot up. That tone always meant a surprise was coming. He forgot all about the cookies as she set a box on the table.

"I thought we could do crafts." She lifted the lid, reaching inside and pulling out....

"You bought me building sticks!" Excitement shivered through him as she set out each item. Glue... markers... and stickers!

"What do you think? Shall we build a fort? Or a castle?"

He shook his head. "I wanna build a house for you, and we'll live there forever."

"I would love that. Here's the deal. You build the house..." His eager gaze followed as she picked up a marker and tapped it gently against the tip of his nose. "...and I'll make it pretty."

He pulled the red marker from her hand, replacing it with a blue one. "This one."

"Blue it is. Have you decided which cookie?"

Knees on the chair, elbows on the table, he rocked back and forth, savoring the aroma of his favorite treats. Chocolate chip or oatmeal raisin. He stretched out a hand, waving it round and round over the plate before zeroing in on his selection.

"Chocolate chip is your favorite today?"

The first bite was a hug inside his mouth, warm and sweet. He shook his head, swallowing. "All your cookies are the best."

"All your cookies are the best," Rhys said.

Dana turned, spatula in hand. She'd just transferred the final cookie to the cooling rack. "What did you say?"

Something was wrong. She gleaned it from the quiet way he sat, his focus centered on the plate in front of him. When he lifted his gaze, anguish filled the depths of his dark green eyes as he pushed the plate to one side.

"I used to say that to my mother. She died when I was young." He gestured toward the plate. "She made the most incredible cookies."

She was no stranger to that sort of pain. Regardless of the time spent together or the time since passed, the void always existed. A part of the heart shut away for eternity for the loss of a loved one.

The rapport between the two of them had been nearly instantaneous, evolving into a mutual friendship. Words wouldn't heal his pain, but maybe she could offer a measure of comfort to ease his burden. She circled the island, then stopped. His red-rimmed eyes stared at her as he continued.

"I was four years old when it happened. One day she was with me, the next day she was gone. She died in a car wreck."

Heat rushed through her, feathering into her arms and legs. She braced her hands against the counter behind her, struggling to contain the trembling. "Our conversation reminded you of that."

Rhys pushed back the chair to stand. A harsh scraping rippled through the room. "It happened in Chesapeake on old Militia Road twenty-three years ago."

Don't say it! Don't say the date!

"May eighth. The description of the car jogged my memory. I went home and found this." He pulled a photograph from his pocket, but she couldn't look at it.

Dear God, no. Please…

The salty sting of hot tears flooded her eyes, rolling unchecked down her cheeks. "When I came out of the coma, no one would tell me anything. They told me to just concentrate on

135

getting better so I could go home to my son."

She cursed herself for uttering such lame excuses. Home to *her* son, while Rhys was left without a mother.

"I killed her, didn't I? That's what you're telling me." A fearful dread swelled in her chest, rising into her throat. She choked, forcing out her fears. "I'm the reason you grew up without your mother." Her knees weakened. She slid down the side of the island, hands pressed to her face. "Oh, God, Rhys, I'm sorry! I am… so sorry!"

Rhys's hand cupped her elbow, drawing her upward. "You need to see this."

I can't!

But she had to. She didn't have a choice but to face her actions. She wiped a hand across her eyes, clearing her vision enough to look at the photograph.

She recognized his face even at that young age. Happy, secure, a touch of mischievousness. *Oh, baby, how much longer did you have your mother after this photo was taken?*

His hand jiggled the photo. "The car."

The car? What about…? The vehicle was not new but appeared well-cared for. The candy-apple exterior was clean and shiny; the ebony upholstery gleamed.

Her heart pounded in a thunderous beat as her words echoed back to her. *The hood of my car was red, the dash was black.*

"I don't know how, but a switch occurred. This photograph proves it. Dana, you didn't kill my mother. You *are* my mother."

She stared into his face, and for an instant saw the image of the little boy from the photograph. Or was it from another place and time? A gray haze descended, leaving her with the memory of a child's face and a laughing peal of joy. Her knees buckled, and she groped for the counter.

I remember you.

Rhys bit back a curse, catching Dana as she collapsed. *Could you have been any clumsier?*

He carried her into the living room, eased her onto the couch. Grabbing a nearby pillow, he elevated her legs, then dropped to his knees beside her. She lay there, unmoving. Pale and quiet, so unlike her usual vivacious self.

But indomitable. Within seconds, she stirred. Eyelashes fluttered, a weak hand lifted.

Rhys breathed a sigh of thankfulness. He clasped her other hand between his palms, waiting, watching as she slowly gained awareness. Her eyes opened, and she stared up at him.

He smiled and spoke the words he hadn't said in over two decades.

"Hi, Mom."

Chapter Twelve

Mom.

No other word could have pulled her to awareness so fully. Joshua needed her. The final step from dark to light was instantaneous. Her son's face came into focus.

But it wasn't Joshua kneeling beside her. It was Rhys.

Not Joshua. Not her son.

She pushed a tumble of curls from her face and struggled to sit up. "You called me Mom." He was wrong. He was mistaken.

"Careful. Maybe you should…."

"Help me up." She hated asking for help, hated even more admitting that she needed it.

With Rhys's arm around her shoulders, Dana maneuvered into an upright position. She shifted slightly to the side as he slid onto the cushion beside her. His face brimmed with excitement. A desperate, lonely part of her wanted to believe his crazy claim. To know that she wasn't alone in the world. That despite Joshua's refusal to communicate, she still had someone she could call family.

"What you're saying can't be true. That photograph isn't proof. A red car with a black interior is not uncommon."

She expected disappointment or even anger over her denial. Certainly not a boyish grin that sent a pang through her heart. *Why am I looking for reasons to believe him?* It wasn't true; it couldn't be. As fervently as Rhys was advocating this story, he was destined to be hurt.

And her heart would shatter as well.

Rhys twisted to one side, nabbing a packet from the end table and extending it to her. "These do prove it."

Dana turned the envelope over in her hands. Her breath stilled as she read the name on the label. "Catherine McCall. That was your mother's name?"

She saw he wanted to correct her. To insist that Catherine was her name. Rhys had never mentioned his mother's first name, so why was it familiar? He simply nodded and gestured to her to continue.

She opened the flap, shook the envelope, and the photographs tumbled into her hands. Her heart beat faster as she viewed each photo. It was her. Younger—so much younger! And it was Rhys with an adorable grin and those brilliant green eyes. Her hungry gaze devoured each image as proof of what her mind still rejected.

A butterfly painted on her check, a hot air balloon on his.

Riding the merry-go-round.

Eating cotton candy.

Sliding down a watery flume in a log-shaped car.

Resting on a bench; his eyes closed, her cheek nestled against the top of his head.

A deep, keening cry burst through her lips. The photos tumbled into her lap as she buried her face in her hands. Her body shook with unrestrained sobs.

My baby. My little boy.

Through the fog, a pair of strong arms wrapped around her. Anchoring her, providing shelter and comfort as Rhys's voice, hoarse with tears of his own, filtered through her grief.

"Please don't be sorry."

Sorry?

She pulled back to look up at him. The apprehension on his face—that precious face—ignited a fresh rush of tears. She stroked a hand across his cheek, brushing away the dampness.

"Why would I be sorry? This is the most incredible gift." She dashed tears from her own cheeks as a nervous laugh spilled from her lips. "I was never crazy after all."

Rhys frowned as he gathered the photographs that had spilled across the couch and placed them in the envelope. "What do you mean?"

"I remembered doing things like this with a little boy. But that couldn't have happened. Joshua was only two when the car accident occurred, too young to do so many of the things I remembered. Everyone told me it was my imagination or phantom memories. But they weren't." She struggled to keep her voice from breaking. "I was remembering you."

"I never knew…." He stopped, rubbing a hand across his neck. "Listen, how about something to drink? Iced tea, lemonade, coffee?"

A diversion. Something to break the moment until they could regroup. Her son—*her son!*—was a fixer like her. "There's lemonade in the fridge."

He bounded to his feet. "Great. I'll get a couple glasses along with that plate of cookies. Then you can tell me what else you remember about these photos."

She watched him cross the room, his long legs moving with an easy grace. Her heart bumped again as she remembered the toddler who'd once skipped by her side.

Oh, honey. How do we find our way through this?

She picked up the packet of photographs. What else could she remember? A county fair? An amusement park? But who took the pictures? She flipped through the images again, this time finding one of Rhys with another woman and a little boy. Who was she? A friend? A relative or neighbor? She wondered if Rhys would remember his childhood friend's name.

Why didn't I see the resemblance right away?

Because everyone told you that little boy didn't exist.

She choked back the tears once again threatening to erupt. How could she celebrate when the specter of lost years loomed over everything else? But to have never known…? Rhys's entreaty now made sense. The pain tearing her apart now was transitory. Joy soon would overweigh everything else.

Everything would change. Jamie and Paige would be shocked but happy. Nick? How would he react? And Joshua. Did she find one son to make up for losing the other? One thing for certain, Rhys would have to be the one to tell…

…that rat bastard.

Damn you, Erik McCall. You knew!

It explained his reaction when he'd first seen her with Rhys on the street. It also explained those ambivalent feelings about James when she'd first regained consciousness. But why would either man have allowed the deception to continue?

Dana glanced in the direction of the kitchen. Drawers opening and closing. Glasses clinking. Water running in the sink. She couldn't put Rhys in the middle. He would return any moment, and his quick mind would jump to the same conclusion.

She shook her head. The first confrontation belonged to her. Shoving the photographs back into the envelope, she scurried into the foyer and shoved her feet into her shoes.

"Going somewhere? Maybe to see my dad?"

She jumped, whirling around to see Rhys standing at the other end of the hall, serving tray in hand. He nodded to the doorway that led to the living room. With a muffled grumble, Dana walked back into the room as well. She dropped back onto the couch, toeing off her shoes.

"Busted," he said, setting the tray on the table and seating himself beside her. "By the way, I somehow knew exactly where the glasses and silverware were kept."

"You used to help set the table." She jerked as the memory came instinctively to mind.

"Partners even then, huh?" He poured a glass of lemonade and handed it to her. Grabbed a cookie for himself. "You reached the same conclusion I did, didn't you?"

"That your father recognized me? Yes, and I intend to confront him."

"Alone? No."

"It's going to be ugly—"

"It's been ugly between us for some time. I thought his behavior was about taking back control. Now I think it's been about hiding the truth." He grunted, a harsh sound that sent a chill through her. "How this for a news flash? My own father fired me from the company."

Her mouth dropped open. Erik McCall's viciousness shocked her, but in a strange way, the cold-hearted retaliation seemed almost familiar.

The glass trembled in her grasp. She leaned forward, placing it on the tray. "We both need to confront him, and I would love to have you with me."

"Then let's go hear what he has to say." He stood, holding his hand out to her.

Dana slipped on her shoes, then took his hand. She picked up the packet of photographs, and together they walked to the front door.

"Hold on a second." Rhys turned back to the living room, snatched a cookie from the tray, then raced back to her side. Catching her look, he shrugged as he opened the door. "Your cookies are the best. Oh, and I'm driving."

She blinked back another rush of tears. No time for that. She had an ass-kicking to deliver.

Dana charged into Erik's office. She beat Rhys only because he paused to direct Stacy to hold any calls or visitors.

The rat bastard was seated at his desk. His head jerked upward at the intrusion. Something—shock, fear, anger—flashed across his face. She didn't give a good damn which it was. His rage didn't scare her, and as for fear, he needed a huge dose for what she was about to unload.

He shot to his feet. "What the hell do you think you're doing, busting into my office? I told you…."

She slapped her hands on the desktop. "It's what you *didn't* say!"

He stiffened, gaze locked upon her as one hand snaked toward the phone. "You can leave now, or the sheriff can remove you."

"Fine. Call the sheriff and tell him your *wife* is… hmm, what should we call it? Disturbing the peace? Trespassing? Back from the dead?"

The door slammed as Rhys entered the room.

Erik pulled his hand back to his side. His steely gray glare glittered with contempt. "Whatever scam you're trying to pull isn't going to work with me. As for you—" His gaze shifted to Rhys. "Are you lame-brained enough to fall for her line of—"

"Careful what you say, Dad. I'm as furious with you as I have ever been in my entire life."

"Because some con artist spun a story? Where's the proof?"

"Right here." Dana held up the packet of photographs.

Rhys took the package, turned the label to face his father. "Yeah, Dad, turns out you didn't destroy all the pictures of Mom after all."

Dear God. It really was Kate standing before him.

Erik folded his arms across his chest, glaring at his accusers. Bad enough to have to see that damn woman's face again, but having Rhys standing there beside her—defending her—cut him to the core.

"I'm telling you for the last time. As far as I knew, Catherine died in that automobile accident."

"What about when I first arrived? When we met on the street? You didn't question that?"

Erik grunted. "Seeing a face I never wanted to see again— even if it was a hell of a lot older? Gave me a start, but why would I think anything other than it was some bad cosmic joke. How would I know you'd been living in adultery under an assumed identity?"

Kate stiffened, glaring at him. "I didn't choose that situation."

"As for these photographs, doesn't prove a thing. Find a picture of Dana Canfield prior to the time of the accident, and you might prove your point. But while you're pleading amnesia and throwing out all these accusations, let me pose a question to you? Why didn't Canfield say anything? He must have known he was sleeping with a woman who wasn't his wife."

Bull's-eye.

Color washed out of Kate's face, her dark eyes glistening as she glared back at him. Good. She damn well deserved it for all the hell she'd put him through in those few short years.

"We're not discussing James. We're talking about you."

"I was told you were dead, and that was all I needed to know. I got my son and brought him home where he belonged." Erik shot a look at Rhys. "You know what she'd planned to do?"

Rhys shook his head. "Why would I? You refused to talk about my mother and dared me to ask questions."

Erik waved a dismissing hand. "I was working part-time on the mainland but mostly on PI. Kate was living in some crummy student housing apartment and refused to move here.

Tells me she's transferring out of state and taking you with her. When I heard about the accident, I wasn't the least bit sorry. Saved me the cost of a divorce and a custody suit."

"You cold-hearted bastard."

Erik snorted at Kate's pronouncement. Like he hadn't been called *that* before. He narrowed his eyes as Rhys stepped in front of the woman. Figures, she already had him taking her side. Playing the victim as usual.

"Dad, that's enough. Even if you didn't care to find out for sure back then, you should have told me about the resemblance when Dana arrived."

"What good would that have done? You even remember what she looked like?" The stunned look on Rhys's face pleased him. "Nope, didn't think so." He jabbed a finger in Kate's direction. "As for what you believe, I don't give a damn."

"You never did." She snatched up the packet of photographs from the top of the desk. "This is useless."

She stormed toward the door, stopping to deliver another one of her snotty glares. God, he hated that look. Seeing Rhys fall into step behind Catherine, Erik held back his next volley. He didn't need his son feeling more protective than he did already. Rhys didn't understand the true nature of that woman.

"Son. Wait."

Rhys's reluctance showed in the set of his son's shoulders, the hesitant pause and slow turn to face him.

Erik forced his hands to relax, to uncurl from their angry clench, but he couldn't hide the anguish that he knew spilled across his features. "I didn't know."

A flicker of belief. A glimmer of trust. That's all he would need to know he hadn't lost his son to that woman.

But he saw nothing. Neither condemnation nor acceptance. For the first time in his life, Erik couldn't read his son's emotions.

Damn you, Kate. It wasn't enough for you to ruin my life once, was it?

Twenty-three years ago

Erik collapsed into the hard plastic chair in the hallway of the hospital emergency ward. He pressed a fist against his chest, trying to control the furious beat of his heart. Thank God his son hadn't been in the car when Kate had torn off to wherever. If Rhys had been hurt...well, he would have finished the woman off himself. She'd been nothing but a pain in the ass from the moment they'd met.

He'd lost April before even having a chance to fight for her. By the time he'd recuperated from the beating Davis and his buddies had delivered, he was too late to halt April and Mitch's elopement. Erik had returned to Virginia but couldn't force himself to board the ferry to PI. Instead he'd stopped at a local pub, finding the noisy exuberance of the college crowd to be just what he'd needed to dull the pain of his failures.

And there he'd met Catherine.

Mouthy, with brown eyes, dimples, and a halo of black curls, she was the antithesis of April, and at that moment, antithesis was exactly what he'd needed. She'd resisted at first and called him a flirt. In time, he'd won her over—just to prove that he could.

Barely twenty-two when Rhys was born, he hadn't planned on becoming a father yet. After seeing that helpless scrap of humanity, a child he hadn't even wanted, he'd lost his heart immediately. He didn't give a good damn that Kate was the mother. The boy was *his son*, a McCall. He'd convinced her their child needed the security of legitimacy, and they'd married. It was the legal nail he needed to ensure no one else took someone he loved away from him.

Caught now in a whirl of mechanical beeps and antiseptic odors, he sat and waited. And he prayed. Prayed that his wife either succumbed or recovered on her own. *Don't make me have to make a decision.* Damn it! He shouldn't be dealing with this bullshit. None of this was his fault.

The squeak of rubber-soled shoes caught his attention. He looked up, his gaze following a fine set of legs as a nurse walked briskly down the opposite end of the hallway.

"Mr. McCall?"

Erik jolted. His heart stopped, then started, racing as he turned his head. His eyes narrowed at the sight of an older man now standing before him. Gold watch. Custom-tailored suit and silk tie. Dark hair peppered with touches of gray swept back from a golf-course tanned face.

"My name is Nathan Stoddard. I'm an attorney for the Canfield family." He gestured to the empty chair. "May I?"

Erik shrugged, looking away. "Help yourself."

"Terrible day for everyone. I apologize for intruding. Do you have any family who could be here with you?"

The man's voice was rich, commanding, yet gentle. Erik wasn't an imaginative man, but even he could hear the beauty in those melodic tones. It was a voice that could soothe a troubled spirit or convince a sucker that selling his soul was a fine idea.

He turned his head again. Suspicion died away at the compassion reflected in the man's blue eyes. "I only have a son. He just turned four."

A hand rested briefly on Erik's knee. Not long enough to be intrusive, but enough to convey comfort. "I apologize if this seems insensitive, but there are matters that need to be discussed. James—Mr. Canfield—was out of town when we received the news of the accident. He's on his way back now. However, I am entrusted to act on his behalf."

Cynicism replaced that momentary sympathetic connection. *Lawyer. Figures, and here comes the pitch.*

"I want to assure you that all medical expenses will be covered, including compensatory consideration for you and your son. I also would like to offer my assistance with making the final arrangements for your wife."

Final—what? For a moment, he couldn't move, couldn't think, could barely breathe. He swallowed hard. Pushed a fist against his chest, forcing air back into his lungs. "What do you mean? Are you talking about Catherine?"

Shock etched its way across the attorney's face. He drew several deep breaths before speaking. "Mr. McCall, I apologize. I was certain the doctor had informed you immediately of your wife's passing." He bit his lip, shook his head. "My client's wife was the one who suffered the head injury. It was your wife Catherine who sustained the worst of the injuries. If it's any consolation, I can assure you that the doctors were diligent in their attempts to save her."

The black cloud of guilt faded away, replaced by a euphoria he hadn't felt in ages. *I'm free, and I have my boy.*

"Are you all right?" A comforting hand rested on his shoulder.

Erik dipped his head, hiding any hint of joy. "I was thinking about my son. I suppose I should talk to someone about the arrangements." He took a deep swallow before looking up at his companion. Something about the man's demeanor made him feel he could confide in him.

"Kate and I—we weren't close. We got married because she got herself pregnant. I did the best I knew how, but it was never good enough for her. I always did right by my boy." He lifted a shoulder in a small half-shrug. "I never expected things to end this way."

"None of us expected to be where we are today. Let me take some of that burden off you and tend to your wife's final arrangements."

The cynic in him couldn't let go completely. He'd worked and sweated for anything and everything he'd had in this life. Good things didn't happen this easily. "Why are you doing this? Kate, me—we're nothing to you."

A shimmer of moisture glistened in the man's cool blue eyes. "The cause of the accident is yet to be determined by the police. Investigations, accusations, lawsuits. I'm sure those will all be forthcoming. For now, the living must deal with what happened today."

Stoddard slid a hand into the inner breast pocket of his suit jacket and pulled out a slip of paper. "Please take this. Regardless of the issues with your wife, your son lost his mother. Money can't replace her, but perhaps it can provide a fresh start for you and your boy."

Erik took the check, his breath catching as he counted the number of zeros. Relief, guilt, and suspicion warred within him. "You're just giving me this money? You want something signed, right?"

The older man glanced down the hallway, then back to him. "I have a confession...."

Here we go.

"Based on my conversations with the police, the early indications are that my client's wife may have been at fault. It's not prudent of me to admit that but, for everyone's sake, it would be best to avoid any long, drawn-out legal battles. I'm certain you want to return to your life with your son, and James needs to do that as well." He hauled in a huge breath of air, releasing it with a whoosh. "So, no, I don't need a waiver signed. I trust you to understand I'm dealing in good faith and with good intentions. If you find yourself in further need, you only have to ask."

The accident had to be the other woman's fault. A lawyer wouldn't pony up a ready-made check for this amount unless he was trying to head off a massive lawsuit. Better yet, this meant Kate wasn't at fault, and nobody could come back at him claiming damages.

A cold chill having nothing to do with the blast from the A/C enveloped him. Angels and devils were tap-dancing across his shoulders. Right now, he wasn't sure which ones were leading, but he heard one of them whisper *Take the money.*

He folded the check, then stood, sliding the paper into the front pocket of his jeans. "Maybe I would be due more depending on whose fault is determined, and you certainly look like you could afford it. But I won't be asking for a cent more, sir. Though if you could see your way to making those arrangements, I'd surely appreciate it."

The attorney nodded his head. "Do you have any preferences?"

"Like I said, we weren't in a good place. Just something respectful. I won't be here for it. I'm taking my son back home with me, with no plans to come back to this place again."

The man rose, his tanned face wreathed in a benevolent smile. "Clean break and a fresh start. Consider it done."

Erik hesitated, then extended his hand. "I appreciate all you're doing. I couldn't have handled it myself."

Stoddard's hand was warm, the clasp firm. "Good luck to you, Mr. McCall."

With a final nod to the man who'd showed him such kindness, Erik turned and walked away. The girl he'd loved was lost to him while the girl he'd married was waiting to be laid to rest. A few short hours ago, he'd been close to dead broke and at risk of losing his child. Now he had a couple hundred Gs in his pocket and sole custody of his son.

This day couldn't get any better.

Current Time

Erik crossed the room, sinking down onto the couch. Resting his head against the back cushion, he pressed the heels of both hands against his brow.

Should he have known? Of course not. Whatever deception had occurred, it had been cultivated for over twenty-years. It had happened outside his knowledge, beyond his control.

Not my fault.

When he'd seen the woman on the street, it was like a ghost had come back to haunt him. Those eyes staring at him as if she had every right to be there. She hadn't recognized him, hadn't confronted him. Why shouldn't he conclude it was a bad twist of fate the woman looked exactly like his biggest regret? The name Canfield? Long faded from his memory after all these years.

He'd be the one to pay for it. Catherine would make sure of that. She'd already siphoned Rhys's loyalty away from him. Her influence explained why his son had abandoned his heritage at McCall to work with a total stranger. Not that Rhys was entirely blameless. His resentment of Kevin's presence had also added to the estrangement.

Tough love hadn't succeeded in bringing Rhys around. Not unexpected. The boy always had been too stubborn for his own good. Sensitive too. Took after his mother in that way. Still, if tender feelings were needed to bring his son back, then he'd become the most sensitive SOB on all of PI.

Family. That's what would draw Rhys back. The black cloud of rage faded, replaced by the dream he'd once thought lost forever.

April as his wife, by his side as it should have been all these years. April would provide a much-needed maternal touch, and Kevin would welcome Rhys as a brother, once their initial rivalry was resolved.

Rhys, Kevin—my sons. The three of them working together under his guidance.

Erik pushed up from the couch. He stretched, then walked to the wall of windows behind his desk where downtown PI lay before him. There were no limits to what he and his boys could achieve.

As expected, Keg was waiting at the bar, halfway through his drink when Nick arrived at the restaurant. Eyeing the man's unsteady walk as they followed the hostess to their table, Nick wondered how many drinks Keg had consumed so far.

Relieved that Keg didn't order a refill when they placed their dinner order, Nick settled back in his chair. Talk of poker, Megan, baseball, and general BS filled the time until their food arrived.

Keg cut into a steak so rare it looked as if the horns had been knocked off just before it was served. "You're looking good, Nicky. Life on PI agreeing with you?"

"Good enough. Wish I had a prettier face sitting across from me. You look like you've been to hell and back."

Age, the job, stress—something was taking a toll on Keg. Deep lines worried the corners of his eyes and the sides of his mouth. The man had a good ten years on Nick, but right now, it could have been twenty.

"Thanks a lot, buddy. You try working twelve-hour shifts day after day. Not just the hours that kill you. It's all the crazy shit that goes down. It's enough to suck the soul right out of a guy. Put one dirtbag away, and ten more take his place. Used to be worth it. Saw a difference made in the end. Now, I'm biding my time 'til it all gets loaded into the handbasket."

Keg's bitching about his job was a poker-night tradition. But the depth of his attitude was something new. "Sounds like some vacation time might be in order."

"Damn straight." He jerked his chin in Nick's direction. "Shoulda been like you. Haul ass to some quaint little island. Hang out all day playing with cars and watching the tide go in and out. Not having to give a damn about anyone but yourself. Good life, huh?"

Nick schooled his face as Keg shot a narrow-eyed glance in his direction. "I'm content running my garage."

"And investigating James Canfield's shooting? Sounds to me like you're getting bored." The glare shifted to a sneer. "I'm deducing you've met the Widow Canfield. Pretty little thing, isn't she?"

Nick shrugged off the glib dismissal of his job, but the flip description of Dana had him biting back a fierce retort. "We've met. Wouldn't mind checking out that car of hers. BMW convertible."

Keg snorted. "The lady made quite a haul from her husband's death. Canfield was an estate lawyer. Handled a variety of accounts, very lucrative ones. And before you ask, never a hint of impropriety. Anyway, he and the missus supposedly had a solid marriage."

Nick took a long sip of iced tea, hoping the glass hid his expression. He wanted cold, hard facts, not a recap of half-assed gossip. Especially when it centered on Dana. "Supposedly?"

Keg waved his hand. "Getting there, Nicky. Their son Joshua takes off for parts unknown. The Canfields make a few obligatory appearances at some social functions but otherwise are off the social scene. Most popular rumor is Mrs. C was having an affair."

Nick poked his fork into the grilled salmon, a selection that had lifted the other man's eyebrows when he'd ordered it. Steak was on the menu tomorrow. Not that Keg needed to know that. "Why not suspect Canfield of having the affair? Supposing that either of them were."

Lansing shrugged. "Who knows? Canfield was a workaholic, but that was nothing compared to the additional hours he started working after the kid took off. Story goes that he was reorganizing his assets in preparation for a divorce. What also made Mrs. C the likely candidate was all the so-called decorating she was doing at the alleged lover's house. None other than Judge Hannaman."

Nick's hand stalled over his plate. "A judge?"

"Exactly. Hannaman refers a friend of his to Canfield to handle the guy's divorce. Not Canfield's area of expertise, but for whatever reason, he agrees. Day of the hearing, Canfield, the client, and a bystander get shot."

Nick stared down at his half-eaten dinner, his appetite gone. He pushed the plate away. Keg's story, even if it was gossip and rumor, sounded damning, but it didn't account for the other incidents that Dana mentioned. Someone had wanted James Canfield dead. It might have been Hannaman, but it damn sure wasn't Dana.

"Coincidental, but nothing conclusive."

"Connect the dots, Nicky. Mrs. C inherits a whopping ton of cash, gets out of a marriage that had run its course, and skips town to work on some vanity project on PI."

"Hardly a vanity project. It's a revitalization effort. Guy named McCall is running the project."

Lansing swallowed the last piece of steak, shrugging. "Hope McCall doesn't end up like Canfield."

Nick batted away the thought of Rhys McCall and his obvious crush on Dana. "Did you recheck the file?"

Keg grunted, sinking back in his chair. "I took a gander at it, but didn't see any red flags or clues. I don't know what happened with Canfield, but I'm not putting a target on my back by checking out a copy."

Nick's temper flared. Keg could have refused over the phone. The entire trip to the mainland was a waste. "You're okay with someone getting away with murder?"

"No, I'm not okay with it, but I have over a dozen open cases on my desk. Burglary, assault, and more crazy-ass shit than you can imagine. That's my reality." Keg tossed his napkin on the table. He pushed back his chair and stood, pulling keys from his jacket pocket.

"You intending to drive? Let me call a cab." Nick held out his hand for the keys. "Or I'll drop you off."

"Yeah, yeah. A cab. Right smart idea, Nicky. I can hook one just down the block." A smirk crept across Keg's lips. "While we're handing out advice, here's a few words for you to take to heart. Steer clear of this one."

Not a chance. If Canfield had been the intended target rather than a bystander, Dana was in danger as well.

The waitress returned, sending a glance at Keg lumbering through the dining room before addressing Nick. "Leave room for dessert?"

Nick shot a quick glance at his watch. "No, thanks, Brenda. If I leave now, I can catch the last ferry back to PI."

Brenda shook her head as she gathered the used plates and tableware. "Not tonight. Fog's rolled in. They've suspended crossings until tomorrow morning. I'll be back in a moment with your check."

Dinner tab. No inside information. No way home tonight. Screwed all around.

Chapter Thirteen

"You won't want dinner if you keep eating those cookies."

After the confrontation with Erik, Dana and Rhys had returned to her house. Nestled on the sofa, she laughed as Rhys popped another cookie into his mouth. He plopped onto the couch, shifting to face her.

"We should celebrate. How about pizza for dinner?"

"We could order pizza, or I could cook." She struggled to recall the word from their past. "Maybe... fizgetti?"

"Fiz... spaghetti?" Rhys's eyes widened. "You remember what I called it?"

"I never forgot." Her smile faded. "Joshua would get so mad when I called it that. Even as a toddler, he had the most precise enunciation."

She looked up when Rhys failed to respond. Her words, a sudden memory casually mentioned, had shattered his mood. "Honey, I didn't—"

"I know. It's just... he had all those years with you. Years I—" He ran a hand over his mouth. Moisture glistened in his dark green eyes, and the sorrow on his face scorched her heart.

She gripped his hand between hers. "You were my life and my happiness. Every time I thought of the things we did, I was filled with joy. When I was told that precious little boy didn't exist, I wanted to go back to that long sleep so we could be together again. I dreamed about us. Each time I woke, I had to face that things weren't that way and never would be. It makes sense now why that life seemed more real than the one I was living." A choked laugh broke loose. "I went to so many psychiatrists to help—how did they put it? 'Assimilate back into reality.' Crazy, huh?"

He shook his head. "No, never crazy."

"No wonder I never remembered anything about my so-called life as Dana Canfield prior to the wreck. I never lived it. Regardless of any fallout, I will never regret learning the truth." She cupped his face, marveling how she could discern traces of the child she'd long thought was an illusion. "I have you back."

Although... maybe it wasn't quite the same for Rhys. Her shoulders sagged, and she dropped her hands into her lap. "What about you? You're a grown man and certainly don't need a mother dropping into your life."

"I might not need a mother." He slid across the cushion, closing the distance between them. Hand beneath her chin, he tilted her head so their gazes met. "But I surely do need a Mom."

You were right, Toddy. Whether it was a mom or a mother, a boy always needed one. She pressed a kiss to those work-roughened fingers. "Did you have a stepmother growing up?"

He settled back, stretching out his legs. "No. In fact, Dad rarely brought around any of the women he dated. I knew about some of them. Most didn't last very long. I stayed with Paige's family whenever he was away overnight. Had dinner with them most nights as well. The Carsons fixed a permanent bedroom for me since I stayed there so often."

Thank you, God. He hadn't been alone all those years. "They were your family, weren't they?"

"Dad wasn't a traditional parent. These days he'd probably have had social services called on him. I went to work with him when I was a kid. I had my own junior hammer when I was four. At five, he guided me making my first cut of wood with an electric saw. We went camping, fishing, boating. I learned how to be self-sufficient. I probably would have been a complete Neanderthal if not for Mom Carson. She taught me table manners, etiquette, rules of the household. Pop Carson taught me about ethics and honor. As I got older, I realized Dad's pride in me was needing to see a reflection of himself. I don't know what the story was between him and Pop, but Dad always backed down to him."

Not perfect, but at least his childhood had some happiness and normality. She hesitated. Her next question was born out of sheer selfishness.

"Did you remember me?" She steeled herself for his denial as Rhys looked away. He had been so young and so much time had passed. Why should she expect otherwise?

When he turned back, his eyes were rimmed with red.

"I remembered you every day for the longest time. I remembered drawing pictures. You read to me. We played in the rain. You made life an adventure. Dad refused to let me talk about you. The Carsons were sympathetic, but more concerned about helping me cope with my new life." He shrugged. "They did what they thought was right. As far as anyone knew, that was the best thing for me. But at night…" His voice faltered, then with a deep breath, he continued. "Memories were my bedtime stories. Finally, I stopped reliving them because it was too difficult when I'd wake up and those times were no longer my reality. Just like you had to do."

Tears ran unchecked down her cheeks. Both of them had suffered. Both had coped in the only way they could. "How did you happen to have those photographs? I'm surprised Erik didn't destroy them."

"Pop saved all the things from our old apartment before Dad could throw them out. He stored them at his home until I bought my own house. If he hadn't, those pictures would have been lost forever. As it was, Dad destroyed all the ones he had of you." He bowed his head. "I hated him for the longest time for that."

"If not for Mr. Carson's intervention, you would have been left believing I drove the car that killed your mother."

"I have to believe we'd have discovered the truth. There was an immediate connection when we met. I think instinctively we recognized each other." He paused for a brief moment. "I believe Dad when he said he didn't know that you were alive."

His admission stung, but the hurt on his features was too evident for her to be angry. "Why would you believe him?"

"Because he heard what he wanted, and it was convenient. I'm not excusing him. What he did was negligent and cruel. He owed both of us the responsibility of confirming that information." He swallowed, but a tremor lingered in his words. "I never knew where my mother was buried. I never had the closure of leaving flowers or saying a prayer at her grave. I never had anything except for memories I fought to keep alive."

A hesitant look crossed his features before he spoke again. "He isn't the only one to blame."

She knew exactly what he meant. "James. You're right. He's guilty too." A horrible thought hit her. "Toddy!"

Rhys shook his head. "Who is Toddy?"

"James's godfather. He's like a grandfather to Josh. I consider him more of an eccentric uncle. He's been my anchor this past year. I can't believe he knows anything about this… but he *has* to know too." She struggled again with tears that seemed to have no end. "I can be furious with Erik, but James…"

"Was he good to you? Were you happy?"

That question took her to a place she wasn't ready to explore. She needed time to remember and process. She studied Rhys's face, saw his own mixed emotions. Hoping she had a happy life but, if even selfishly, sad that her life had been lived without him. She didn't blame him. Those same thoughts raged within her.

"Happy, no. Not at first. Not for a long time. My husband was a stranger. My child was afraid of me. I was told the memories I did have were my imagination. Products of the head injury or medications." A harsh laugh spilled from her lips. "I was so afraid James would become irritated with my lack of progress. That he'd leave and take Joshua from me. I had no reason to think that, other than I must have been remembering how things were with Erik. He was always threatening to take you away from me. But James wasn't like that. He was kind and patient… and so sad for the longest time."

"Was it grief for his wife? Or guilt over his lie?"

She surprised herself by how quickly that answer came. "I don't know what kind of relationship he had with her. As for the lie, I just don't know. He once told me he couldn't be happy until he knew I was happy. I realized I had to try harder."

"To live his lie."

His bitter tone cut, but she understood. Rhys had no reason to think kindly of the man he deemed just as guilty as his own father. She could never tell him that was the same moment she'd started to fall in love with James Canfield.

Good effin' morning to me.

Nick paced the width of the garage in a futile attempt to work off a case of mad. So much for his bright idea to drop by Dana's for a morning cup of coffee on his way home from the ferry. Stopping at the intersection of Magnolia and Astoria, he'd thrown a glance toward her place. The large white house glistened in the morning sunlight. To his surprise, a red SUV was parked in the driveway.

Within seconds, the front door opened and Rhys McCall walked out onto the porch, followed by Dana. The kid stopped on the top step, turning to rest one foot on the edge of the porch. Dana, looking like a teenager in a pair of snug cropped pants and oversized T-shirt, smiled down at him, then leaned forward into the kid's outstretched arms.

...rumor was Mrs. C was having an affair... a whopping ton of cash... marriage had run its course...

He'd whipped the truck onto Magnolia—in the opposite direction of Dana's house—and headed home.

A quick shower later, he was back downstairs, wandering around in search of some task to occupy his mind. He leaned back against the workbench, eyeing the empty bays. Good time to clean out and reorganize the garage.

Bullshit on that. It was Saturday. Time to kick back and... what?

He spied the ceramic T-Bird tucked to the back edge of his desk. Picking it up, he jerked the dying flowers from the container and dropped them into the trash. He'd keep the car as a reminder about trusting women. He sure hadn't expected Dana to be a Callie-clone.

He started up the staircase, stopping on the third step as the buzzer sounded at the rear entrance. *Damn it. Forgot to lock the door.* He turned, retracing his steps.

"Nick! Oh, there you are!" Dana rushed into the building, dark curls flying. "You'll never guess what's happened."

Nick halted on the bottom of the landing, ticked at the way his heart beat a little faster on seeing her slender curves decked in a bright blue summer dress. Her pretty face was flushed, and the brilliant smile she sent his way *almost* nudged him into a better mood. He gave himself a mental slap back into a well-deserved anger. "I bet I could, but right now I'm too busy for games."

Guilt delivered a slap of its own as Dana's smile dropped. With a slight nod, she gave a cool survey of the empty bays. "I can see you're up to your neck in work. Want to share what brought on this attitude?"

Attitude? Oh, hell, he *was the one with the right to have attitude.*

He stalked midway across the garage. The scent of her perfume reminded him of when he'd held her in his arms after the near hit-and-run, when they'd danced together at Eddie's, and when she'd spent the night in his arms after the break-in. Where was the scent of grease and oil when he needed it?

Feet planted, he shoved both hands into his pockets and gave her the scowl he usually saved for Megan's indiscretions.

Dana's right eyebrow telegraphed a silent *Really?*

"I made a totally wasted trip to the mainland last night. Couldn't get back to PI because the ferry shut down due to fog. Driving home this morning, I decided to go by your house."

Her eyebrow lifted a fraction higher. "And?"

"And I see you having cougar time on your front porch, cuddled up with that damn pretty boy who's half your age. For chrissake, Dana, he's young enough to be your son."

Explain that one, lady.

Dana's icy glare dropped another fifteen degrees. She hefted the strap of her purse onto her shoulder, pivoting toward the exit. "I came here to tell you that Rhys—that pretty boy—*is* my son." She pushed the door open, swinging around to add, "Oh, and you're an ass."

Nick snorted, glaring as the door glided shut. No doubt Dana expected it to slam shut but—booyah—hydraulics showed her. Did she think he was stu—*Son?*

He bolted for the exit, shoving the door open in time to hear the purr of the BMW as it headed toward the front gate of the parking lot. He slammed a fist against the remote on the wall. The gate slid shut just as the car drew even with the side of the garage.

Storming onto the driveway, he cast a leery look in Dana's

direction. He wasn't at all sure she wouldn't consider giving him a nudge with the vehicle.

"Open the gate, Nick!"

"Get out of the car. We need to talk."

"Open the gate."

"Forget the gate card, sweetheart?" He had the upper hand, and from the look on her face, she knew it too. He didn't bother to conceal a victory smirk as she shifted into Park and shut off the engine.

Dana exited the car and fired another glare in his direction. "Fine. My car can sit here all day blocking your driveway."

He snorted. "Like I can't start a car without a key?"

"Don't you *dare* touch my car!"

"You can't get out on foot, sweetheart. The gate's locked, and I don't see you slamming that pretty little car through the fence."

She whirled, storming over in front of him. "You are—"

Enough. Nick snatched the purse out of her hand and jammed it under one arm. Tucking one shoulder into her belly, he lifted her off her feet. "Yeah, I know. I'm an ass."

Back inside the garage, he tossed the purse onto the workbench, then flipped the lock on the door. A sharp kick landed on his thigh. One knee buckled, and with a grunt, he regained his balance. With a quick brush of his hand, he flicked both of her shoes to the ground, then headed for the stairs. Two more kicks landed in quick succession.

"Put me down! Wherever you got the idea you can manhandle—"

He laid a palm across her hip, steadying her as he started up the steps. "Tell me all about it when we get upstairs. And I suggest you stop kicking if you don't want to send us both tumbling."

Dangling over Nick's shoulder, Dana fumed. *You are in so much trouble, Nick Warden. I came here to share happy news, and what do you do? Act like—*

His pace slowed as his hand moved from her back. The click of the door latch was followed by the echo of Nick's boots on a wooden floor, softening as he stepped on a large area rug. His hand returned to her back, and the world spun as he lowered her onto the couch.

"If you think... Oh, my God. This couch is amazing!" She shifted on the cushion, running an appreciative hand over the sleek black leather. Luxurious and sinfully soft, the behemoth cradled her in a seductive embrace.

She looked up, confused. "Why do you have such a huge sofa?"

"Because I wanted a big-ass sofa." He jerked his thumb toward the wall behind him. "Just like I wanted a big-ass TV." A forefinger stabbed the air toward the opposite side of the room. "And I'd be more than happy to introduce to you to the big-ass bed in the corner."

She sniffed. "In your dreams."

"Every night of my life." He dropped down onto the couch, his heated gaze robbing her of speech.

She wanted to stay mad. He *deserved* that and more. But she couldn't deny the sincerity in his dead-on gaze nor the squishy feeling his outrageous confession generated. She flopped back on the sofa—that gorgeous, deliciously comfortable sofa—folding her arms over her chest. "Did you even *consider* that Rhys was there because of another break-in?"

"No, ma'am. You would have called me if there had been another incident. Now what's this about the kid being your son? Oh, and sorry about the cougar crack."

The goodwill he'd gained flitted away, replaced by another layer of exasperation. "That's your apology? *Oh, sorry*?"

Nick slid off the couch, dropping onto one knee. She caught her breath as a work-roughened hand cupped the side of her face. Biting the inside of her lip, she refused to nestle her cheek into the warm flesh of his palm.

"I am truly sorry. I was tired and—"

"—and jealous."

He rolled his eyes. "And not in the best of moods. I shouldn't have doubted you, and I apologize."

His sincerity begged her forgiveness; the soft kiss delivered to her forehead sealed the deal. "Accepted. Now, come up here. I can't wait to tell you what happened."

Barely waiting until Nick planted himself back on the

cushion beside her, she swiveled, bent knee nudging his thigh. When his hand closed over her knee, she let it linger, resting her own on top of his as she related what Rhys had discovered.

"Rhys and I ended up talking well into the night, and he stayed over. We had breakfast this morning, talked more. It was—you don't believe me?"

He hadn't said a word during the entire story. Except for the faint frown creasing his brow, his features remained expressionless. With her question, he jerked, blinking. "Of course I do. I was just trying to make sense of it."

Dana straightened her leg, scooting closer to him. When Nick wrapped an arm around her shoulders, she gave in to temptation and rested her head against his chest. A contented sigh escaped as she indulged in the comfort of his strong solid embrace.

"None of it makes sense. Why would James tie himself to a stranger? I didn't have any money. Did he even care I had a child of my own, and what about his child? After I came home, Joshua wouldn't have anything to do with me. He cried constantly. He kept saying 'You're not my Mommy,' and James kept insisting I was. What would motivate him to lie to his own child?"

A thumb ran gently across her face, wiping away her tears. "All good questions, sweetheart, but the fellow who has those answers isn't here to tell us."

"Someone has to know. It explains the missing wedding photographs. And why he never wanted to renew our wedding vows or go back to Seattle."

"You're from Seattle?"

"*They* were from there, unless that was a lie too. I have no idea where I'm from. Or what my maiden name was." The uncertainty from all those years of confusion crashed back into her consciousness. "Nick, I don't even know who I *am*."

His palm stroked down her arm, soothing her rising agitation. "You're the lady who seduced me through the windshield of her car in five seconds flat. You like to line-dance. Love seafood. Got a killer pair of legs. Probably know the name of every paint chip in the hardware store. Have the most beautiful brown eyes I've ever seen. And have no problem going toe-to-toe with me when I act like an ass. So whether you call yourself Dana or Kate... or even Rose, you're you."

Talk about cutting through the bull. She could dance around her feelings. She could call it an affair. But the truth? She was falling in love with Nick Warden. If it took an awkward Shakespeare reference to tip her decision over the edge, that didn't seem the least bit bizarre. Nick was right. She was that strong, determined woman who'd driven off the ferry days ago, eager to start a new life. The past? That was a mystery she'd have to solve.

"There's no way I'm asking Erik. If he did answer, it probably would be a lie sending me off in the wrong direction." She pressed a hand against his chest and sat up. "Wait! My maiden name would be on Rhys's birth certificate. He has belongings from our old apartment. There might be records there. Maybe even my marriage license to Erik."

Nick groaned. "Sorry, but I'm still trying to wrap my head around the fact you were married to McCall. Met the guy once. A real SOB."

Dana nodded. "That's a totally accurate description." Seeing another question forming on his lips, she headed the conversation back to her original point. "If Rhys does have any records, I can gather a lot of information on my own first before hiring an investigator."

Nick's hands landed on her shoulders, twisting her around to face him. "Until we get a better feel for the situation, it's not wise to bring in an outsider."

"A detective would be required to maintain confidentiality."

"If he can be trusted."

He wasn't kidding. The solemn expression on his face clearly communicated that message. "You're scaring me, Nick. I'm going to start being suspicious of everyone."

"Canfield was an attorney. No doubt he had friends in law enforcement plus contacts at the courthouse. We don't know who was involved in this cover-up."

"You keep saying *we*. You don't have to get involved in this."

His frown made her laugh, bringing a reluctant chuckle from him as well. "You remember the day I brought lunch by your office?"

"Vividly." Thursday, the day she'd decided to sleep with him.

"I unloaded on you about that female onslaught at the

garage and the text supposedly from Megan. Now, it's your turn to lean on me."

"Hardly the same thing. My baggage is a lot more intense—and definitely dangerous."

"All the more reason for *we.*"

Her heart gave another blip, tumbling further toward the finishing line. "You're right. I need to think this over first."

Nick heaved a sigh. "Good. I also need to tell you—"

A beep from Dana's watch interrupted him. She glanced at the dial, then ran a final lingering hand over the soft leather before pushing to her feet. "I have an appointment in fifteen minutes. Are we still on for tonight?"

Nick stood, an odd expression crossing his features before he shrugged. "Ah, yeah. About tonight."

"Do not tell me you're canceling again." Her warning tone and stony glare must have been fiercer than she realized, and it cheered her to see Nick take a cautious half-step back.

"Not at all. I have some serious making up to do, so you need to leave everything up to me." His hand shot up, stopping her protest. "All I need from you is a promise not to go near the back of the house or look out until I get there."

She eyed him warily. "What are you planning?"

He flashed a killer smile. *Damn him.*

"A surprise. Oh, and I need the keys to your patio gate and the back door."

"The key?" She tapped a forefinger against one cheek. "Hmm, that would be in my purse, which is downstairs. Along with my shoes."

Nick chuckled. "So it is. Need some help getting down the steps?"

"I'll manage." She paused in the doorway, gazing back at the bed in the far corner of Nick's apartment. "It is big, isn't it?"

The startled look on his face was even more satisfying than having the last word.

Nick strode into Carson's, his boots echoing on the wooden floor as he approached the counter. As requested, Paige and Jamie were waiting, and the spitfire didn't look happy.

"I don't know what this is about, Mr. Warden, but I'm not open for business yet on Saturdays. Jamie and I have plans—"

"All the more reason I appreciate you meeting me." He pulled a sheet of paper from his shirt pocket, tossing it onto the counter. "I need your help planning a dinner for Dana."

Paige picked up the list, then looked up, eyes wide. "All this? What did you do to tick her off?"

Irritated at her half-correct assumption, he loomed forward over the counter. "Maybe I just want to do something nice for her. It's not like I can take her somewhere fancy locally because of that poster—"

Paige took a step back. "Let's not go there, besides—"

"And I might be grateful enough to consider our lunch deal paid in full if you'll help me out on this."

She waved the sheet of paper. "*This* is going to take all day."

"The remainder of our lunch deal is three more weeks. Take your pick. Keep in mind that I'll probably get very hungry over those next few weeks."

"Knock it off, you two." Jamie slipped the paper from Paige's hand. "This doesn't seem too bad. Come on, Paige. It'll be fun, and it's for Dana."

Paige glared at Jamie, then back to him. "New deal is we help you set up this dinner—"

"According to plan."

"According to *plan*, and we're even." She plucked the paper back from Jamie's hand. "What will you be doing while we're taking care of all this?"

He patted his shirt pocket. "Taking care of my own list. We'll meet back here at four, then go over to Dana's to set up."

Paige shook her head "We'll meet you there. You and Jamie can keep working until it's time for me to come back over here to finish the food. Then I'll transport it over. You know cars, but I know food. If we're doing this, then this part will be done my way."

Nick swallowed back the growl rising in his throat. Damn it, he had the perfect surprise planned for Dana, and he needed Paige's help. Maybe she was right, but no doubt she would have argued anyway for sheer contrariness.

"Fine," he said through gritted teeth.

"Fine it is."

"Oh, give it a rest!" Jamie slid off the stool. "We have a lot to get done."

He tipped his head in Jamie's direction. "Right you are. I'll meet you at Dana's at four o'clock."

He turned toward the door, pausing to hold up a warning finger. "Mess this up, and it'll be two months of free lunches."

The beginning of a screech reached his ears before the door swung shut behind him. A chuckle broke loose. Something about that girl just sparked the orneriness in both of them.

Speaking of ornery... No answer from Megan. Which meant a call to Callie, and now he was really ticked off.

"Those two look way too happy to be on their first drink."

Rhys followed Sam's nod toward the table where Paige and Jamie sat waiting for them. As they crossed the pavilion at the Lighthouse Cantina, Rhys agreed. Euphoric appeared to be trotting close on the heels of happy. "Looks like both of us are designated drivers tonight."

He pulled out the chair opposite Jamie, the two of them exchanging shy, flirty smiles.

Sam dropped into the remaining empty chair across from Paige, fixing her with a steely glint in his eye. "Started the party early, did you?"

The women exchanged glances, then burst into giggles. Paige waved a hand, taking a sip from her glass before regaining her composure. "We are not drunk. We're relaxed."

Rhys jabbed an elbow into Sam's arm. "I've seen her this way before. She's giddy because of something the two of them got up to today."

Paige curled her lip. "Don't be so judgmental. We were doing good deeds, weren't we, Jamie?"

"It's true. We're Cupid's helpers."

Another shared look, another eruption of giggles. The server arrived at the table, a hesitant look on her face. Rhys eased the two margarita glasses in front of him, then motioned the server to his side of the table. "Tara, just bring us our usual, but with soft drinks instead this time. And take these away, will you?"

Tara smiled and nabbed the glasses in a quick, efficient

motion. "Sure, Rhys. I'll have your drinks right out."

Paige's hands fluttered in protest. "I wasn't finished with that!"

"You are more than finished with it." Rhys turned to Sam. "She gets plowed on a thimbleful of liquor."

"Good to know." Sam stretched out his legs under the table. "So, into whose ass did Cupid fire an arrow?"

"It's actually quite romantic," Jamie said. "Mr. Warden—"

"Nick Warden?" Rhys exclaimed, a bare moment before the same words bolted out of Sam's mouth. He eyed the sheriff suspiciously. "What—"

"Do you want to hear our story or not?" Paige glared at both men, then grinned. "Mr. Warden asked Jamie and me to help set up a dinner for Dana. Total romance on the patio at her house. Flowers everywhere, bit of a French sidewalk café vibe. Best of all, I am off the hook for those free lunches, and who knows? Maybe Mr. Warden will get lucky and have a better attitude."

"I don't think so!" Rhys bolted to his feet, the words spilling out of his mouth before he could think. "I'm going over there and break that up."

Three shocked faces stared up at him. *Shit. That was hardly subtle.*

"What I meant...."

The spell broke, and all three began talking. It was Jamie's quiet "Sit down, Rhys" that broke through his haze. He dropped into the chair, refusing to meet any of their curious gazes.

Tara arrived, delivering their soft drinks and a fresh basket of chips and salsa. Rhys snatched up a chip and shoved it into his mouth.

Paige tapped a forefinger on the table top. "Spill it."

He chewed, swallowed, took a drink. Their steady glares confirmed he couldn't avoid an explanation. "She barely knows this guy. What kind of man makes moves on a woman who's been a widow for only a year?"

Jamie shook her head. "Mr. Warden's been sweet on Dana since they met. I think he just wanted to do something— platonically—romantic."

Sam snorted. "Platonic and romantic? Isn't that a bit of an oxymoron?"

Jamie shot a disgusted look in the sheriff's direction. "No, think of it like courting."

Rhys caught his breath as Jamie's gaze met his. He did *not* want to think of Dana and Nick Warden in those terms. It was one thing when she was a business associate, but now?

She's my mom!

Sam spluttered, grabbing a napkin to catch the liquid spewing from his mouth. Jamie's mouth dropped open. Paige choked, spewing bits of corn chip across the table.

Oh, hell. He'd said it out loud.

Chapter Fourteen

Nestled on the chaise lounge in her bedroom, Dana watched for Nick's arrival. The activity earlier in the afternoon had taken her by surprise. The request to stay away from the back section of the house indicated that the surprise had something to do with the patio area. No doubt the star of the evening being the grill.

She'd made no promise about the front windows. Not that she'd learned much other than seeing Jamie arrive with Nick. Then she'd had only a glance as his vehicle continued along the side driveway to the back. Even more surprising was Paige arriving shortly afterwards. They stayed and left at various intervals, leaving her no clues as to what was being planned other than some tempting aromas from the kitchen.

Finally giving up—and not wanting to ruin her own surprise—she took refuge in the large soaker tub in her bathroom and spent the rest of the afternoon pampering herself.

She swept her curls into a loose arrangement. The dress was one she hadn't had an opportunity to wear yet. Black, form-fitting, ending several inches above her knees. Shot with threads of gold, the shimmering material glistened as she moved. She paired it with shoes that seemed little more than stiletto heels and thin leather straps.

She wanted to knock Nick's socks off when he saw her. The

rest of his clothing… she planned on taking that off him piece by piece.

The roar of a powerful engine and the crunch of tires on the driveway signaled his arrival. Doubting he could see her through the sheer draperies, Dana took full opportunity to watch as he exited the vehicle.

The fit of his dark gray suit won her feminine admiration. The pause to adjust his tie and run a hand over his hair won a smile. She saw him take a deep breath before passing out of her sight. Seconds later the doorbell rang.

She rose from the lounge, walking over to pick up her cell phone from the bureau. She tapped a quick message.

Heard the bell. Ok to come downstairs in my own house?

She grinned as his response arrived seconds later.

If you please.

"Oh, yes, Nick. I very much plan to please you tonight."

His expression was everything she'd wanted when she opened the door. Heat rose from deep within as his dark eyes scanned her from head to toe and back again. She took his hand, and he stepped inside, gaze still locked on her.

"You look amazing." He closed the door behind him with a gentle sweep of his arm.

"You look very handsome yourself, Mr. Warden. Obviously, you're not planning on manning the grill in that suit." Dana slid both hands up the front of his jacket, then traced a finger down the length of his tie. "Nice tie."

"I am a man of my word." He reached out a hand, toying with one of her dainty chandelier earrings. "Change of plans, as you no doubt guessed from the activity this afternoon."

"Plus that amazing aroma from the kitchen." An impish giggle broke free. "I'm dying to see what you've planned."

He crooked an elbow, and she slid her arm through his. He escorted her through the living room, pausing to open the French doors leading to the patio.

Dana expected something special—tablecloth, roses, a candle or two. But what she saw was beyond anything she could have imagined.

Garden containers encircled the perimeter of the main patio. White miniature roses, blushing petunias, vivid purple begonias, and yellow dahlias mixed and mingled, transforming the terrace into a joyous riot of color. Strings of tiny decorative lights wound around the deck railing, adding an additional glow to the evening sunlight. Noticing the citronella torches set around the area, she smiled. He really had thought of everything.

She whirled and launched herself into his arms. "No one ever has ever done anything like this for me before."

"Now someone has." The soft exhale of his breath breezed across her neck, a light chuckle following it. "Someone who's very relieved you like it."

She took a half-step back, resting her hands on his chest. "I adore it."

He dropped a light kiss onto her lips. "And there's more to come."

She caught her breath for the second time as Nick led her to the wrought-iron patio table and pulled out a chair. Covered by a pale green linen cloth, the table was set for two with gold-trimmed white china and crystal glasses. Candles nestled in cracked-glass holders etched in gold flanked tea roses set in a miniature vase. She couldn't help caressing the deep red petals.

"You've been busy." Her gaze followed him as he pulled a bottle of wine from a silver bucket sitting on a side table.

Nick poured a glass, then handed it to her with a smile. After filling his own, he took the seat opposite her. "I had helpers."

"I heard voices." She wasn't about to rat herself out completely. Besides, Nick had said nothing about looking out the front windows.

"Jamie and Paige pitched in. Couldn't have done it without them."

His honesty in acknowledging their help impressed her as much as his appreciation for their efforts.

Nick lifted his glass. "To…?"

She touched the rim of her glass lightly against his, the ring of the crystal pure and clear. "To where this takes us."

"And beyond."

Switching out the courses throughout the dinner took some maneuvering on Nick's part. He must have worked as a waiter at some time, or maybe it was his customary deftness with his hands that allowed him to handle the plates and cutlery so skillfully. Any restaurant experience he'd had obviously hadn't extended to the kitchen. Over the course of the evening, several muttered curses drifted through the screened doors.

How long had they lingered over dinner? Long enough that the sun had set. She switched on the outside lights, dimming them to maintain the romantic mood. However long the meal had lasted, they'd found enough topics to discuss without talking about her tangled past.

I feel like me again. Alive, alert, and filled with passion for life—and for the man returning to the table. She studied the dessert glass filled with a mixture of chilled fruit topped with a dollop of whipped cream.

"Thought we'd go with something light for dessert."

"It's perfect. And thank you for not choosing strawberries and chocolate."

Spoon halfway to his mouth, Nick froze for a second, then burst out laughing. "Paige and I went a couple of rounds over that very subject. Any special reason?"

"It's a lame cliché. It's supposed to be sexy, and maybe at one time it was. Now it just seems trite." She spooned up several mixed berries. "This shows imagination. It's light, refreshing, and colorful. Each bite has a slightly different flavor."

Nick shook his head. "Damn, I'm good."

"And you get me."

Surprise flashed across Nick's face, and Dana wondered if she'd just committed TMI. Pushing the bowl—and etiquette—aside, she rested her elbows on the table, palms cupping her cheeks. "You understand me better than anyone ever has. I don't know why, since we haven't known each other that long. But I'm glad I met you, happy I have you in my life."

He'd held her gaze the entire time she spoke. When she fell silent, the quiet didn't alarm her. Instead, it filled her with hope. He stretched a hand across the table, and she took it without hesitation.

"I never made any secret that I'm attracted to you. And despite some clumsy attempts on my part, you always gave me chances to show you I care." He glanced away for a second, then back to her. "That toast you gave—to where things take us. That's happening. It's here, it's now, and it's us."

Holding his gaze, Dana extended her glass. "Us."

He held out his glass and gave her a knowing wink. "We."

The crystal chimed again. In the night air filled with

shimmering lights and the fragrance of summer flowers, it was magic.

After finishing dessert, they worked together clearing the table and returning used dishes to the kitchen. Dana stored the leftover food in the refrigerator, then wiped down the countertops. Glancing out the window, she watched Nick extinguish the torches. Her gaze moved to the riotous collection of potted plants that lined the perimeter of the patio.

He gave me a garden.

Every part of the evening showed his touch, his thoughtfulness, in the design and the execution. She couldn't count the number of flowers she'd received from James. Simple bouquets to elaborate designs. All from the hands of an elite florist. Special dinners at home were the work of a hired caterer. To his credit, James never forgot a birthday or anniversary. Only it hadn't been *her* birthday or *their* anniversary.

But why? They'd lived together for over twenty years. She *knew* James was an innately good man. Why had he allowed both of them—*allowed their son*—to live a lie all those years?

The patio doors rattled, and she glanced into the living room. Nick latched each panel, checked it a second time. He took a half-step toward the kitchen, then pivoted, heading into the living room. He'd apparently taken her at her word that he was banished from any further kitchen duties.

Wistfulness swept through her as she looked around the kitchen. *This is what marriage should be. Sharing, protecting, caring. Knowing the person you love is waiting for you just a few steps away.*

Marriage. Wow. Where had that come from? Considering her track record with Erik and James, that should be the last thing on her mind.

But this is Nick.

He'd captured her attention at first glance. Made her laugh and experience emotions that had been buried for longer than she'd like to admit. Made her feel cherished and secure.

The man I love.

She walked to the edge of the kitchen to lean against the doorframe and watch him. He'd shed his jacket earlier. Tie loosened, top two buttons of his shirt undone, sleeves rolled up. Yearning stirred within her as he eased his long body into a chair.

I want to come home to this every night. To you and me.

She just didn't know what Nick wanted.

Despite the earlier set-to with Dana and her "it's a boy" surprise, the rest of the day had fallen right into place. Seeing the look on her face, followed by that spontaneous leap into his arms, ignited Nick's hopes about a future together.

He'd even enjoyed the time spent with Jamie and Paige as they'd worked together. Paige—he shook his head—that girl sure reminded him of Megan.

He pulled out his cell phone, checking for a message he knew wouldn't be there. No answer from Callie either. He calculated the time difference and debated calling versus sending another text. If she was at work, he wouldn't hear back immediately anyway. One thing for sure. If Megan *had* decided to sever their relationship after all these years, she was going to tell him herself.

Although, the "dad" text message may well have been the work of Callie or Gary. Meaning Megan may not have access to her phone. Still, she had to have at least one friend who'd let her borrow a phone to call.

Too many ifs, and all of them didn't sit well. One way or another, he was getting an answer. Even if meant hopping a plane to Denver.

He stopped in the midst of texting as Dana appeared in the doorway. A few curls had escaped to dance around her neck, and a gentle smile framed her lips.

Desire, hot and fierce, shot into his gut. He'd wanted her from the first time he'd laid eyes on her. But this yearning went beyond a physical need. He wanted evenings cuddling on the couch in front of the fireplace. Waking up every morning to see her sweet face. Spending holidays with their patchwork families around that ugly dining room table. Even the thought of household chores—and he was sure Dana could create a monster honey-do list—didn't faze him.

She wanted him too. No question about that, but she also was a mite skittish. No surprise there. Putting her life back together, and certainly not counting on starting up a new relationship. That word though didn't quite do justice to the powerful connection between them. Attraction, chemistry, romance—whatever it was called, it had "I do" written all over it.

I want a life with you. But if Dana needed more time, that's what he'd give her.

Reluctantly, he stood, slipping the phone into his pocket. He'd finish the text when he got home. "Getting late. I should take off."

Dana pushed away from the doorframe. She crossed the room in a slow glide, stopping mere inches in front of him. Her hands traveled up his chest, then onward to twine around his neck.

"I'd rather you stay."

Stunned, he took a half-step back. The whisper of air between them did nothing to cool his heated skin, and the imprint of her body against his was a temptation he couldn't push away. It was damn hard to remember his vow of restraint while Dana's hand toyed with his belt buckle.

"I want to make love with you more than anything. If we take this step, there's no going back."

"Really, Nick. Do you want to stand around and debate whether I know my own mind?" The look she cast him from beneath her lashes was bold and filled with passion. Wrapping a fist around his tie, she tugged slightly. "Or do you want to go upstairs?"

"Upstairs—definitely."

She grabbed his hand and pulled him toward the steps.

Bossy little thing. A smile quirked the corner of his mouth as he trailed behind her. He'd planned on carrying her up the stairs—the right way this time. But he couldn't complain about the view as she climbed the steps in front of him. The sway of her hips, the flex of her firm buttocks, and those world-class legs served as a nice piece of visual foreplay. If Dana thought she was setting the pace for the remainder of the evening, well, it was her turn for the next surprise.

Rounding the railing on the second floor, he halted. Before

Dana could protest, he scooped her into his arms. He smiled at her startled expression. "In a hurry?"

A light blush swept across Dana's face. "Oh, well… yes, I am."

"Nothing wrong with that." He captured her mouth in a hard, demanding kiss, then strode briskly to the room she indicated. He toed the door open, heeled it shut, and headed for the bed.

A single lamp provided a soft glow in the darkened room. The comforter was folded neatly to the foot of the large sleigh bed. Several foil-wrapped packets waited on the nightstand.

It was a bit obvious compared to the patio garden Nick had provided. Still, it wasn't as if she'd had time to run upstairs and light candles. Judging by the appreciative smile on Nick's face, he didn't seem to mind a bit.

"You've been busy today too." He set her gently onto her feet.

"A few things to keep me occupied." Lifting both hands, Dana unclipped the barrette holding her hair. She shook her head, letting the dark curls spill around her neck.

"There's my lady," Nick murmured. He took the clasp from her hand and gave it a cursory look before setting it on the vanity.

Her breath caught as he turned his gaze back to her. The passion that filled his eyes moments ago remained, but it was banked now behind a gleam of exquisite tenderness. Work-roughened palms cupped her face. He lowered his head, brushed his lips against hers.

"Be sure."

The whispered entreaty shot straight to her soul, and she understood. It was not just her heart at risk; it was his as well. His words echoed in her mind. *If we take this step, there's no going back.*

I want to go forward, Nick. With you.

"Dana, I need to tell you—"

"I love you, Nick!" The words burst from her lips. She couldn't hold back telling him for another second.

His hands dropped to his sides, and he grunted in exasperation. "Seriously, Dana? You couldn't let me finish and say it first?" The smile in his eyes belied the irritation in his tone.

She huffed back at him. "It's not a competition. And how was I to know you planned on saying it?"

Nick shook his head, a deep chuckle rumbling through his chest. "We're even going to argue over this, huh?"

"It's a spirited discussion." She busied herself with removing his tie, unbuttoning his shirt. "Besides, you started it."

He ran a hand through his hair, a few strands spiking up in protest. The amusement on his face faded, replaced with an infinite gentleness. "I love you, Dana. We wouldn't be here in this room if we both didn't feel that way." His gaze shot over to the bed, then back to her face. "Deep down, I've loved you from the start. I just didn't have a name for it. Each time we were together, another vacant spot in my heart was filled. I didn't even realize how empty I was until you came along."

Tears welled in her eyes, his heartfelt confession stealing away any lingering doubts. "I had no intention of getting involved with anyone ever again. You've made me aware of what I'd been missing in my life. It scared me. I didn't want to go through losing someone again. But the greater loss would be not having you at all."

His hands caught her hips, drawing her close. Dana leaned into him, reveling in the feel of his hard, muscled body and the security of his firm embrace.

I'm home.

Her new beginning wasn't a house or an office or a project. It was this man, and he lifted her spirits to heights she'd never known.

Nick.

She slid her palms upward to cup his face. "I love you."

The soft lights from the bedside lamp reflected in the rich darkness of his eyes. "And, you my dear," he murmured, shifting slightly to trace a forefinger down the length of the zipper on her dress, "have been driving me crazy with this dress. It's been tempting me all evening, wondering how I'd unzip you if I got the chance. Do I take it down inch by inch, or zero to sixty…?"

Dana bit her bottom lip as he prolonged the suspense, at last lowering the tab slowly and steadily. Cool air rushed in as the back of her dress opened, and she shivered at the contrast when his warm hands touched her skin. He parted the panels and with a quick flip, unhooked her bra. Once again, his finger trailed down her back, tracing each pearl of her spine.

Her heart raced as his touch grew bolder, sliding inside the garment. Across her stomach, then upward to cup one breast. She stiffened, pressing backward into his solid form as he captured one nipple, rolling it gently between thumb and forefinger. She'd never felt so naked without removing a single stitch of clothing.

But not for long.

His palms moved to her shoulders, and with a gentle sweep, he slid the dress and bra from her body. The garments pooled around her feet, leaving her standing in the briefest scrap of silk. She turned, meeting Nick's gaze with a bold one of her own. It took several seconds for his gaze to travel up her body to her eyes.

He scooped her into his arms. Carried her to the bed and laid her gently on the mattress. He lifted one foot and eased off her shoe.

"Just so you know," he said, slipping the second shoe off. He dropped it to the floor to join the first one. Her soft moan filled the silence as his thumbs massaged the arch of her foot. "I plan on touching every inch of your body before the night is over."

She tugged her foot free from his grasp and rolled onto her knees. Gripping either side of the open shirt, she pushed it off his shoulders, and he shrugged it the rest of the way to the floor.

Her arms circled his neck, and her breasts flattened against his chest.

"Just so you know." Her teeth lightly nipped at his earlobe. "I intend to do the same for you."

Chapter Fifteen

Twenty-three years ago

Nathan Stoddard watched until Erik McCall turned the corner. His benevolent smile faded as a wave of satisfaction coursed through him. *Fortunately for you, Mr. McCall, you handled the situation perfectly.*

Life was all about control. Taking it and keeping it. This morning had been a monumental disaster, but gradually each piece was settling back into place. He walked briskly down the hall, pausing in the crossways as two police officers approached from the oncoming direction. Nathan held up his hand, catching their attention.

"Officer Mallory. Officer Lansing. I wanted to offer my thanks for all you did today. Your compassion is much appreciated."

Mallory dipped his head in acknowledgment as his partner responded. "You're welcome, sir. I'm pleased to know we made things somewhat easier for you."

"You have indeed." With a nod, Nathan turned to the right and entered Exam Room 2.

A white sheet covered the body of James's wife. Only hours ago, that same body had been alive, defiant, and headstrong. Now it lay destroyed—broken and battered—not even viable enough to harvest organs to save some other poor soul.

Nathan shook his head, a deep sigh rushing through his lips. Such waste was deplorable. He drew the sheet down to the shoulders and winced. Very little of her face remained recognizable. "All your rebellion came to this."

Not as if she hadn't been warned about that temper. That kind of recklessness would have brought trouble to all of them eventually. He'd offer a toast to Karma later tonight for her timely intervention.

Hands in pockets, he rocked on his heels, chuckling. "Have you heard the news? We have a new Dana, and I think she's going to work out splendidly."

He flipped the sheet back into place and walked to the door, pausing for a last good-bye. "Good luck at the crematorium, *Catherine.*"

Despite the required medical equipment, the private hospital room could have been mistaken for an upscale hotel suite. Next to the bed, a cozy seating area had been set up. Leather chair. Side table holding a bucket of ice and a silver serving tray with bottles of sparkling water and a saucer of sliced lemons. Several newspapers and magazines lay to one side.

Nathan gave an approving nod. He could be quite comfortable for the time he spent here. He sent the private duty nurse on a dinner break, explaining that he wanted to spend time with Dana before leaving for the evening.

Nathan studied the woman's still features. In truth, she was better off under his protection. He'd recognized Erik McCall instantly as a no-good bullshitter. No man worth his salt would have left his deceased wife, regardless of the state of their relationship, for someone else to bury. As the mother of his child, she was due respect for that, if nothing else. It was money well spent to know that McCall would never look back nor question the events that had transpired today.

"You'll have a husband who'll cherish you. A son who will as well, as soon as he understands that Mommy looks a little different."

Fortunately, James's few family members lived far away and rarely visited. None of them were familiar enough with James's wife to question any differences. Especially with the automobile accident to explain any physical alterations.

She bore more than a passing resemblance to the other one. Her features were more delicate, with no sign of vile indulgences. Nathan smoothed back the unruly curls that tumbled around her face with a gentle brush of his hand. "I look forward to a rewarding relationship, Dana."

Nathan circled the bed, studying the pole holding the IV bags. He slipped a hand into his jacket pocket, removing a hypodermic syringe. Within seconds, he'd dispensed the drug into the IV line. "It's said that patients in an unconscious state can hear conversations around them. Whether you can or not, we'll proceed as if that's true."

He slid the syringe back into his pocket, then returned to the opposite side of the bed. He settled into the leather chair.

"I have a story to tell you. One you'll hear often while you're recovering. It's to help you step back into your life once you go home." He slid a hand through the railing of the hospital bed, linking his fingers with those of the silent woman.

"Your name is Dana Canfield...."

Chapter Sixteen

Dawn seeped through the windowpanes, edging its way across the floor. Dana shifted, glancing at the clock. It was seven. Even a night of mind-blowing, multiple orgasms couldn't override her internal alarm. She stretched languidly, then rolled over onto one elbow.

If her body stirred at the unobscured sight of Nick asleep on his back and half-aroused, her heart was three beats ahead.

He'd done much more than keep his promise to touch her body. He'd touched her heart. Caressed it with a passion born from those very stars that had watched over them the night before and filled her spirit with a joy she'd thought she'd never recapture.

I love you, Nick Warden.

She stroked a hand across his chest, fingers trailing through the dark mat of hair. Her palm traced downward to his stomach, and the sudden change in his breathing alerted her that he was waking.

And watching her with sleep-heavy eyes. Eyebrow cocked, a smirk creasing his lips. "See something you like?"

She skimmed her fingers downward. "I like everything I see." A swift arm twined around her waist, hauling her against him.

His lips caught hers, and she melted into the pleasure of a good-morning kiss. His sleep-graveled tone rumbled in the still

182

silence of the morning. "Right back at you, sugar."

He rolled back onto the mattress, taking her with him. Head resting in the hollow of his shoulder, Dana sighed in contentment as Nick's fingers danced across her back.

"So breakfast…?"

A chuckle tickled her throat. Seemed like reality was rearing its head as well this morning. The man *did* deserve a hearty breakfast, but just how hungry was he?

She reached across to the nightstand for the remaining foil package and flipped it onto Nick's bare chest. "I could be persuaded to fix homemade waffles."

Nick wiggled the packet between two fingers and grinned. "Deal."

"Finally!" Paige rushed around the counter as Jamie entered the restaurant not long after the Monday lunch rush had subsided. She grabbed Jamie by the wrist and tugged her back to her station. "So? What did Dana say? How did she look? Did she like the dinner?"

Jamie shook her arm free. "Really, Paige, I'm surprised you didn't come to the office and ask her yourself."

"I would have, except Aaron called off, and I couldn't leave Karen by herself. I've been dying all weekend to find out how it went. So…?"

"Dana loved everything. She plans on stopping by before you close to thank you herself. It's been a crazy morning. The ribbon cutting for the start of construction is being held on Main Street—"

"What about Mr. Warden. What did she say about him? Did he… did they…?"

A shocked gasp escaped Jamie's lips. "Paige, I'm not going to hint around if they… you know."

"Had sex. You know they did. His car was still at her house at midnight when we drove by."

"I can't believe you talked me into doing that. What if he had been leaving right then and caught us?"

"Pssh! It's a public road. We had every right to drive that route."

"Coasting at five miles an hour and staring at the house?"

Paige dismissed the protest with a wave of her hand. "Did you get a chance to talk with Rhys this morning?"

"Just in passing before he left for the ceremony." She shook her head. "I can't believe his father destroyed everything that belonged to Dana."

Paige rolled her eyes. "I can. He's a first class a-hole."

Jamie's lips quivered, laughter warring—and winning—against her disapproval. "I haven't met Mr. McCall yet, but from what I've heard, he's not the warm and fuzzy type. Anyway, I really need to get back to the office. Do you have my lunch ready?"

"Yes, but since everyone's still over on Main Street, why don't you eat here?"

"Because Nick is about to cross the street, and I don't want to be here when you get where I know you're going."

Paige pushed onto her tiptoes, craning her neck to look out the window. "Target in sight. Mr. Warden, you and your wallet are all mine."

Satisfaction coursed through her at the thought of Nick Warden *finally* paying for his lunch. Her smile faded as a frown crossed Jamie's face. Paige narrowed her eyes. "What?"

"He really does like you, Paige. We talked quite a bit after you came back here to finish the food prep. He said that you remind him of his daughter."

Yeah, well, he's not my dad. Pain shot through her heart, and she blinked away the sudden tears. Pop hadn't given quarter to her attitude either. He'd loved her but never hesitated to step in when he felt she was on the wrong track.

Swallowing back the lump in her throat, she asked, "Where is his daughter?"

"With her mother in Colorado. I don't know the entire story. He didn't offer, and I didn't feel I could ask. I shouldn't repeat it, but I thought you should know that much." Jamie's firm stare pinned her in place. "He said you both were spirited, hard-working, full of life. He's a good guy, Paige. You wouldn't have encouraged him toward Dana if you didn't think so."

He's not my dad… but he is a dad. And if his daughter was far away, he had to be hurting as well. "I know. Pop used to tease me, push my buttons to get a reaction. Sometimes it was fun, other times it irritated me. I'd give anything to have that back."

Karen appeared from the kitchen, setting several bags on the front counter. Paige mulled over this new insight about Nick Warden as she rang up Jamie's purchase. "Thanks for letting me know."

Jamie picked up her lunch and turned toward the door. "Just keep that in mind."

Paige watched her friend depart, then turned her attention to Mr. Warden, studying him through the window. It was cute the way he went gooey-eyed when he was around Dana. All in all, her instincts had been right to maneuver a relationship between them. Not that she was interfering. Just setting the stage so nature could take its course.

Jamie was right. Nick Warden was a good guy. He had the same solid sense of dependability that Pop had had. Despite whatever dustups occurred between her and Mr. Warden, she knew he would come to her aid in a heartbeat. He'd even given her an out for the remaining three weeks on their lunch deal and in such a way as to save her pride.

Lesson learned.

He entered the building and made his way to the counter with a loose-hipped stride.

Oh, yeah. He got some.

Swallowing back a snicker, she summoned a smile. "Hi, Mr. Warden. How are you today?"

A slow smile crossed his lips as he nodded. "Good. Thanks again for your help. By the way, I'm picking up Wallace's lunch too."

Paige frowned. "Why?"

"We have a lunch meeting." His glance shifted to the waiting bags as he dug his wallet from the back pocket of his jeans.

Hmm. Interesting.

"So, how was dinner Saturday night? Everything turned out okay?"

"Perfect." He paused, lifted a brow. "Dana particularly liked the dessert."

Jamie's warning echoed in her thoughts but—*darn it*—he'd just taken the opening shot. She nudged the boxes out of his reach. "And it was such a nice night to sit outside, wasn't it? We had dinner at the Cantina. Sat out on the deck until it closed.

Nice night for a drive. Took the long way home a little after midnight. Out Magnolia to the crossroads."

Nick tapped his wallet against the edge of the counter. "Is there something specific you want to know?"

Paige sniffed. Nick Warden didn't intimidate her—much. She slid the lunches across the counter. "As a matter of fact, yes. Cash or debit?"

Tucking the wallet into his back pocket, Nick nabbed the two containers from the counter. "Put it on my tab." He turned on a boot heel and paced toward the door.

Her mouth dropped open. "Damn it!"

"Go on back, Nick." Molly nodded her head in greeting, holding out a visitor's pass. "Sam's on a call in his office, but said to make yourself at home in the conference room. First door on the right down this corridor."

Nick followed the directions and entered a tiny space generously labeled on the door as a conference room. A small table with a half dozen chairs filled the majority of the floor space. He set the lunches on the table and smiled at the bulletin board hanging slightly askew on one wall. Basic, functional—he wondered what magic Dana could work with this space.

Running a two-bay garage on a small island off the coast of Virginia hadn't been a glimmer in his life's plan. Taking a crazy opportunity like this seemed like the cure he'd needed. A business of his own, time for fishing, maybe sailing. In that casual plan for the second half of his life, he'd never expected to meet the woman of his dreams.

The corners of his mouth turned up in a smile. He'd been doing a lot of that these days. Dana made him feel younger than he had in years—even before they'd hit the sheets.

Boot steps sounded in the hallway. Nick turned around as Sam entered the room.

"Thanks for bringing over lunch."

"No problem. I told Paige to put it on my tab."

Sam tossed two thick folders on the table, then dropped onto the closest chair. "Didn't know she ran a tab."

Nick grinned, sitting down on the opposite side of the table.

"Neither did she."

Sam snorted in amusement, then pushed the folders across the table. "Dana Canfield's accident file. James Canfield's murder file." He flipped open the lid to his pizza box.

"You do quick work."

"I have a contact with Sutton PD who was willing to make copies for me. I made a trip over yesterday and picked them up. Don't worry. He's discreet."

"I appreciate the urgency." Nick took a hefty bite of his sandwich, then set it to one side.

"Rhys tells me Dana is his mother. That's quite a story in itself. You think it's connected to Canfield's shooting?"

Nick nodded while he chewed then swallowed. "If an honest mistake had been made about the two women's identities, Canfield could have cleared that up immediately. He had to know the woman identified as Dana was not his wife. Which leads me to believe that for some reason 'Dana Canfield' had to remain a living person."

"All indications were Canfield was scrupulously honest in his estate and investment accounts."

Nick shrugged off that assessment. "He was a cheat and liar when it came to his personal life."

"What if one or more of the accounts he was managing was a front? Something hidden deep. He discovers it, but before he can report it to the police, he's killed. The murder is made to seem like a custody case gone bad, so no red flags are warranted for an in-depth audit." Sam thought a moment, then shook his head. "Nope. Doesn't explain the tie to Dana."

"Not to our Dana, but maybe to the other woman. At the time of the accident, Canfield would have been starting out. He wouldn't have had the clout or the funds for a cover-up like this. But someone else did. Another thing—whoever took over managing Canfield's cases must have been satisfied with the final audit. If one or more of those accounts was used to launder funds or hide assets, someone should have pushed for an independent audit."

"Possibly." Sam flipped an uneaten pizza crust into the box. He wiped his hands on a paper napkin, then opened the accident file. He flipped through the pages, shaking his head. "Not the most thorough investigation. Best bet would be to start with the responding officers if they can be located. Mallory and Lansing."

A chill stole through Nick's veins. "Let me see that." He held out a hand, surprised it remained steady. It should have been shaking from the rage rolling in his gut.

Sam slid the folder across the table. Nick thumbed through the pages. He scanned the final page, dread rising in his core as he read the signature of the lead officer on the case—Kyle Lansing.

Keg.

"Find something?"

Nick pushed the open file back across the table. "I know this guy Lansing. He's a detective now."

"Detective? Whoa—I didn't catch the name when I reviewed Canfield's case. Take a look at this."

Nick took the paper from Sam, gaze scanning down the report. "Lead detective was Allen Cooper. Oh, hell! Keg was first responder." He sank back in his chair. "That's why he called me out of the blue."

"He must have somehow learned you were involved with Dana." Sam nodded toward the paper in Nick's hand. "According to that report, he was at the courthouse to testify in a separate case. Just happened to be first one on the scene. All the witnesses were killed, the shooter stayed out of range of the security camera, and—"

"—And Lansing was the only one able to provide a partial description." Rage drove Nick to his feet. He shoved the chair so hard against the table it ricocheted into the wall. "That bastard stole twenty years of Dana's life, and at the least he's an accessory to Canfield's murder."

"We can't—" Sam broke off as a tap sounded on the door. "Come in."

The door opened, and Molly stepped into the room. She extended a paper toward Sam. "This just came in. I thought you should see it right away."

"Thanks, Molly."

With a smile and a nod, she closed the door behind her.

Nick sat down and waited as Sam read the report. His senses tingled as the lawman's brows lifted. Sam leaned forward.

"Abe Clancy's truck was found out on Cavalier. Body found too."

Nick's gut tightened. "Abe?"

Sam shook his head. "Tom recognized the guy. We've been trying to locate him. A print we lifted from one of the burglary sites matched his file."

"Someone local?"

Whatever Sam was about to say was lost as his cell phone buzzed. "Hold on."

The conversation continued for several minutes, and Nick shifted restlessly. His patience waned with each glance Sam sent his way.

At last, Sam ended the conversation. "Okay, Tom, I'm on my way."

Nick was on his feet a split second before Sam stood. "And?"

"You'd hear this eventually." He let out a deep sigh. "Yeah, a local. Buzz Grainger. If you hadn't made his acquaintance, you're luckier than most. Truck was headed back toward town. Mike found a flyer for the Main Street event on the front seat."

Nick knew who the guy was. Lowlife from the lower end of PI. Always ready to drink, even more eager to fight. "So what happened? Driving drunk and ran off the road?"

"Truck was parked at the side of the road. Body was found next to the vehicle. Gunshot. Three times."

Nausea rose in Nick's throat. "This is not some falling out between petty thieves. This has Keg's name all over it."

Sam looked sick. "And he could have had the files flagged for him to be notified if they were checked out."

"This means he's here on PI covering his tracks." Nick whirled and bolted for the door. "Dana's at the Main Street ribbon cutting. I have to get to her."

Sam grabbed a sheet from the case folder. "I'll have Molly send a BOLO out with Lansing's photo, and I'll get a couple more deputies over to Main Street."

If the sheriff expected him to wait for that conversation to take place, Nick fully intended to disappoint him. He raced through the lobby as a shout followed.

"Warden, if you see any sign of Lansing, do *not* engage. Call me."

Nick ignored the order and raced out of the building. He had to get to Dana.

The ceremonial ribbon cutting had taken mere moments. The party planned by the mayor's office consumed the remainder of the morning. The celebration provided good publicity, and with the stores closed for the occasion, all the shop owners were able to attend. The afternoon's efforts would fall to the city and McCall's workers, prepping the area to initiate the new traffic flow and designate the new parking areas.

Dana watched as Rhys was approached by several merchants. Each one received his full attention, and by his gestures and expressions, she knew his answers were thoughtful and precise. Her chest swelled with pride, warring with the ever-present sorrow for all the years she'd never had with her son. She scanned the crowd, her gaze landing on Erik, who also watched Rhys. She caught a glimpse of regret in his expression, but felt no pity for the man. He'd carelessly thrown away years she would have treasured.

A whirlwind of perfume swept up behind her, followed by a one-armed hug from April. "Dana! Isn't this exciting?"

Dana returned the hug and smiled at the other woman's exuberance. "It's going very well."

"I'm so proud of Kevin. Wasn't his speech wonderful?"

Dana dampened an instinctive urge to boast about her own son's contributions. *She doesn't know.* With Rhys determined to acknowledge her as his mother, the truth would be revealed soon, but now wasn't the time.

The party finally subsided to the point where she could leave, and Dana headed back to her office. She debated stopping at Carson's to speak with Paige, then decided to check in with Jamie first.

She entered through the back entrance, the tapping of a keyboard growing louder as she approached Jamie's desk in the reception area. She set her tablet on the corner of the desk. "How's everything here?"

Jamie straightened, stretching her arms overhead. "Quiet. I updated the project plan and work schedules."

"You didn't have to leave the event so early. This work could have waited."

"I didn't mind." Jamie pushed her chair back from the desk. "Are you going to be in the office for a while? Alison from the Chamber asked me to go with her on a final test run on the valet buses from the ferry to the drop-off area for the Main Street shops."

Dana waved a hand. "Absolutely. Take all the time you need, then go home. I'll handle anything that comes up."

"You rock." Jamie flashed a brilliant smile. "Oh, and I emailed you some suggestions for a Main Street website." Within moments, she shut down her computer, grabbed her purse, and with a "Have a good evening," was out the door.

Dana walked over to the sofa and sank down onto the cushions. She kicked off her shoes, then tucked one leg under the other. She should be working—inputting the updates from Jamie into the master project plan, downloading the photographs from the ceremony, checking in with Paige. But she couldn't get motivated at the moment to do any of that.

Of all the plans she'd made for her new life on Providence Island, none had included hiring the World's Best Assistant, finding her lost son, and having mind-blowing sex with a handsome, hard-bodied mechanic. And so what if the only renovations on her house so far consisted of a new patio door?

Pulling her cell phone from her jacket pocket, she scrolled down the list of emails and missed calls.

One from Glaser. Three from Main Street merchants. Hmm, one from Nick. She wouldn't mind seeing him tonight. Or every night.

She dropped the phone onto her lap. Five minutes, she promised. Just a short break to sit quietly and revel in the silence. Less than a minute passed before the front door opened.

With a silent sigh, she rose to greet the gray-haired man who entered. Her welcoming smile faded as she recognized him. "Detective Lansing?"

Kyle Lansing offered a polite smile. "Hello, Mrs. Canfield. I'm probably the last person you expected, aren't I?"

"I certainly didn't expect to see you again, Detective Lansing." Dana's fingers tightened around the cell phone. "Is Detective Cooper no longer assigned to my husband's case?"

She'd never liked Lansing. He was brash and impertinent. Quick to play the witness card as the last person to see James alive and interjecting himself into the investigation even after it was assigned to Allen Cooper. The murder of an attorney at the courthouse was high-profile, and Lansing obviously resented his first-on-the-scene status being discounted for the lead investigator role.

He took his time before answering. His eyes scanned the reception area, then down the hallway, then back to where she stood. With a jerk of his head, he walked toward her. "The case is still open, and Cooper's still assigned. I came across some interesting developments. Thought I'd pop over to PI and get your take on them."

Dana gestured to one of the chairs. Lansing paused for the briefest moment, then seated himself. She took the sofa. "Shouldn't you discuss those developments with Detective Cooper?"

"This particular information came directly to my attention. Figured I'd check it out myself first. That break-in at your home last week. Any reason why you didn't report that?"

"I reported it to the local sheriff's department. You're not...." A finger of panic rose into her chest. She took a deep breath, swallowing hard. "Are you saying the break-in is connected to James's murder?"

Her cell phone rang, and she jumped. She glanced at the screen. *Rhys.* "I'm sorry. Let me switch my phone to vibrate so we can talk."

She swiped and tapped, then dropped the phone onto the cushion beside her. Settling her hands onto her lap, she nodded to the detective to continue. "What new evidence is so important that you made a trip all the way to my office, Detective Lansing?"

Chapter Seventeen

The streets were packed.

"Like a damn circus," Nick grumbled as he shouldered his way through the crowds. His gaze darted over the area, searching for a glimpse of Dana's dark cloud of hair. A tall figure at the edge of the crowd caught his attention.

Nick bolted across the street at a diagonal, racing to catch up to Rhys as he walked toward a makeshift parking area. "McCall! Wait up!"

The younger man paused and turned, a look of irritation flashing across his face. Nick ignored it. He didn't have time to deal with the kid's attitude right now.

"Where's Dana?"

"Probably at her office. I'm on my—" His eyes narrowed. "What's wrong?"

Nick scrubbed a hand across the nape of his neck. "I need to find her. She could be in danger."

He gave the kid credit. He didn't waste time asking questions or demanding explanations.

"Hold on. I'll call her." Rhys pulled out his cell phone and tapped the screen to put the call on speaker. A frown creased his brow as a rustling noise sounded over the line. "Mom? Where are—"

"What new evidence is so important you made a trip all the way to my office, Detective Lansing?"

Nick tugged at Rhys's arm. "We have to get over there now!"

Rhys motioned to the nearby lot. "My truck's right there."

Both men sprinted across the area designated for construction vehicles. They jumped into the truck, Nick barely closing his door before Rhys engaged the vehicle.

"Who is this detective?" Rhys asked as the truck jolted off the lot. The cell phone rested in the console between the two seats.

"Name's Lansing. Sutton PD. If I'm right, he shot James Canfield. Or at least is an accessory. He also may have been involved with Dana's car accident."

A shocked breath hissed through Rhys's lips. "Damn it."

"I'm calling Wallace." Nick scrambled for his phone. The sheriff answered before the second ring. "Sam, Lansing is at Dana's office. Get someone over there now." He dropped the phone back into his shirt pocket.

Dana was smart. She was brave. And she was a miracle he'd never expected. But Lansing was desperate.

Hang in there, sweetheart. We're on our way. I'm not going to lose you now.

"I can't lose her."

Nick shot a glance at Rhys, who'd just echoed his own words. The kid's face was pale and tight.

Dana held a part of each of their hearts. From the expression on the Rhys's face, he was just as willing as Nick to put his life on the line to save her.

Dana frowned as a sly smile crossed Detective Lansing's face. He seemed too pleased with himself for the news to be anything positive.

Lansing shook his head and a chuckle spilled out of his mouth. "I'm surprised Nick hasn't filled you in yet. When we talked last Friday night, it made me more than a little curious what his connection is to all this."

Nick? The more Lansing talked, the less sense he made. She studied his posture and the clearness of his eyes for signs of drinking. All she could discern was his usual smug demeanor. "If you're talking about Nick Warden, he operates a garage here on the island. I have no idea why he spoke to you about this. How do you even know him?"

Lansing's sneer deepened. "Possibly he's working for the people who killed your husband—"

Not Nick. As the words echoed through her mind, she wondered if she was denouncing his lie or praying for it not to be true. That wayward moment of indecision dissolved. She trusted Nick, and she definitely didn't trust Detective Lansing.

"Or, perhaps, you're not being truthful about your collusion with Warden. I always knew you had something to do with your husband's murder. Just never knew who your partner in crime was. In any case, I need you to accompany me back to the station—"

"I have no intention of going anywhere with you, Detective. If there's new and valid evidence that needs to be discussed, have Allen Cooper contact me." Dana stood, gesturing toward the exit. "You need to leave."

Lansing shook his head, slowly rising. "You refuse to make things easy." With a smooth motion, he slid a hand beneath his jacket and drew out a revolver.

Dana's mouth went dry. She took a slow breath to steel herself against the trembling coursing through her arms and legs. "You don't need a gun, Detective. Let's call Sheriff Wallace...."

"You have the right to remain silent, Mrs. Canfield. At least until we get to where we need to go. At that point, you have the obligation of answering my questions. Let's go quietly out the back door."

She read the threat in his eyes, heard the promise in his voice. She'd never make it to the Sutton Police Department. Leaving with this man would be as good as signing her death warrant. If the weasel thought she would go peacefully, he was in for a disappointment.

She stepped casually toward the wall nearest her office, pausing to trace her fingertips along the glossy top of the accent table. "There's a snag in your plan, Detective."

"Not interested in your games, Mrs. Canfield." He gestured toward the hallway. "Move."

"I don't play games. When that call came in a few minutes ago, I didn't turn off my phone. Someone's been listening this entire time. The sheriff's department should be on its way."

Lansing shot a furious glance at the cell phone lying on the sofa cushion. Dana seized that moment of distraction. She grabbed the hummingbird statue from the side table and swung the metal statue in a sharp arc. The motion caught Lansing's attention at the last second, and he threw up one arm in an instinctive defense.

The blow slammed against his upraised arm. An anguished howl burst from the man's lips, and the gun fell from his hand. Dana swung again, this time catching the detective in the chest. As Lansing stumbled backward, she dropped the sculpture and snatched up the gun.

"Don't move." Keeping the gun trained on the man, she stepped backward toward the sofa for her phone.

"Goddamn bitch!" Lansing struggled to his feet, cupping his injured arm. "You'll beg for death before I finish with you. But before you die, you will tell me where Canfield hid his files."

Dana tightened her grip on the gun, arms extended. "I will shoot."

A shadow fell across the front windows. She caught of glimpse of blonde hair. *Jamie? Not Jamie, but who…?*

A moment later, sunlight spilled into the lobby as the front door swung open. The entry wall blocked the newcomer from her sight. As Lansing cast a glance over one shoulder, Dana stepped back, increasing the distance between them. She didn't have much room to retreat, but each inch might make a difference in saving her life.

The detective stiffened, turning toward the unseen person. "What are you doing here, Ham—"

Two shots, fired in rapid sequence, struck Lansing in the torso. A third shot followed, this time to the head. Blood sprayed as Lansing dropped to the floor.

Oh, my God!

Her knees trembled and her arms shook as she struggled to hold the gun steady.

Sunlight spilled once more in the lobby entrance. A rush of air and sounds from outside drifted inward as the shadow of the shooter moved away. The door closed, cutting off the sunlight.

What—? Her heart beat a furious tattoo as she waited.

Silence. Whoever it was had left.

A sob broke loose as she stared at Lansing's motionless form. Blood soaked the carpet as it seeped from his body; the smell of death filled the air. She set the gun on the table. Dropping to her knees in front of the couch, she grabbed the cell phone, clutching it like a lifeline.

"Rhys, are you there? Can you hear me?"

"Mom, I'm here." The gentle tones reached her seconds before his hands settled on her shoulders and lifted her to her feet. "You're safe."

Safe? Maybe for now. But someone else is out there. Someone who's been watching me. Someone with a gun.

"What do you want?" The whisper slipped from her lips.

"Mom, what is it?"

She barely registered the question as Nick approached. She held up one hand to stop him. "Lansing said you knew each other. You met with him Friday night." She wanted to scream the accusation at him, but the words that fell out of her mouth were as numb and lifeless as she felt inside. "That you talked about me."

Rhys stiffened, taking a protective half-step forward.

Nick shook his head. "I didn't know he was involved with your husband's murder until this afternoon. Wallace and I made the connection. I went over to the Main Street site to find you." He broke off the explanation as Wallace and Deputy Winslow rushed through the front entrance.

"Mike, secure the area around the body until the technician arrives." Sam glanced at Lansing as if to confirm his demise before walking into the room. "Mrs. Canfield, are you hurt? Do you need a doctor?"

"No, just—" She shook her head and slipped from Rhys's embrace to wrap both arms around her waist. "Just scared."

He pawed his notebook and pen from his shirt pocket. "Can you tell me what happened?"

"Detective Lansing—he's with the police department in Sutton. He asked why I hadn't reported the break-in at my house. I don't know how he knew about that." She caught the look that passed between the sheriff and Nick. "He mentioned having dinner with Nick the other night."

When Nick offered only a nod of acknowledgment, she returned her attention to Sam. "He told me I had to go with

him. He said to the police department, but I didn't trust him."
She realized the cell phone was still in her hand, and she held it
up. "I felt uncomfortable with Detective Lansing's reasons for
being here from the start. When Rhys called, I placed the phone
on speaker so he could hear. I also hit record."

Approval swept across Sam's face. He called for an evidence
bag from the deputy. Holding it out, he nodded for her to drop
the phone into the bag. "What about the gun on the table? Is
that the one you used to shoot Lansing?"

"I didn't shoot him. Someone came in the front door. I
couldn't see who it was because of the entry wall. Detective
Lansing recognized whoever it was. He didn't seem pleased. He
started to say something when the person shot him."

"Three times," Mike said, walking over to join them.

"That's right. Two—"

"Two in the body and one in the head. Just like Grainger."

Sam nodded. "And from the looks of that cannon on the
table, it wasn't the one used in either shooting."

"What other shooting?" Her head swiveled from Sam to
Mike then back. "Who is Grainger?"

"From what we've put together, it seems Lansing hired a
local named Grainger. He was found dead next to Abe Clancy's
truck. Shot the same way as the detective here. We suspect
Grainger's the one who tried to run you down your first day here
and broke into your house. We also have preliminary evidence
that Grainger was involved in those other break-ins as well." A
brief pause followed before Sam continued. "And it appears that
Lansing may have been responsible for your husband's
shooting."

A gray haze ebbed and flowed across her vision. She'd been
in the same room as the man who killed James. A man who
wanted her dead for reasons she didn't even know. A man lying
dead mere feet away from her.

Bile surged in her throat. "Sheriff, I need to leave."

Sam shook his head. "I'm sorry, Mrs. Canfield, but I need to
finish this line of questioning."

Rhys spoke up. "She had nothing to do with this shooting.
She's the victim here. We heard everything on the call as we
were driving over. Lansing started to talk to someone else, then
Mom screamed when those shots were fired."

"Grainger was shot in the same manner as Lansing." Nick nodded to the body of the detective. "That also suggests someone else was here."

Wallace broke in. "What it means is there's a killer on PI who shot two people. Chances are he's already headed for the ferry." One hand shot up to forestall any questions. "And, yes, we're checking the ferry. But it's also possible he's holed up here at one of the local B&Bs or still walking the streets. I have a deputy checking the businesses in the area to see if they noticed anything suspicious."

Her fists clenched at Wallace's words. *That person could still be here. Watching.*

She met Sam's gaze, and his expression softened. "I don't expect you to stay here in this room. Is there an office where we can talk?"

"There's an empty office down the hall." Dana nodded toward the corridor.

"We'll talk there." Sam gestured for her to proceed him. Once she passed, he shifted positions, blocking anyone else from following. "Nick, Rhys, both of you need to head on over to my office. Tom's on his way there now to take your statements. Mike, secure the front entrance. Everyone uses the back door."

Protests and arguments buzzed behind her, a cacophony of sounds that made no sense. Again. It was happening again. Questions, innuendos, veiled accusations. The same as when James was murdered. It didn't matter that she was the target this time.

She led the way into the spare office. The room held a few pieces of furniture. She gestured to one of the armchairs before seating herself.

"I didn't shoot Detective Lansing." The words burst out before she could stop them. She gulped a deep breath, forcing the panic from her voice.

"I don't think you did either. But I still need to ask you about the events that led up to the shooting."

She wondered if that soothing tone was the same one he used when dealing with drunk and disorderly calls. It certainly settled a measure of calm upon her. At least what she could achieve under the circumstances.

"The recording will give you most of the encounter. You'll

find several other injuries on Detective Lansing's body. The hummingbird statue. On the floor. You saw it?" With Sam's nod, she continued. "I hit him twice. Once on the forearm, the second time on his chest. It was the only way I could disarm him. That's when I got his gun. I could have shot him. I would have shot him if that other person hadn't beaten me to it."

"No one would blame you for protecting yourself. It still stands you're the only person who can give us any information about the person who did shoot Lansing."

A flash of sunlight, a flicker by the window, a clip of a name. She couldn't see how the sheriff could find any clues in those few facts.

"Did you see anyone outside the window before the shooter entered the building?"

"I thought it was Jamie coming back to the office." She would never have forgiven herself if that bright, vivacious girl had been hurt.

"Why did you think it was Jamie?"

"I caught a glimpse of blonde hair through the window." She closed her eyes, trying to recapture that quick glance to the window. "But in that instant, I realized it wasn't Jamie. The hair was shorter and a darker shade… and it was a man."

Wallace's mouth curved in a soft smile. "Blonde. That helps. When the person entered, was there a shadow? That might help us determine height."

"I didn't see a shadow. Just daylight spilling in."

"You're sure?"

"Almost positive." She shook her head. "It was a brief glance. I was trying to keep my attention on Lansing."

"For a brief glance, this is good. Anything else?"

Dana closed her eyes, forcing herself to replay the memory of that scene. When she opened her eyes, she saw the sheriff leaned back in his chair, patiently waiting.

"I think he must have been left-handed."

Wallace sat forward. "Why?"

"The entry area isn't that large. From where Lansing was standing, this person would have had to step past the entry wall to fire his gun if he were right-handed."

"We'll check that out. That's all for now, Mrs. Canfield. I know going through this was difficult." Sam stood and walked to the door. "Before I let you go, we'll need to swab your hands for gunshot residue—"

The tenuous thread controlling her patience snapped. She jumped to her feet. "I told you I didn't shoot him!"

Wallace lifted one hand, halting her protest. "I believe your story, Mrs. Canfield. However, I need to cover all bases, and this is for your benefit as well. Negative results will eliminate you from any future accusations. Mike will come back here to take the swab. After that, he'll drive you home. We'll keep a watch on your house for at least a day or two until we get a better feel if the shooter's still on PI."

The sheriff was right, but it didn't mean she had to like it. She didn't. Not one bit.

She sank back in the chair and gave a grudging nod. "Then what? I'm terrified this man is still on PI and that people I care about are in danger."

Sam rested a shoulder against the doorframe. "You gave us a good start. Hopefully, we can pick up some additional details as we continue investigating. I advise you to remain cautious and aware of your surroundings and not go out alone. Gut impression, Mrs. Canfield, I don't think you're in any immediate danger from this person."

Her mouth dropped open. "How can you say that?"

"Whoever this person is, he shot the man who tried to run you down in Abe Clancy's truck. He shot the man who held a gun on you." He straightened, resting his hand on the doorknob. "What it comes down to is I need to find the person who's willing to kill to keep you safe."

Dana shook her head, denying his assessment. "You mean, until he longer needs me."

Her first act after returning to her house was a long scrubbing in a hot shower. Clad now in comfortable faded blue jeans and a white T-shirt, Dana curled up on one corner of the couch in her living room, bare feet tucked beneath her. At the opposite end of the sofa, Rhys lounged, watching her with a protective gaze.

He'd ignored the sheriff's edict to meet with Deputy Hunter and was waiting at her house when she arrived. One look at his face, and she'd swallowed any protests about needing help. *He* needed *her.* And, truth to tell, she needed him as well. He'd coordinated a handoff of her car keys to Jamie, who drove the BMW, followed by Paige. Both girls had rushed into the house, needing to confirm with their own eyes that she was all right. They hugged; they cried. She fed them cookies, then sent them on their way. Except for Rhys. Now it was time to let him go as well.

She stretched out one arm, capturing his hand in hers, and marveled at the unfamiliar sight of his adult hand in hers. For those few short years they'd had together, she'd held his tiny hand so many times. First steps, holding a spoon, crossing the street, saying prayers. Protecting and giving comfort.

"I'll be okay. You don't have to stay."

"I'm not even close to okay. I could have lost you again." Rhys stirred restlessly on the cushion beside her. "Other than the break-in at your house, I had no idea anything was going on until Warden showed up at Main Street looking for you."

Dana sniffed. "Apparently, there's a lot that Nick and Sheriff Wallace haven't shared with me either."

"He was scared. Both of us were. Listening to that call, hearing that guy threaten you and not knowing if we could reach you in time."

"I wasn't going to let Lansing win without a fight."

"I wish I'd gotten there in time to see you hit him with that statue." One side of his mouth quirked in a grin. "You are one bad-ass Mother."

An unexpected laugh burst through her lips. "You always could make me smile."

"You remember?" A hopeful gleam shone in his dark green eyes.

She pressed a fist to her breast. "My heart remembers."

Rhys glanced out the window. "Warden just pulled in to the driveway."

"Your cue to leave." Dana stood, waiting for her son to follow suit. She needed to have the upcoming conversation with Nick in private.

Rhys rose to his feet, then hesitated. "Maybe I should stay—"

She left him no choice. She took his hand, and they walked to the foyer. "I'll take care of it."

"I don't doubt it." He paused by the front door. "I'll call you later."

"Uh, no phone."

"Damn it. Here, take mine. I'll check with Sam to see when you can get yours back."

"Rhys...." She accepted the phone but gave him a warning look in return.

"Right." He held up both hands in surrender. "Just because you can, doesn't mean you have to. I'm here."

Those damn tears again. She swiped them away, then kissed his cheek. "I know, sweetheart."

Rhys turned and opened the front door just as Nick reached the porch. They side-stepped one another with a bare nod of heads.

"Warden."

"McCall."

Men.

Dana returned to the living room, not waiting for Nick. When he entered the room, he held up a red leather portfolio. "Thought you might want this."

Her tablet. Untouched because she'd left it on Jamie's desk.

"Thank you for bringing that by. But you need to leave."

He set the case on the side table, then heaved a sigh. "I understand you're upset with me—"

She delivered a glare that should have fried him into oblivion. "You have *no* idea how I feel!"

"Judging by your tone, I'd say you're pretty pissed off."

His cavalier attitude severed the last sliver of her patience. "I am beyond pissed, Nick. I'm furious, and I'm disappointed in you. You of all people should have realized how important trust is for me. Erik abandoned me to strangers and stole my son. James manipulated my life for over twenty years. Now you go behind my back and investigate my life without even telling me."

Nick's jaw tightened. "When you told me about the incidents after your husband's death, I suspected there was a connection to what was happening here. After you found out about your son and started remembering your past, I wondered if that was connected too. I didn't want to alarm you until I'd gathered more information."

"The end result is that you took it upon yourself to decide

what was best for me." Tears welled in her eyes, and she blinked them away. "You could have told me what you suspected. I might have gotten upset, but I would have been prepared. I can't—I *won't*—be with someone who disrespects me this way."

Nick's face flushed a dark red. "Dana—"

"Don't." Her hand sliced the air, punctuating the word. "Just... don't."

He leaned against the doorframe, staring at the floor for several seconds. When he looked up, her heart sank at the sadness darkening his strong features.

"All I wanted to do was protect you. But I get it, what you said about making decisions for you. And I was wrong." His foot scuffed the floor in front of him. Another glance down then back to her, followed by a deep breath. "But so are you."

Her mouth fell open. "Don't you dare—"

He pushed off the doorframe with a nudge of his shoulder. "I'm not the guy who took your son and left you with strangers. I'm not the guy who spent years conning you into living someone else's life. When I said I loved you, that means everything I do is built from that love. Doesn't mean I won't make mistakes, but they won't be made out of selfishness or greed."

Hands shoved into the back pockets of his jeans, he stood in that same hip-shot stance as the first day she'd laid eyes on him. The memory tugged her heart as fervently as any she'd reclaimed of Rhys as a child. The humor that typically simmered in his whiskey-brown eyes was missing for the first time.

"I'm going to step aside and give you time to think about—and feel—what I've said." A faint smile creased his mouth. "When you're ready to talk, you know where to find me. I'm not going anywhere."

He turned and walked away. The click of the door shutting told her she was alone.

She sank down onto the couch, forcing herself not to look out the window as he drove away. Her gaze fell on the tablet lying on the table. She picked it up, hugging it to her chest.

Everything I do is built from that love.

Dana pushed off the couch. No sulking or pouting. She was,

as Nick hadn't hesitated to point out, wrong, and he deserved an apology.

And a whole lot of loving.

Chapter Eighteen

Benjamin Hampshire walked partway back to the ferry. Stopped for a cup of coffee, bought a book so he'd have a bag to carry. He caught the trolley the rest of the way, attaching himself to a large group of shoppers. Just another tourist heading back to the mainland.

Ten minutes into the trip, he dropped the gun's magazine over the port side of the boat. Several miles later, he moved to starboard and released the gun barrel into the water. By the time the ferry docked, all pieces of the handgun that had killed Buzz Grainger and Keg Lansing had been consigned to the Atlantic Ocean.

Luring Grainger to the remote area had been child's play. The idiot's promise to make good on killing Dana Canfield had barely passed his lips before Ben fired three shots. Two center mass, one to the head.

'Cause that's how I roll.

The dipstick would have been dead several days sooner if his original attempt, a lame hit-and-run—*in front of the sheriff's department!*—had been successful. The brief extension of Grainger's life had been granted only until they'd confirmed Kyle Lansing's involvement in hiring the local.

Mr. Stoddard had not been pleased with that piece of information. Permission had been granted to eliminate James Canfield. Going rogue on the lady? Death warrant. Lansing had been so frantic to eliminate any chance of Canfield's death coming back on him, he'd made stupid mistakes. The biggest one? Not trusting Mr. Stoddard to protect him.

Ben gave a grunt of satisfaction. A job was a job, but popping a trifecta into Lansing put a glow on his day.

He walked down the gangplank toward his car. If traffic cooperated, he'd be back at the office before five o'clock. Sufficient time to report to Mr. Stoddard that his mission had been completed successfully and still make his dinner date by seven.

Chapter Nineteen

Ominous gray-black clouds slid across the horizon before rolling into one solid mass. Hot lightning streaked the sky, followed by a vicious roll of thunder. Nick stared out the oversize windows at the front of his apartment. He'd left the lights off, preferring to watch the storm in the dark.

Raging weather, fireplace, glass of wine, cozy bed. Perfect night to slide between the sheets with a certain dark-haired lady. If he only had the fireplace, the wine, and Dana.

Looks like the only *I need you* coming his way tonight would be from some idiot foolish enough to test the roads in this weather.

Give it time.

Problem being patience wasn't his strong suit when it came to Dana. In less than two weeks, they'd zoomed from zero to sixty. Still, she should have trusted that everything he'd done was to keep her safe.

Yeah, well, good intentions, paved roads.

He'd forced himself to remain calm at her house. She'd been through hell and didn't need the rough edge of his temper. Understanding her position didn't take the sting out of her accusations. He was nothing like Erik McCall. He'd met him only once, but that was enough to get a measure of the man. As for Canfield, he'd let Dana live a lie for over twenty years. *At least what I did was to keep her—*

Safe.

And maybe, just maybe, that's what James Canfield's intentions had been. Whether Canfield had acted as a pawn or protector, twenty-plus years was a long time to sustain that kind of a lie without tender feelings on both sides.

Keg. Now *there* was a pawn. A dirty cop. As paranoid as Keg had been the night they'd met for dinner, Nick had to agree with Sam's supposition. The case files had been flagged to notify him if someone requested them. A connection between Grainger and Keg had been established by a note scribbled on the back of the flyer found in Abe's truck.

KL, 11am, Cavalier

Who, when, and where. Obviously more info than Grainger wanted to trust to memory.

The theory that Keg killed Grainger was dropped when the detective met the same fate just hours later. After listening to Nick's statement and the recorded call, Sam had to agree that a third party had been the shooter.

Which meant Dana was safe only as long as that unknown manipulator deemed her life necessary. Or else, why hadn't he killed her too?

A mechanical beep shattered the momentary stillness. Nick jerked, head swiveling toward the security system panel where several indicators flashed yellow. The side gate to the parking lot had been opened. He hustled to the back of the apartment, glancing out in time to see a figure darting toward the rear entrance.

He slid the lock to the stairwell door open, then eased down the steps to the work bay. The lights on the downstairs panel switched to green as the alarm deactivated. The door opened, and in the glow of the outside lights, the intruder entered the garage.

With a flick of one finger, Nick flipped the light switch.

"Hello, Dana."

She jerked, freezing midstep at the sudden illumination. Eyes wide, lower lip caught between her teeth, she seemed less than her usual confident self.

Good. About time he had the advantage in one of their conversations.

"Car trouble?"

He swallowed back a smile as a hint of irritation flashed across Dana's face. She lifted one hand and waved the key card he'd given her.

"You said to use this if I needed."

His heart jumped, and he cautioned himself. She was too calm, too controlled for something dire to have occurred. "Something happen?"

"I had an epiphany."

He descended the final steps, then stopped, propping an elbow on the stair rail. "Must have been a doozy to bring you out with a storm about to break."

Dana cast a brief glance through the glass door, then gave a shrug. Her hands closed around the key card, rubbing it between her palms. "It wasn't that bad when I left home."

His gaze dropped to her hands, and he wondered if she realized the suggestive way she was stroking the plastic card. Probably not, but it was playing hell with his concentration. "So, why the visit?"

"This is where I knew I'd find you."

Hope broke into a tap dance as she echoed his earlier words back to him. Not that he was letting her off the hook that easily. "What does that mean?

"That I owe you an apology. I was wrong to accuse you of manipulating my life." She took a step forward. "But it's important I know we're equal partners. Fifty-fifty in all ways."

Nick took his own stride forward. Step by step. Each of them giving, taking.

"Few things are fifty-fifty, sweetheart. Forty-sixty, twenty-eighty. Sometimes even zero-one hundred. Whatever the split, you have my word it'll be a mutual decision."

A deep roll of thunder rattled the windows. Sheets of rain broke loose, beating against the pavement outside. Luck just flipped in his favor. "You can't go back out in this."

Dana's dark eyes sparkled with unspoken suggestions. "No, it wouldn't be wise."

Nick crossed to the exit. Relocked the door, reset the alarm. He turned, easing behind her. So close he felt her shiver as the gap between their bodies disappeared. A light floral fragrance mixed with the scent of rain drifted into his nostrils. Hunger for her kicked into full gear.

"I do have one *tiny* condition."

He choked back a snort of laughter. Never easy with Dana. "Go on."

She shifted to face him and tossed the key card onto the counter. "You let me take as much time as needed tonight to make it up to you."

He bit his lip, shook his head. "I don't know. I'm pretty hurt over this whole thing. It could take all night."

"What luck. I have all night available."

He smoothed back those wayward curls to expose the delicate curve of her neck. Dipped his head and traced his lips across her soft skin. "In that case, what say we go upstairs and check out my big-ass bed?"

Those lips he loved curved into a gentle smile. "I would love that."

With a quick dip, he hefted her over one shoulder and headed for the stairs. Her startled squeal gave him his best chuckle of the day.

"You *know* I hate when you do this!"

Nick stroked a hand over her backside. "And yet…."

It took a special kind of man to turn a woman on and tick her off all at the same time. But Nick was just that kind of guy. He might think he was playing Big Bad, but Dana knew better by the tender way he set her on her feet, keeping an arm around her while she regained her balance. Even if he did cop a feel of her butt with one hand while flipping on the lights with the other.

His fingers settled onto the curves of her hips, and he stood watching. Waiting for her to make the next move. She cupped the sides of his face, rubbing a thumb over the bristles along his jaw. She might have gone the rest of her life never knowing this man. Chance, fate—whatever had brought them together—left no doubts he was her future.

"You mentioned something about a big-ass bed."

A deep chuckle sent a quiver racing through her. "So I did." Firm lips brushed hers, lingering a second time.

His hand closed over hers, then he led the way across the

room. When they reached the bedside, Nick grabbed a remote control from the side table with his other hand.

Really? "You're turning on the television?"

He grinned, aiming the device backward over his head. In tandem, the window blinds descended.

She snatched the remote from his hands, eyeing it with a fierce greed. "I've seen these in catalogs but—Hey!"

He scooped the remote from her hand, tossing it… somewhere. "Later."

Any protest she might have made was lost in the folds of her sweater as Nick eased it over her head. Fair enough. She went to work unfastening the buttons on Nick's shirt.

"I was thinking." She pushed the front of his shirt open and slid her palms up the hard planes of his chest. "That zero-to-sixty thing?"

"Uh-huh." His nimble fingers flicked open the clasp of her bra. From the look on his face, she wondered if he was even listening.

"That's who we are. It doesn't make sense to wait."

"Nope. Sure doesn't." His hot breath scored a path behind her ear, down her neck.

She arched into him as he cupped one breast, took a nipple into his mouth, his teeth giving a gentle tug. Her knees weakened, and she clutched his shoulders for support.

"So will you mar—"

"No!" He jerked upward, laying a finger on her lips. "If anyone asks that question, it'll be me."

Dana drew back, an exasperated huff sending her breasts bobbing. "Really, Nick, does it matter who asks?"

She waited patiently as his gaze dipped downward, lingered, then drifted back to her face.

He grinned, totally unapologetic. The smile faded, and his gaze shifted into a tenderness that captured her heart. "It matters a lot. You deserve a real proposal."

That quiet affirmation silenced her. She didn't remember, but odds were Erik hadn't gotten down on one knee to propose. James? His proposal had been for the woman whose life she'd lived for all those years.

She blinked back a rush of tears. "How do you know me so well? Know what I need, when I need it?"

"I love you."

The simple truth of those three words reflected in his eyes. An oath promising his soul, his heart, and his honor to her for eternity.

"I think I've been waiting for you all my life." She stepped forward, and with a swift glide of her hands, slid the shirt off his shoulders. She was reaching for the zipper to his jeans when his cell phone buzzed. Her exasperated exclamation nearly drowned out the hearty curse that dropped from Nick's lips.

The glare he threw at the cell phone should have set the device on fire. "Sorry, I'm on call." He grabbed up the phone, eyes widening as he read the display. "It's Megan."

Dana's disappointment washed away, supplanted by the joy of seeing Nick's face radiate with happiness. She urged him with a nod to answer the call.

"Megan, sweetheart. I've missed hearing from you. Did you get the birthday present I sent?"

She snatched his shirt from the floor, tugged it on as she moved to explore the small built-in kitchen on the other side of the room. Functional. Neat. Efficient. She could do a lot with this space. Then again... even if Nick did insist on proposing in his own time, that didn't mean she couldn't suggest moving in together.

Her house, of course.

Nick's voice, filled with anger, broke into her musings. "Callie, I'll call you back if I hear from her."

Dana stiffened at the sound of Nick's ex-wife's name. She whirled—privacy be damned—then froze, stunned at the anguish on his face. "What happened?"

Instead of answering, he walked to the couch and dropped onto one of the cushions. Dana followed, easing down beside him.

"Is Megan all right?"

"No idea. Callie started out saying Megan had disappeared. I asked why she had Megan's phone. Didn't get an answer, but it turns out Megan left by choice. She packed her clothes and a few other belongings while Callie and Gary were out to dinner and left a note saying she was moving out."

He jumped to his feet, pacing. "Damn it. While Callie's bragging about how Megan won't get far with an empty checking account and no cell phone, Gary's in the background cussing about what an ungrateful brat Megan is."

Her heart echoed his pain. *I know what you're feeling. Not knowing if your child is safe.* The situation with Megan though was not quite the same as it had been with Joshua, especially in light of one comment she'd overheard during Nick's call.

"When is Megan's birthday?"

He stopped midstep, head pivoting to stare down at her. Parental love flashed across his face, momentarily wiping away his despair. He dropped back onto the couch, this time next to her. She snuggled into his chest as he wrapped an arm around her shoulders.

"Tomorrow. Eighteen years old, and this'll be the first birthday we haven't celebrated together."

"I heard you mention a present. What did you send her?"

A chuckle rumbled from his chest. "Usually her present was something we'd do together. I wanted her to have memories, not just possessions. This year, I wasn't sure what she wanted or needed, so I sent a check along with a suggestion to come for a visit this summer."

"That's exactly what Megan is doing." She rolled out of his embrace, sitting up. "Whatever that situation is in Denver, she stuck it out until she legally, or within a few hours of legal, could walk out the door. That's why Callie called you. She knew exactly where Megan was headed."

"She could have gone to a friend's house. She could even be hooked up with some guy, for all I know."

"Hey." She cupped his face. "Your daughter is coming home to you."

"I hope you're—" He broke off as his cell phone rang. His face brightened as he checked the display. "Denver area code."

She wished he had put the call on speaker, but the smile that grew broader as each second passed told its own story. When the call ended, he set the phone on the side table.

"Megan's friend Amber. My girl is on a plane headed this way. Megan didn't want her to call until the plane took off. Something about plausible deniability for when Callie called."

"I knew it!" She bounced onto her knees, throwing both arms around his neck. "When does she arrive?"

"Layover in Detroit, then arrival in Richmond at nine-thirty tomorrow morning. I'll drive up to get her. I can't wait for you two to meet."

She didn't expect to be invited along for the ride. The meeting needed to be between Nick and Megan. *Wow.* Nick's daughter, possibly her daughter as well one day. But would Megan accept another woman in Nick's life?

His hand slipped over hers, entwining their fingers. "Joshua will come home one day too."

A boy always needs his mom. Peace settled in her heart. She'd continue her attempts to connect with Joshua, always sending her love. When—not if—he chose to return home, she'd welcome him with open arms.

He squeezed her hand. "I seem to remember you owe me an apology."

"That would be correct."

A wicked gleam flickered in his eyes. "Need me to carry you?"

"Don't you dare!" She scrambled off his lap, stumbling around the side of the sofa.

The room wasn't big, her legs were shorter than his, and Nick Warden was a determined man. When he swung her up into his arms, she turned a startled gaze on him.

"Oh, you meant this way?"

"Yes, ma'am. And if you run out of ways to apologize during the night, I have a few suggestions in store."

"Can't wait to hear them," she said as he set her gently onto her feet.

"I love you."

His vow mingled with her pledge, three words echoing the wish of two hearts. One shared life ahead of them.

As for the secrets in her past, she and Nick would solve those mysteries. Together.

THE END

ABOUT THE AUTHOR

Dianna Wilkes is an award-winning contemporary romance author. *Main Street*, the first book in the Providence Island series, was a finalist in the 2015 Maggie Awards and 2016 Molly Awards, 3rd place winner in the 2016 Lone Star Awards, and 1st place winner in the Orange Rose Awards.

Reading has always been an important part of her life. "My mom taught me to read when I was four years old," she said. "Writing my own stories seemed a natural progression."

A West Virginia native now living in Delaware, Dianna has a B.A. in Visual Communication and a M.Ed. in Instructional Technology and works as an Education Consultant. Despite all that nerdy stuff, she loves creating stories of romance and mystery with touches of humor.

When she isn't writing or working, Dianna is deep in researching various twigs and branches on her family tree or fulfilling entries on her travel bucket list.

Facebook: www.facebook.com/DiannaWilkesAuthor/
Website: www.diannawilkes.com

MORE BY THIS AUTHOR

The story continues in *Towne Square* (Providence Island Book 2):

Jamie Danvers's luck changed for the better when she was hired to handle marketing and communications for a Providence Island design firm. Although she's learned from her past mistakes, her family continues to believe the worst about her. On PI, she's making a fresh start—a home, good friends, and a challenging career. Her boss, Dana Canfield, believes in her, something Jamie hasn't experienced for a long time. Falling in love with architect Rhys McCall wasn't in Jamie's plan, especially since he's Dana's son. Can she trust her instincts this time that Rhys might be The One?

Workaholic Rhys McCall put off having a personal life for too long. A fractured family life growing up left him cynical about finding eternal love. Jamie's beauty catches his interest from the beginning. Her clever mind and quick wit keeps him on his toes, and he's ready to become a believer in Forever After. She's the perfect fit for him—personally and professionally.

But the path to love isn't going to be easy. A killer roams the streets of PI. He's murdered two people already, and Rhys appears to be next in his sights. Until Rhys discovers who's targeting him, he can't put Jamie's life at risk. But Jamie's not about to let Rhys shut her out. Will her determination to save their relationship put them both in jeopardy?

Turn the page to read a short excerpt from *Towne Square*.

EXCERPT FROM
TOWNE SQUARE

Providence Island, Virginia

Damn it, Kate. Why couldn't you stay dead?

Erik McCall stormed across the second level of the downtown parking garage. His footsteps echoed in sharp, steady beats, keeping pace with the pounding at his temples.

He stopped next to the stairwell, gazing out at the downtown streets. Not even seven o'clock, and the sun had already burned off all but a few lingering wisps of fog.

Looking out over his kingdom usually put a shine on the start of his day. For more than four generations, McCall Construction had built or renovated the majority of the downtown buildings. Their reach spanned even further if he counted in all the residential work.

He had every right to brag. He'd worked hard, gotten his hands dirty, and now owned one of the largest businesses on the island.

No way would he let Kate destroy the life he'd built.

Marrying Kate had been the biggest mistake of his life. His luckiest break had come when a two-car accident on the mainland sent her off to the afterlife. For more than two decades since then, she'd ceased to exist in his life even as a memory.

So what if he hadn't watched her being planted six feet under?

Dead was dead.

Except Kate hadn't died. For some reason, her identity had been switched at the hospital with that of the woman in the other vehicle. First indications suggested the other driver had been at fault, and her family obviously wanted to avoid a lawsuit. Otherwise, why would the Canfield family lawyer have approached him at the hospital and offered a check with more zeros than he'd seen in his lifetime and an offer to take care of Kate's burial?

Erik had taken the money and returned to PI with the four-year old son Kate had tried to keep away from him. Rhys was a McCall, and he belonged with his father.

End of story.

Except Kate was here now on PI—his turf—and calling herself Dana Canfield.

Just his damn luck that a random remark from that woman sent Rhys off searching for one of the few photographs of his mother Erik hadn't destroyed years ago. Had Rhys come to him? Faced him man-to-man and asked for an explanation? Nope, he'd gone straight to Kate, who'd claimed she'd had amnesia and had spun a sob story.

Two decades of doing his damnedest to raise his son, and what was his reward? In a heartbeat, Rhys had turned his back on his own father for a woman he could barely remember.

Kate certainly hadn't suffered while living Dana Canfield's life. Attorney husband with a trust-fund client list. Society life. A so-called job decorating houses for idiots with more money than brains, and raising the other guy's kid as her own.

I'm not the bad guy here.

If anyone was to blame, it was the hospital for not catching the mistake in the beginning. Or Canfield and his lawyer for letting it continue. Why hadn't her fake husband corrected the mistake all those years ago?

He snorted. For all her considerable faults, Kate did have some serious talent between the sheets. Must have been good enough to keep Canfield satisfied all these years. Until a bullet sent him to the beyond and put Kate on a collision course back into his life.

When Kate was around, there was always trouble.

Erik stepped away from the overlook and into the stairwell. The flicker of a shadow gave him a split-second warning before pain exploded just above his right ear.

Who the hell—?

He caught a glimpse of the crowbar seconds before it slammed against his ribs. His knees buckled. Bile surged into his throat. Sweat and blood ran down his face as he grabbed blindly for the assailant's shirt. If he could pull the punk off-balance....

The punk retaliated with a swift punch to Erik's jaw, followed by an elbow shot to his chest.

Erik toppled down the remaining steps, landing flat on his

back. His head slammed into the concrete. The throbbing in his ribs and the shattering pain ripping along his spine left him struggling to breathe.

A gray haze swept over his vision as he stared up the stairwell at the blurry image of a man who stood silent and still, the crowbar lowered to his side. A deep throated chuckle filtered its way through the sound of his own labored breathing.

He was broken, not beaten. He still had fight left in him. Just let the punk get close enough for him to get in one good shot. He blinked...

...and the man was gone.

Cell phone.

If only his damn hand would cooperate. Dizziness washed over him, leaving time for one final thought before claiming the last of his consciousness.

Kate was back, and so was trouble.

65412402R00141

Made in the USA
San Bernardino, CA
02 January 2018